Dual Flame

Betsy Tate

Published by Betsy Tate, 2024.

This is a work of fiction. Similarities to real people, places, or events are entirely coincidental.

DUAL FLAME

First edition. November 11, 2024.

Copyright © 2024 Betsy Tate.

ISBN: 979-8227696526

Written by Betsy Tate.

Chapter 1: The Reluctant Spark

He leaned back in his chair, a self-assured smirk playing at the corners of his mouth, and I could practically hear the gears whirring in his mind as he calculated his next move. The rain pattered rhythmically against the window, a gentle reminder of the storm brewing not just outside but between us. I could almost taste the tension, a bitter cocktail of ambition and unspoken attraction that hung thick in the air.

"Are you always this combative, or is it just because you're facing me?" Reid quipped, his deep voice slicing through my focus like a knife. There was a mischievous glint in his eye, one that hinted at a game I didn't want to play. My office was a sanctuary—my sanctuary—and I had fought hard for every piece of furniture, every framed degree hanging on the wall. Yet here he was, a dark cloud hovering over my meticulously curated haven.

"Only when I have to deal with someone who thinks they can outsmart me," I shot back, crossing my arms defiantly. The air crackled, not just with our heated words but with the underlying chemistry that I'd rather deny. It was absurd, really. This was a professional setting, and yet, every time I caught a glimpse of him, my heart did a little dance, as if betraying the steely resolve I'd cultivated over years in this unforgiving world of family law.

As the conversation spiraled into the depths of our clients' lives—twists of betrayal and shattered dreams—my mind struggled to maintain its clarity. Each piece of evidence he presented was expertly crafted, but I could see the cracks, the opportunism bleeding through the cracks of his polished exterior. My instincts screamed at me to stay grounded, to guard my emotions against this man who thrived on discord, yet he drew me in with every word, every calculated glance.

"Do you ever think about the people behind these numbers, Reid?" I challenged, my voice softer now, almost vulnerable. "These aren't just assets and debts. They're lives we're dismantling." I hated how earnest I sounded, how easy it was to slip into that space where personal stories tangled with legal disputes. It was the reason I became a lawyer in the first place—to help people find resolution, not just victory.

He paused, a flicker of surprise crossing his sharp features, as if I'd jabbed a finger into a soft spot. "I think about them all the time," he replied, his voice suddenly stripped of its bravado. "But the moment you let their emotions dictate the negotiation, you lose control. This is a battlefield, and I fight to win."

His words hung in the air like a palpable weight, and I could see how he carried that philosophy in the lines etched on his face, the way he adjusted his cuffs like a soldier preparing for war. I wanted to tell him that sometimes, it wasn't about winning; it was about healing. But the words wouldn't come, trapped behind the wall I'd built around my heart.

I felt the urge to shift the conversation, to ground myself in the present rather than spiraling into the complexity of our mutual disdain and unexpected intrigue. "Then perhaps it's time to reconsider your strategy," I said, allowing a playful lilt to enter my tone, a tactic I often employed to disarm opponents. "You might find that understanding can be more powerful than winning."

He leaned forward, his dark eyes glinting with amusement. "Is that your way of saying I should play nice?"

"I'm saying you might discover that people respond better to kindness than to aggression. You catch more flies with honey, you know?" I shot back, a smile tugging at my lips, emboldened by the fleeting moment of connection. But the smile faltered when I noticed the way his expression shifted, the amusement replaced by something darker, more calculated.

"Kindness doesn't pay the bills, nor does it win cases," he replied, a hard edge creeping back into his tone. "And in this business, we have to be ready to sacrifice a little kindness for the sake of our clients."

Something stirred deep within me at his words, a realization that perhaps I was clinging too tightly to my ideals in a world that thrived on cynicism. I had always believed in the better nature of humanity, yet here was Reid, embodying the very opposite of what I stood for. He was a reflection of every cold, calculated maneuver I had fought against in my career, yet there was an undeniable magnetism about him that drew me in, despite my better judgment.

The negotiations wore on, each round punctuated by sharp exchanges that crackled with unacknowledged tension. Every time I shifted in my seat, every slight movement drew his attention, and I could feel my heart race as I became acutely aware of the distance between us. It was a dangerous dance, one that left my mind reeling, and yet I couldn't look away. I couldn't let this man—this beautiful, infuriating man—derail me.

"Let's take a break," I finally said, my voice steadier than I felt. The moment the words escaped my lips, I regretted them. I needed to stay focused, to maintain the upper hand, but my heart, that traitorous little thing, had other ideas. I stood up, my chair scraping against the floor, a sound that broke the tension like a fragile bubble bursting.

As I walked toward the coffee machine in the corner of the room, I could sense him watching me, his gaze a tangible force. I poured myself a cup, hoping to ground myself in the familiar routine of caffeine and distraction. But even the rich aroma of freshly brewed coffee couldn't chase away the swirling thoughts that had taken residence in my mind.

"Coffee isn't going to help you win this case," he called, his voice teasing but laced with something deeper, something I couldn't quite place.

"Maybe not, but it's a hell of a lot better than dealing with your brand of logic." I shot back, turning to face him, mug in hand, adrenaline still coursing through my veins.

His laugh, low and rich, echoed through the room, sending an unexpected thrill down my spine. "Then I'll have to think of a way to make you a little less hostile, won't I?"

For a fleeting moment, the world outside faded, leaving just the two of us locked in an unspoken understanding. Perhaps this negotiation was only the beginning, a mere prelude to a much larger conflict that lay ahead—a battle of wills and hearts that neither of us were prepared to face.

The coffee had barely cooled in my mug when Reid rose from his chair, a predatory grace in his movements that felt disarmingly intimate. He strolled across the room, his presence both unsettling and intriguing. As he leaned against the edge of my desk, casually insouciant, I felt the air thicken between us, charged with a current I couldn't ignore.

"Do you believe in fate, or is that just another fairy tale you like to sell your clients?" he asked, tilting his head slightly as if genuinely curious. I blinked, caught off guard by the unexpected question that slipped past our contentious negotiations.

"I prefer to deal in reality," I replied, gathering my composure, but the answer felt flimsy in the face of his piercing gaze. "Fairy tales might be comforting, but they rarely pay the bills." The moment the words left my lips, I regretted the retort. It was too defensive, too revealing. I needed to keep my emotional cards close, yet here I was, laying them out like a poorly played hand at poker.

"Ah, so pragmatism is your armor," he mused, a flicker of respect in his eyes that sent a ripple of warmth through me. "That's quite a choice, considering what you're up against." The way he spoke made it sound as though he knew something about the odds I faced that I didn't.

"Everyone has their methods," I replied, raising an eyebrow, hoping to appear nonchalant. "Some prefer to play nice; others, like you, thrive on chaos."

He chuckled, a low, rich sound that sent a thrill through my spine. "Chaos, or strategy? It depends on who's defining the terms." I could feel the challenge in his tone, and my pulse quickened. He wasn't just here to negotiate; he was here to test me, to see how far I'd bend before breaking.

Before I could respond, the door swung open, and my assistant, Molly, poked her head in, her eyes darting between us like a hawk spotting prey. "Sorry to interrupt, but there's a call from Mr. Jenkins about the Willoughby case."

"Thank you, Molly," I said, forcing a smile. "I'll take it in my office."

Reid's expression shifted, an eyebrow arching, as if he found the interruption fortuitous. "I suppose I should be grateful for a momentary reprieve," he said, a smirk tugging at the corner of his mouth.

"Oh, don't worry," I shot back, a playful lilt creeping into my voice. "I'm sure I'll return shortly, perhaps with a few more surprises to share."

With that, I stepped into my office, the door closing behind me with a soft click. As I answered the call, I could still feel the weight of Reid's gaze lingering, as if he had left a piece of himself behind in the room with me. The conversation with Mr. Jenkins blurred into a haze of legal jargon and procedural nuances, my mind wandering back to Reid's mischievous smile, the warmth of his laugh.

After the call ended, I took a moment to collect myself, staring out the window at the drizzling rain. It was soothing, the kind of weather that made the world feel muted and introspective. I leaned against the cool glass, my thoughts swirling like the raindrops racing down the pane.

What was happening? I was supposed to be focused, navigating this complex divorce settlement with sharp precision, yet Reid's presence had infiltrated my mind in ways I hadn't anticipated. I glanced at the clock—time was slipping away.

I returned to the conference room, heart racing slightly as I prepared to confront him again. "I'm back," I announced, my voice steadier than I felt. Reid was still leaning against my desk, a relaxed facade that belied the tension simmering just beneath the surface.

"Good to know you haven't run off," he replied, his tone teasing yet sincere. "I was beginning to think you'd abandoned the field."

"Hardly," I shot back, a smile breaking through despite my best efforts to maintain a stern facade. "I wouldn't leave without ensuring I have the upper hand."

"Let's hope that's the case," he replied, straightening up, the playful banter fading into the charged atmosphere once more. "Shall we dive back in?"

The negotiations resumed, our voices rising and falling like the rhythm of the rain outside. Each point of contention was a volley in our unspoken battle, and I found myself both challenged and exhilarated by his presence. Every argument he presented was an intricately woven thread of logic, and I had to navigate them carefully, unraveling his intentions while weaving my own strategy.

At one point, Reid leaned closer, the scent of his cologne—a mix of cedar and something more elusive—filling my senses. "You really care about your clients, don't you?" he asked, a genuine curiosity underlying his words. "Most attorneys would rather churn out settlements than worry about feelings."

"It's not just about the paperwork," I replied, heart racing at the sudden intimacy of his tone. "These are real people, Reid. They deserve someone who understands what's at stake."

His gaze softened for a fraction of a second before the walls returned, that practiced neutrality descending once more. "Then perhaps we should find common ground. Clients aren't the only ones with stakes in this game."

I nodded slowly, feeling the shifting dynamics in the room. It was as if we were two dancers caught in a complicated tango, each of us stepping forward and back, testing boundaries while drawn inexplicably closer together.

The negotiations drew to a close for the day, but as we gathered our papers, I sensed an unresolved tension that hung in the air like a storm cloud waiting to break. "So, what now?" I asked, trying to keep my tone light, though my heart raced with uncertainty.

"I'll think about your proposal," Reid said, a hint of a challenge in his voice. "And perhaps you'll find that I'm not quite the villain you've painted me to be."

"Perhaps I'll find you more insufferable than I thought," I countered, a playful smirk crossing my lips.

"Touché," he replied, his laughter echoing through the room, warming the space between us. "Until next time, then."

As he walked out, the door closing softly behind him, I couldn't shake the feeling that this was only the beginning of something far more complicated than I had anticipated. The game was afoot, and whether I liked it or not, I was already in deep.

The days that followed Reid's unexpected exit from my office blurred into a whirlwind of paperwork, meetings, and more legal jargon than I cared to count. Yet, despite my best efforts to stay focused, my thoughts kept drifting back to him—his sharp wit, that confident stance, and the way he had challenged me not just in negotiation but in ideals. Every time I passed the conference room,

I half-expected to find him waiting, his dark suit a stark contrast to the light, airy decor of my office.

It was on a particularly dreary Wednesday that I found myself staring out the window, rain streaking the glass like tears. My phone buzzed with a message, jolting me from my reverie. I grabbed it, a flicker of excitement bubbling up inside me. Maybe it was Reid, maybe it was a client, or perhaps it was just Molly reminding me of my lunch appointment—nothing ever quite so exhilarating as a chance encounter, yet I hoped for something more.

The message lit up my screen: "Can we talk? — Reid."

My heart did a little somersault. I took a moment to steady my breath, wrestling with the urge to respond immediately versus the rational part of my brain that cautioned me to tread carefully. But there was a thrill in uncertainty, one that I hadn't realized I craved until now. I quickly typed back, my fingers hovering over the keys as I considered my response.

"About what? The case or something more personal?"

His reply came almost instantly: "Both. Meet me at Brix in an hour?"

I glanced at the clock, then at my half-eaten lunch, feeling a surge of adrenaline. Brix was a cozy little café down the street, known for its artisanal sandwiches and intimate ambiance. It was the kind of place where secrets could be shared, and I couldn't shake the feeling that this meeting would be anything but ordinary. I straightened my blouse, took a deep breath, and with a final glance at my scattered papers, I headed out.

As I entered Brix, the familiar scent of freshly baked bread and rich coffee enveloped me, instantly easing some of the tension that had wound tightly in my chest. The café was sparsely populated, a few scattered patrons lost in their own worlds. I spotted Reid at a corner table, his back to the wall, the low light casting a warm glow on his chiseled features. He looked up as I approached, and a smile—genuine and surprisingly disarming—broke across his face.

"Glad you could make it," he said, gesturing to the empty chair across from him. I settled into my seat, trying to ignore the flutter of nerves that accompanied his presence.

"I had to check if you were pulling my leg. You know how much I enjoy legal games," I replied, offering a teasing smile that masked my genuine curiosity.

"Not this time," he said, his tone earnest. "I wanted to talk about the case, but I also wanted to get to know the woman behind the attorney. You've made quite an impression."

"Impression or annoyance?" I countered, arching an eyebrow playfully.

"Definitely an impression," he said, leaning in slightly. "You're refreshingly different from most lawyers I deal with. You actually care."

"Flattery will get you nowhere," I replied, the corner of my mouth twitching into a reluctant smile. "But thank you. I take my work seriously."

"I can tell." His expression shifted slightly, a shadow passing over his features. "And that's why I wanted to talk. The case is complicated, and I think we might actually have a chance to resolve it amicably if we work together."

A flicker of surprise coursed through me. "Are you suggesting we collaborate?"

"Collaborate, compromise—call it what you will," he said, his tone teasing but the underlying sincerity unmistakable. "We both know our clients would be better served by a settlement rather than dragging this through the courts. Plus, it'll make for a good story."

"A good story? Please, enlighten me."

"Two fierce attorneys, once rivals, joining forces to help their clients achieve peace and understanding." He chuckled, and the sound sent a wave of warmth washing over me. "That's the kind of headline I'd like to see."

I contemplated his proposal, feeling the weight of the decision pressing down on me. Was I really ready to trust him? I could still feel the electric tension between us, and I wasn't sure if it was a spark of competition or something deeper. "I don't know, Reid. This isn't exactly the norm for either of us."

"Isn't that what makes it intriguing?" he challenged, his gaze unwavering. "Maybe this is our chance to rewrite the rules."

"What's in it for you?" I asked, suddenly suspicious. "I can't help but wonder if you have an ulterior motive."

"Fair point," he admitted, leaning back in his chair. "Maybe I'm tired of the usual back-and-forth. Maybe I'm curious about you. You're not like the others, and I find that refreshing."

"Refreshingly reckless, perhaps," I said, allowing a teasing lilt to my voice. But beneath the jest, I felt my resolve beginning to crumble. What was I getting myself into?

He smiled, a soft, genuine smile that crinkled the corners of his eyes. "Let's not be reckless. Let's be strategic."

We talked for the next hour, bouncing ideas back and forth, laughing at the absurdity of our initial encounters. The chemistry was undeniable, crackling like static electricity in the air, and I found myself leaning closer, drawn in by his passion and charisma. It was exhilarating yet terrifying, like standing on the edge of a precipice.

As our discussion wound down, Reid suddenly leaned forward, his expression serious. "There's something else you should know," he said, his voice dropping to a whisper that sent a shiver down my spine. "I've been approached about a potential conflict that could affect both of us."

My heart raced. "What do you mean?"

"There are elements at play in this case that are more complex than we realized. It involves our clients' backgrounds—things they haven't disclosed."

"Such as?" I pressed, the gravity of his words hitting me like a slap.

"Things that could change the entire landscape of this negotiation. If we're going to work together, we need to be on the same page."

Just then, the café door swung open with a loud chime, drawing my attention away from Reid. A figure stepped inside, drenched from the rain, shaking off an umbrella like a dog. My breath hitched when I recognized the familiar silhouette. It was my client, Amanda, her expression a mix of frustration and urgency.

"Julia!" she called out, her voice slicing through the warmth of the café. "I need to talk to you. Now!"

Reid's eyes widened, the tension in the air suddenly thickening with uncertainty. I glanced between Amanda and him, a rush of anxiety flooding through me. What had I just stepped into?

"Hold on," I said, standing up, my heart racing. "What's going on?"

As I approached Amanda, her face turned pale, and in that instant, I knew this was only the beginning of a much bigger storm—one that threatened to engulf us all.

Chapter 2: A Cold Evening in Manhattan

Outside, New York hummed with life, the cacophony of honking cars intermingling with the chatter of late-night diners crowding into nearby restaurants. The scent of street food wafted through the air, mingling with the sharp, earthy aroma of rain-soaked asphalt. I had just stepped out of the office, my shoulders still tight with the weight of another exhausting day, ready to hail a cab and retreat to my cozy, albeit cluttered, apartment in Astoria. But as I turned the corner, I spotted Reid standing on the sidewalk, a solitary figure draped in a dark trench coat, the rain slanting against the pavement like silver needles.

    He looked as if he were lost in thought, his brow furrowed, hands shoved deep into his pockets as if he were anchoring himself to the ground. The city buzzed around him, a vibrant whirl of color and sound, but he remained still, almost impervious to the chaos that enveloped him. For a moment, I considered slipping away into the night, avoiding the magnetic pull that his presence always exerted on me. But as if sensing my hesitation, he lifted his gaze, locking eyes with mine. The world around us blurred into a hazy backdrop, the cacophony fading to a muted murmur.

    I could feel the tug of something unnameable between us, a mixture of tension and curiosity that had simmered for months. It was strange how one glance could tether you to someone, making the ground beneath your feet feel suddenly unstable. There was a challenge in his eyes, a silent dare that urged me forward. My feet moved almost of their own accord, guiding me to where he stood. I found myself seeking shelter beneath the awning, a tiny sanctuary from the rain that fell like a curtain around us.

"Coffee?" he asked, his voice low and steady, a rich timbre that vibrated in the damp air. It was less a question and more an invitation, the kind that hinted at shared secrets and unspoken understanding.

"Since when do you indulge in caffeine after dark?" I quipped, trying to mask the sudden flutter in my stomach with a lighthearted jab. "I thought you reserved that for dreary mornings."

He smirked, a glimmer of mischief sparking in his eyes. "Maybe I'm branching out. The night is young, after all. Or is it?" He tilted his head slightly, a mock pondering that made me smile despite myself.

"More like late and soggy, but who's counting?" I replied, leaning against the cool glass of the coffee shop's window. The warmth inside felt inviting, a stark contrast to the chill wrapping around us like a cloak. I could see the barista bustling behind the counter, steam swirling into the air like a cozy embrace, tempting me further.

Reid shifted his weight, watching me as if I were a puzzle he was trying to solve. "You've been working late again," he observed, his tone slipping into something more serious, more concerned. "You know, they'll still have a job for you tomorrow."

I rolled my eyes, but there was a flicker of appreciation for his attentiveness. "I can handle it, Reid. The cases won't solve themselves, and I'm not about to let someone else take the credit for my work."

He chuckled softly, a sound that resonated warmly in the night. "I get it. But you should let someone else help you carry the load once in a while."

"Is that your way of volunteering?" I shot back, my heart racing at the thought. His presence was always a complicated maze of emotions, and I was acutely aware of how easily we slid into a comfortable banter that felt almost natural.

"Only if you promise to keep me entertained," he replied, his eyes glinting with mischief. "And you know I'm a sucker for a good story."

"Then brace yourself," I warned, feigning seriousness. "I have a riveting tale about the printer jamming at the most inopportune moment."

The corner of his mouth twitched up in that familiar way, the one that made my pulse quicken. "Now that's a cliffhanger. But I think I'd prefer something with more... substance."

Our conversation ebbed and flowed, a tide of playful jabs and deeper confessions, the steady rhythm of our words filling the space between us like a melody. I found myself sharing pieces of my life I had long kept tucked away—like the childhood fear of thunderstorms that had plagued me until I realized they were merely nature's symphony. He, in turn, opened up about his late-night drives to clear his head, his voice softening as he spoke of the dark roads winding through the outskirts of the city, illuminated only by flickering streetlamps.

There was a vulnerability in the air, a fragile thread weaving us closer, and with each passing moment, the lines of our friendship blurred into something far more intoxicating. The rain danced around us, a rhythmic patter that seemed to echo our unspoken thoughts, as I caught the glimmer of his intention—a question lingering just beneath the surface, waiting for the right moment to emerge.

As we stood there, lost in conversation, I felt the tension shift, crackling with an electric current that thrummed just beneath my skin. I wondered if he could feel it too, that magnetic pull that kept drawing us together, even as the world outside surged onward. Would we ever dare to step beyond the safe confines of our shared laughter and explore what lay on the other side? The question hung heavily in the air, the city continuing to pulse around us, oblivious to the tiny revolution taking place under this humble awning.

The rain tapped a gentle rhythm on the awning overhead, a soft percussion accompanying our repartee. Each sip of coffee warmed my hands and stirred the embers of conversation between us. I could see the steam rising from his cup, curling into the night air like tendrils of the warmth we were sharing. The streetlights cast a golden glow, illuminating the faint lines of weariness etched around his eyes—a reminder that even the most composed facade can hide fatigue beneath.

"You know," he said, setting his cup down with a decisive thud, "if you keep working these late nights, you'll either become a caffeine addict or a ghost. I'm not sure which would be worse for you."

"Ha! At least ghosts don't have to worry about deadlines," I shot back, enjoying the way his mouth twitched upward at the corners. "And I have my priorities straight. Coffee first, sleep later. I'm on a strict schedule of avoidance."

He leaned in slightly, a conspiratorial glint in his eye. "I think you might be missing the point of the whole 'work-life balance' thing. It's not just about mastering the art of procrastination."

"Are you trying to lecture me?" I challenged, arching an eyebrow. "You, of all people? Last I checked, you've got your own late-night rendezvous with your laptop."

Reid chuckled, the sound warm and rich. "Touché. I suppose we're both guilty as charged. But here's a thought: how about we do something radical? Let's step away from our workaholic tendencies and embrace a night of spontaneity."

"Spontaneity?" I repeated, letting the word roll off my tongue like something exotic. "In New York? Isn't that a bit ambitious? What do you suggest? A midnight tour of the subway system?"

He pretended to ponder it seriously, tapping his chin with exaggerated thoughtfulness. "Actually, that could be intriguing. I hear there's a whole underground world of art. Or we could just go find the best slice of pizza at this hour. A midnight pizza adventure has a nice ring to it."

The idea sparked something in me, a flicker of excitement mingled with the warmth of our shared moment. "You're kidding, right? Pizza is a food group on its own in this city. But I'm in. I can't resist a good slice."

Reid grinned, his expression brightening. "Then it's settled. We'll find the best pizza and declare it our prize for surviving another grueling day. Plus, I have a feeling this could turn into one of those legendary nights we'll talk about for years to come."

I loved his enthusiasm. It was contagious, like a wildfire igniting in dry brush. The prospect of stepping away from my monotonous routine filled me with an energy I hadn't felt in ages. We dashed into the rain, laughing as we splashed through puddles, the night transforming around us. The coffee shop faded into the background, its warm light a distant memory as the cool night air embraced us.

As we navigated through the bustling streets, I was struck by how familiar this felt, as if we were stepping back into a rhythm we hadn't fully realized we'd lost. The vibrant energy of the city pulsed around us, the shouts of street vendors and the distant wail of sirens blending into a symphony of urban life. It was intoxicating, this combination of chaos and thrill, and I found myself stealing glances at Reid, intrigued by the way his smile lit up in the dim streetlights.

"Do you remember the first time we met?" I asked, my curiosity piqued.

"Let's see," he replied, tilting his head in mock contemplation. "You were knee-deep in paperwork, looking like you wanted to throttle the nearest person. I think I was the one who managed to distract you with an impromptu chat about the merits of pizza toppings."

I laughed, shaking my head. "That was my breaking point, not my beginning. I was a shell of a person. But you, with your ridiculous pizza debates, made my day. I thought, 'Who is this insufferable man?'"

"Insufferable?" he repeated, feigning offense. "I prefer the term 'irresistibly charming.'"

"Charming, my foot," I shot back. "You practically ambushed me with your pizza philosophy!"

We rounded a corner, the faint glow of neon lights beckoning us closer. A small pizzeria stood at the end of the block, its sign flickering in the night. The smell of melting cheese and freshly baked dough wafted through the air, wrapping around us like a warm blanket. Reid paused, gesturing dramatically at the establishment as if unveiling a hidden treasure.

"Behold! The culinary gem of Manhattan. I present to you—The Slice of Heaven," he declared, his voice rising in theatrical flair.

"Nice name. I hope it lives up to the hype," I replied, a grin spreading across my face. "Or else I'll be blaming you for my late-night regret."

Inside, the place was alive with the sound of laughter and the hiss of pizza being pulled from the oven. We found a cozy booth in the corner, the walls adorned with photographs of iconic New York moments—Broadway stars, historical events, and, of course, slices of pizza in various stages of consumption.

As we settled in, I noticed Reid's eyes sparkling with excitement, the kind of joy that only comes from genuine passion. He leaned across the table, conspiratorial again. "So, what's your go-to pizza topping? This is essential for our friendship."

"Pineapple," I admitted, watching his reaction closely. "It's a classic, a divisive classic."

His eyebrows shot up in mock horror. "Pineapple? You've just crossed the line. We may need to reassess our dynamic here."

"Don't knock it until you've tried it!" I challenged, waving a hand dismissively. "What's your favorite then?"

"Pepperoni, obviously. It's the king of toppings, a classic for a reason," he declared, his expression all too serious, as if he were presenting an argument for a presidential debate.

We ordered a large pepperoni and a small pineapple for the sake of diplomacy, our laughter blending with the restaurant's buzz. I reveled in the banter, the way it felt easy and fluid, as if we had fallen back into a rhythm we'd unknowingly crafted over countless late-night talks. The pizza arrived, steaming hot, and I couldn't resist the temptation to dive in.

"Okay, here's the true test," Reid said, holding a slice aloft like a trophy. "One bite, and I'll determine if your pizza preferences are valid."

I rolled my eyes, but the challenge was irresistible. "Fine, but only if you promise not to throw up in disgust."

With exaggerated caution, he took a bite, chewing thoughtfully, his face revealing nothing. I leaned in, anticipation buzzing through me. Then he nodded slowly, a smirk breaking through. "Not bad. But let's be clear, it's no pepperoni."

"High praise, coming from you," I retorted, biting into my slice, the sweet tang of the pineapple perfectly balancing the rich cheese. It was heavenly, the flavors dancing on my tongue.

"Now this is a real slice of heaven," I said, unable to hide my glee.

He grinned, and the air between us crackled with an undeniable chemistry. We were lost in the moment, two friends savoring not just the pizza but the shared experience—each laugh echoing against the walls of the tiny pizzeria, creating a bubble around us that felt as warm as the food we devoured. The city outside continued its relentless pace, but for that brief, perfect moment, it was just us against the world, enjoying the sweetness of spontaneity and the unexpected joy of late-night pizza adventures.

The pizza disappeared quickly, slices devoured like cherished secrets revealed in the warmth of the booth. I could feel the tension between us morphing into something deeper, each shared laugh a brick laid in the foundation of an unspoken connection. Reid wiped his hands on a napkin, leaning back as if to relish the moment, his eyes glinting with mischief.

"Alright, I've got a challenge for you," he said, his voice a conspiratorial whisper. "Let's turn this into a little game. You know those silly questions people ask at parties? Let's ask each other the most ridiculous ones we can think of. No holds barred. The loser buys the next round of pizza."

I raised an eyebrow, a smile threatening to break out. "Oh, this could be dangerous. Are you sure you're ready to handle my brand of ridiculous?"

He chuckled, the sound rich and inviting, and nodded with feigned seriousness. "I'm ready. But fair warning, I can be extremely petty when I lose."

"Bring it on, then."

"Okay, first question," he said, tapping his finger on the table for emphasis. "If you could have any superpower, but it had to be completely useless, what would it be?"

"Easy," I replied, leaning in. "I would choose the ability to change the color of my toenails at will. Imagine the possibilities! I could go from electric blue to neon green in seconds. Parties would never be the same."

Reid burst out laughing, shaking his head in disbelief. "That's both completely absurd and oddly specific. I'm impressed. Alright, my turn. If you were a kitchen appliance, which one would you be and why?"

I feigned deep contemplation, placing my hand dramatically against my chin. "Hmm, I'd say a toaster. I mean, I get hot under pressure, but I always manage to deliver a satisfying result. Plus, I'm pretty good at making mornings less bleak with a little bit of warmth."

"Not bad," he conceded, "but a toaster doesn't quite have the same charm as a blender. I mean, blending is where all the fun happens, right? You can whip up smoothies or make margaritas. So many possibilities!"

"Touché," I said, laughing. "But your margarita-making abilities can't compare to my spontaneous dance parties in the kitchen. That's the real superpower."

We volleyed ridiculous questions back and forth, the atmosphere charged with an easy camaraderie. Each query drew us deeper into laughter and storytelling, the outside world fading into the background as we both revealed quirks we rarely shared. He asked about my most embarrassing moments, and I retaliated with his childhood fashion choices. Our banter flowed seamlessly, making the booth feel like a cozy cocoon separate from the bustling city outside.

After a particularly ridiculous exchange involving hypothetical scenarios of living on a deserted island with only a pet goldfish, I leaned back, glancing around the pizzeria as if just now noticing the other diners. "You know," I said, a hint of mischief in my voice, "if we keep this up, people might think we're a couple. The chemistry is palpable."

Reid smirked, his gaze fixed on me with a piercing intensity. "And what if we were? What would that look like in your perfect world?"

The question hung in the air, laden with unspoken possibilities. My heart raced as I met his gaze, a sudden realization dawning on me. I felt the atmosphere shift, the comfortable banter giving way to something more profound. "I guess it would involve late-night pizza adventures, a lot of laughter, and maybe even a spontaneous road trip to—"

"New Jersey?" he interjected, feigning horror. "The horror!"

"Hey, don't knock it until you try it! The shore has its own kind of charm," I shot back, playfully nudging his arm.

"But in all seriousness, what would it look like?" he pressed, leaning forward, the glimmer of curiosity in his eyes sharpening into something more intense.

I swallowed hard, feeling the weight of his question settle in my chest. "I don't know. It would be unpredictable, fun—"

"And complicated?" he added, his tone shifting slightly, the lightness of our previous banter fading.

"Complicated is just another word for exciting, don't you think?" I retorted, trying to keep the mood light, but a knot of tension coiled in my stomach. "I mean, who wants boring?"

Reid's expression softened, a hint of vulnerability creeping into his usually guarded demeanor. "I can handle complicated. But sometimes it feels like you're dancing around something we both know is there."

The vulnerability of his words struck me, igniting a spark of awareness I had tried to ignore. My mind raced, caught in the undertow of my thoughts. What did I want? A part of me longed for the safety of our friendship, yet another part craved the risk of something more. I had never let myself linger in that space before, always opting for the comfort of routine over the thrill of uncertainty. But now, faced with his piercing gaze, the air thick with unspoken possibilities, I felt a shift, a flutter of anticipation that filled the silence between us.

Before I could respond, the door swung open, a blast of cold air sweeping through the cozy pizzeria. A couple rushed in, their laughter filling the room, and for a moment, it was as if the magic surrounding us dissipated into the chatter of the crowd. I felt the warmth of our moment slip through my fingers, and with it, the chance to explore what had been bubbling beneath the surface.

"Should we go?" I blurted, feeling the weight of reality pressing in. "We could take a walk along the pier or—"

"Wait," Reid said, his voice firm yet soft, stopping me mid-sentence. "Let's not run away from this. There's something here, isn't there? Something worth exploring."

My heart raced, uncertainty creeping in like the chill from the street outside. "It's just late-night pizza talk," I said, forcing a smile, the playful façade crumbling beneath the weight of his words.

"Is it?" He leaned in closer, our faces nearly touching, and in that moment, I was acutely aware of every detail—the way his eyes searched mine, the hint of vulnerability dancing in his expression. "Or are we finally being honest about what's really going on?"

Just then, the bell above the door jingled again, and a figure stepped inside. My heart dropped as I recognized the unmistakable silhouette—Clara, my ex-best friend, and the one person I hadn't expected to see tonight. She looked around, her eyes landing on us, and the smile she wore faded into a tight-lipped expression. Time stood still, the air charged with a sudden, electric tension that threatened to shatter everything we had been building in our little bubble.

"Uh-oh," I whispered, my heart thudding in my chest. "This could get awkward."

"Maybe we should talk about this later," Reid said, his expression shifting to one of concern as he watched Clara approach. The moment hung precariously in the air, a cliffhanger that left everything unresolved, the weight of possibilities threatening to tumble into chaos.

Chapter 3: The Glare and the Grace

The morning sunlight streamed through my window, spilling warm gold across my sheets, yet I remained ensconced in a fog of annoyance and intrigue. I could almost hear the rustle of his tailored suit brushing against my mind, a jarring reminder of our last encounter. Reid Stanton had a way of slipping under my skin, his presence a sharp contrast to my carefully curated world. He was infuriatingly charming, with an insufferable confidence that made my blood boil and my heart race in equal measure.

As I made my way to the office, each step felt like a dance on a tightrope, teetering between my professional resolve and the inexplicable curiosity he sparked in me. My thoughts drifted back to the negotiation table, where he had sat across from me, a cocky grin plastered on his face as he dissected my proposals with a precision that was both impressive and maddening. Each word I spoke seemed to dissolve in the air, swallowed by his calculated arguments and that infuriating glint in his eye. The way he leaned back in his chair, arms crossed, made it abundantly clear he saw our clash as a game—and one he was determined to win.

Later that day, I found myself pacing the floor of my office, surrounded by the muted colors of the corporate landscape that usually comforted me. The dull hum of the fluorescent lights felt grating against the backdrop of my tumultuous thoughts. I snatched up my phone, contemplating whether to call Layla, my steadfast anchor in this swirling sea of chaos. I needed her wit, her humor, and most importantly, her ability to yank me back to reality whenever I got lost in my own head.

"Meet me at The Rusty Nail," I texted, the name of our favorite bar slipping from my fingers like a sigh of relief. I could already envision the warm, inviting atmosphere, the intoxicating aroma of craft beer mingling with the laughter of familiar faces. There was something about that place that made it feel like home, and tonight, I needed the familiarity of my best friend's presence.

The Rusty Nail was alive with its usual buzz when I arrived, the low hum of conversations blending seamlessly with the clinking of glasses. Layla spotted me instantly, her bright pink sweater a beacon in the crowd. She raised her glass in salute, a mischievous grin spreading across her face.

"There's my favorite overthinker!" she exclaimed, pulling me into a hug that smelled faintly of lavender and promise. "So, tell me everything about Mr. Stick-Up-His-Backside."

I laughed, shaking my head as we settled into our usual corner booth. "It's not that simple. He's just... annoying, you know? He makes me feel like I'm in a constant duel, and I hate it."

"Oh, please," Layla said, her eyes sparkling with mischief. "You love the challenge. Just admit it; he makes your heart race."

"Only because I want to punch him," I shot back, trying to mask the way my cheeks heated at the thought of Reid's smile—the way it seemed to dance along the edges of my memory, teasing and taunting.

"Sure, sure," she replied, rolling her eyes. "Let's see how many drinks it takes before you confess your undying love for the man who's apparently the villain in your story."

"Undying love?" I scoffed, taking a sip of my own drink, the crisp taste of gin and tonic grounding me. "We're not in a rom-com, Layla. This is reality, where men like him exist solely to make life more difficult for women like me."

"Ah, the classic 'men are trash' mantra. So original," she teased, but I could see the genuine concern beneath her playful banter.

"Fine, I might be a little obsessed," I admitted, unable to suppress the smile that tugged at my lips. "But it's all in the context of loathing. He's infuriating, and yet..."

DUAL FLAME

"Yet what?" Layla leaned in, her expression shifting from playful to genuinely curious.

"Yet, he's fascinating. He knows how to push my buttons in the most irritatingly clever way, and I hate that I respect him for it," I confessed, cringing inwardly at the revelation. "I'm not supposed to admire the enemy."

"Maybe you should rethink that," she suggested, a glint in her eye that told me she was up to no good. "Sometimes, the lines blur between love and hate. You might be onto something here."

"Don't you dare," I said, laughing despite myself. "I refuse to entertain any idea that involves romantic tension with Reid Stanton. He's just—he's just not my type."

"Except he is, whether you want to admit it or not." Layla leaned back, folding her arms with a satisfied smirk.

I rolled my eyes but couldn't shake the lingering feeling that she might have a point. The drinks flowed, laughter echoed through the air, and for a fleeting moment, I allowed myself to forget the chaos of the negotiation table and the man who had so effortlessly disrupted my life. I lost myself in the rhythm of the evening, the warmth of friendship, and the bittersweet tang of possibility.

Yet, even as I reveled in the comfortable familiarity of Layla's company, Reid's image flickered at the edges of my mind, stubbornly refusing to fade. The night spun on, filled with chatter and clinking glasses, but deep down, the battle within me raged on—a swirling storm of disdain and intrigue that left me teetering on the brink of something unexpected.

The next day unfolded with a similar heaviness, as if the air itself conspired to remind me of Reid. I tried to focus on my tasks, but even the most mundane reports felt tainted by his shadow. Each email I composed had a twinge of his mockery embedded in the back of my mind. I found myself looking over my shoulder, half-expecting him to appear in the doorway with that infuriatingly charming smile, ready to dismantle whatever fragile confidence I had managed to rebuild since our last encounter.

During lunch, I sought refuge in a corner café, hoping for solace in a steaming cup of coffee and the gentle hum of chatter around me. I sank into a plush chair, the smell of roasted beans mingling with the faint sweetness of pastries, but the moment I closed my eyes to savor the warmth, I was jolted back to the negotiation room. Reid's voice cut through the air, smooth and unwavering, as he dismantled my carefully crafted arguments one by one. The memory sent a shiver down my spine—not entirely unpleasant.

"You look like someone just ran over your puppy," came a familiar voice, pulling me from my reverie. I opened my eyes to find David, my colleague and a fellow negotiator, standing there with a bemused grin. His disheveled hair and the ever-present hint of sarcasm were comforting in their familiarity.

"Thanks for the support," I replied, managing a smirk. "Just enjoying a delightful episode of corporate warfare, you know."

"Reid again?" he asked, taking the seat across from me, his brow arching with genuine concern. "You need to find a way to deal with that guy. It's like watching a cat play with a mouse. Very entertaining but a bit cruel."

"It's like he has a sixth sense for my weak points," I admitted, taking a sip of my coffee and trying to ignore the heat creeping into my cheeks. "One moment, I'm leading the charge, and the next, I'm left stammering in disbelief as he flips the table."

David chuckled, a deep, rich sound that was oddly soothing. "Maybe you just need to throw him off his game. What's his kryptonite? Does he have any weaknesses? A fear of public speaking? An aversion to puppies?"

I laughed, feeling the weight of the past few days lift just a bit. "If only it were that easy. He seems immune to everything except the sound of his own voice. Besides, who knew a corporate lawyer could be so insufferably charming?"

"Ah, yes. The charm of a snake," he said, leaning back in his chair with exaggerated flair. "Beware the serpent, lest he lure you into the garden of regret."

I rolled my eyes, but his antics pulled me out of my spiral of frustration. "I think you're getting a bit carried away with the metaphors."

"Perhaps, but it's a tempting garden," he mused, a teasing glint in his eye. "What's life without a little danger? Besides, you'd make a great Eve, wouldn't you? Clever, beautiful, and the kind of woman who bites the apple just to see if it's sweet."

"Thanks, I guess?" I replied, feeling a mix of flattery and exasperation. "But I think I'd rather avoid the fallout of any bitten apples for now."

The conversation turned lighter as David launched into a series of outrageous tales from his own negotiation battles, complete with exaggerated hand gestures and dramatic pauses. It was refreshing, the kind of banter that reminded me of why I enjoyed working with him. Yet, even as I laughed, Reid lingered in the recesses of my thoughts, a ghost that refused to be exorcised.

Later that evening, I found myself back at The Rusty Nail, the comforting noise of clinking glasses and laughter wrapping around me like a warm embrace. Layla was already at the bar, her phone in one hand and a cocktail in the other, her laughter cutting through the din.

"Look who finally decided to show up!" she called, waving me over. "I was beginning to think you'd been swallowed by the corporate beast."

"Not yet," I replied, sliding onto the barstool beside her. "But it's a close call. I could use another drink. What are you having?"

"Something fruity and fun. I figured it was a good way to cope with the horror that is adulting," she said, gesturing to her bright pink concoction that seemed to shimmer in the low light.

I ordered a drink of my own and settled into the familiar rhythm of our friendship. We chatted about our work, our lives, and everything in between, the worries of the day dissolving in the warmth of the moment. Just as I was starting to feel at ease, my gaze drifted toward the entrance, and my heart dropped like a stone.

Reid Stanton strode in, his tall frame cutting through the crowd like a ship through fog. He looked effortlessly polished in a navy blazer that highlighted his broad shoulders, and the moment his gaze landed on me, that familiar smirk appeared. My breath hitched, irritation bubbling back to the surface, hot and prickly.

"Of all the bars in the city," he said, his voice smooth as honey as he approached, "I didn't expect to find you here, drowning your sorrows."

I narrowed my eyes, ready with a retort. "And I didn't expect to find you gracing us with your presence. Did you come to gloat, or do you have an actual reason for being here?"

Layla shifted beside me, her interest piqued, clearly enjoying the sudden tension in the air. "This could get interesting," she whispered under her breath, but I barely registered her words, my focus fixated on Reid.

"Gloat? No, that's too predictable," he replied, leaning casually against the bar, as if this were an everyday encounter. "I just wanted to see how you were holding up after our last... discussion. You looked a bit rattled."

"Rattled? Please," I shot back, crossing my arms defiantly. "I'm as steady as they come. If I were a ship, I'd be a battleship."

His laughter rang out, deep and genuine, causing heads to turn in our direction. "A battleship? That's quite a claim. But I can see the waves crashing on the horizon. Just remember, it's not too late to change course."

There was something unsettlingly magnetic about his confidence. I felt it tugging at my defenses, pulling me into a conversation I wasn't entirely sure I wanted to have. "Change course?" I scoffed, leaning in just a fraction closer. "Why would I do that? I've got my eye on the prize."

"Ah, but what if the prize comes with a few unexpected detours?" he challenged, his dark eyes glinting with mischief. "Sometimes the most interesting journeys come from the unplanned routes. Just a thought."

I opened my mouth to retort, but the words fled, replaced by a rising tide of confusion. What did he mean? Why did he seem so infuriatingly compelling? For a fleeting moment, I was caught in the undertow of his charisma, and it terrified me. Just as I was about to regroup and throw a clever remark back at him, the bartender placed my drink in front of me, and I took a fortifying sip.

"Nice to see you two getting along," Layla chimed in, clearly reveling in the tension.

"Getting along?" I echoed, feigning disbelief. "More like battling on a sinking ship."

"Then maybe you should both consider a life raft," Reid suggested, that insufferable grin still in place.

"Oh, please," I shot back, feeling my heart race in a way I didn't quite want to analyze. "I'm perfectly capable of swimming on my own."

He tilted his head, his expression shifting slightly, something more sincere flickering behind the playful banter. "And yet, here we are, both in the same storm. Just think about it—what if we're on the same side after all?"

His words hung in the air between us, charged and uncertain, like an electric current promising something unpredictable. I blinked, the easy repartee stalling, and for the first time, I wasn't entirely sure where this dance would lead.

The atmosphere around us crackled with energy, the kind that stirs the blood and ignites the senses. As Reid leaned casually against the bar, the low light catching the edges of his jawline, I was torn between my instinct to retreat and an undeniable curiosity that made me want to lean in. His presence was magnetic, a potent mix of confidence and charisma that threatened to unravel my carefully woven defenses.

I took a deep breath, trying to shake off the spell he seemed to cast over me. "Let's not pretend this is some grand alliance. I have no interest in teaming up with someone who revels in my failures."

"Ah, but that's where you're wrong," he replied, a playful tilt to his head that sent an unexpected flutter through my stomach. "You see, I admire your tenacity. Most people would have crumbled under the pressure of our last meeting. You stood your ground. That deserves recognition, not disdain."

I raised an eyebrow, skepticism lining my features. "Recognition? Or a condescending compliment dressed up as a backhanded jab?"

"Wouldn't you prefer the former?" His smile deepened, a genuine warmth flickering beneath the surface of his playful banter. "Besides, I think we could both benefit from some collaboration. You have the passion, and I have the expertise. Together, we could achieve something quite remarkable."

"Remarkable or just a disaster waiting to happen?" I shot back, crossing my arms defiantly. The words tumbled from my mouth, but the truth was that the idea was tantalizing, despite how it twisted my insides.

"Why not take a leap?" he countered, his voice low and smooth, dripping with an earnestness that both annoyed and intrigued me. "You'd never know how sweet the fruit is unless you taste it. Or are you afraid of a little risk?"

"Afraid? Hardly. I simply prefer to weigh my options instead of diving headfirst into a pool of sharks," I said, though I felt the tiniest prickle of doubt at the back of my mind. "Besides, what makes you think I'd ever agree to partner with you? The last thing I need is another reason to lose my mind."

"Perhaps you underestimate how much fun it can be to dance with danger," he replied, leaning in closer, the warmth of his voice brushing against me like a tantalizing caress. "After all, the best negotiations often come from the most unlikely partnerships."

I swallowed, caught off guard by the intensity of his gaze. There was a flicker of something deeper behind his playful facade, something that felt achingly sincere. I had to remind myself of the facts: he was my professional rival, not my confidant. Yet, as we exchanged repartees, the lines began to blur, and the tension simmered just below the surface, almost begging to be acknowledged.

"Okay, so say we do this," I said, pushing back against the encroaching warmth that his proximity ignited. "What's in it for you? A chance to gloat? A way to keep me in line?"

"Maybe I see potential in you," he replied, his tone suddenly serious. "Or maybe I just want to prove that you can't judge a book by its cover. You have more in you than you realize."

His sincerity caught me off guard, and I felt the initial thrill of skepticism waver in the face of something warmer. I met his gaze, searching for the signs of deception. "I'm not looking for a hero, Reid. I'm more than capable of standing on my own two feet."

"And yet here we are, both trying to make our way through this corporate maze. Wouldn't it be easier to have someone watching your back?" he pressed, his voice dipping lower as if sharing a secret that only the two of us could understand.

"Fine," I said, exasperation bubbling to the surface. "Let's say we agree to this bizarre proposition. What would be the first step?"

"Let's set up a meeting to discuss our goals," he suggested, the spark of mischief returning to his eyes. "And perhaps a bit of friendly competition to see who can come up with the best strategy?"

"Friendly competition? That's rich coming from you," I scoffed, though the idea rolled around in my mind like a sweetly dangerous thought.

"Life's too short for boring negotiations," he replied, a playful glint in his eye. "And I promise, it won't be all serious business. We'll have some fun along the way."

"Fun?" I echoed, skepticism creeping back in. "That's a dangerous word coming from you. Fun and Reid Stanton should not be in the same sentence."

"Challenge accepted," he shot back, his confidence unshaken. "What do you say? Will you be my reluctant partner in this little adventure?"

I hesitated, the weight of his proposition settling heavily in the air between us. Something in the way he looked at me made it hard to breathe, as if he was peeling away my layers and exposing something raw and unguarded. "This isn't some cheap rom-com, Reid. If we do this, we're going to have to stay professional."

"Of course," he replied, though the glint in his eyes told a different story. "But a little banter never hurt anyone, right?"

Just then, my phone buzzed in my pocket, pulling me from the simmering tension. I fished it out, my heart racing as I saw the caller ID flash across the screen—an unexpected name that sent a jolt of panic through me.

"What's wrong?" Reid asked, sensing my sudden shift in mood.

"It's my boss," I replied, my mind racing as I glanced at the screen again, an unsettling feeling creeping in. "I really should take this."

"Take it, but don't keep me waiting," he said, a teasing lilt in his voice, but I could see the concern lurking beneath.

I stepped away from the bar, the noise of the crowd fading into a dull hum as I answered. "Hello?"

"Where are you?" my boss's voice crackled through the line, sharp and demanding. "We need to discuss the project update, and it can't wait."

I nodded, even though she couldn't see me. "I'll be there shortly."

"Make it fast," she snapped, and the call ended before I could respond.

My heart raced as I slipped my phone back into my pocket, turning back to find Reid watching me with an intensity that made my pulse quicken.

"Looks like you're needed," he said, his expression shifting to one of concern.

"Yeah, I guess I'll have to—"

Before I could finish, the bar door swung open with a sudden force, and a figure stepped inside, silhouetted against the streetlights. My breath caught in my throat as I recognized the face behind the shadows. A familiar face that could alter everything.

Reid's brows furrowed, sensing the shift in my demeanor. "What's going on?"

I couldn't tear my gaze away from the doorway, where a whirlwind of memories and emotions stood waiting. My pulse thrummed in my ears, drowning out the noise of the bar as I faced the impending storm. The night had shifted, and I knew that whatever lay ahead would change everything—again.

Chapter 4: Shadows Beneath the Surface

The courthouse loomed ahead like a grand old ship stranded in a storm of concrete and steel, its marble façade gleaming beneath the pale morning sun. I stepped inside, the familiar scent of polished wood and faint mustiness enveloping me, tinged with the sharpness of freshly printed legal documents. Courtrooms buzzed with the muted conversations of lawyers and clients, each corner echoing with the weight of unresolved disputes and buried truths. I navigated through the labyrinthine hallways, my mind tethered to the upcoming case and the ghost of a different conflict altogether: Reid.

Our last encounter had been charged, each word a sharpened knife that danced dangerously close to the skin. This time, however, the stakes were higher. I could feel his presence even before I spotted him—an undercurrent of tension that crackled in the air. There he was, leaning against the wall like he owned the place, his impeccably tailored suit accentuating the breadth of his shoulders. I couldn't help but admire the way he commanded the space, though my admiration was laced with annoyance. His calm exterior was as meticulously crafted as his arguments, but I could sense the storm swirling beneath.

"Fancy seeing you here again," I said, my tone a blend of sarcasm and genuine surprise as I approached him. I leaned against the wall beside him, our shoulders almost brushing—a subtle reminder of the boundaries we skirted around in our rivalry. "I almost thought you'd take a day off from crushing dreams."

He turned, his blue eyes locking onto mine, and for a fleeting moment, I caught a glimpse of vulnerability before it vanished behind his usual mask of indifference. "Crushing dreams? That's rich coming from you, Ava. Isn't that what you do for a living?" The wry smile that followed was laced with mischief, as if he were enjoying a private joke at my expense.

I couldn't let him see how his words stung. "Touché. But my clients' dreams are usually worth pursuing. Yours, on the other hand..." I let the sentence hang in the air, a taunt meant to poke at his carefully curated façade.

"Careful, or I might think you're concerned about my clients," he replied, a hint of laughter in his voice, but I could see the shift in his expression—how his jaw tightened just slightly as if bracing for an impact he knew was coming.

"Hardly," I shot back, crossing my arms defiantly. "I just find it amusing how far you'll go to win. There must be a line somewhere, Reid. Or do you just dance right over it?"

He straightened, his eyes narrowing slightly as he stepped closer, the distance between us shrinking. "And what if I told you I don't believe in lines?" His voice was low, the challenge clear in his tone. The moment hung, thick with unspoken words and simmering tension.

But then he surprised me. "Why family law, Ava?" The question hung in the air like an unexpected chord in a familiar song, pulling me from the sharpness of our exchange and grounding me in a reality I hadn't wanted to confront. "What's your story?"

The abruptness of his inquiry caught me off guard. I had built my career on carefully constructed walls, each one a defense against prying eyes and probing questions. Yet, here he was, chipping away at those defenses with nothing but a simple question. I hesitated, caught in a tempest of emotions. "I don't think that's any of your business."

"Isn't it?" His voice dripped with something that felt almost like genuine curiosity, and for a moment, I hated him for it. The truth was a fragile thing, and the shadows of my past whispered in my ear, nudging at my resolve.

"Because every case you take on says something about who you are, Ava," he pressed. "You know that as well as I do. So what are you running from?"

I inhaled sharply, his words burrowing into the marrow of my bones. The sound of the gavel echoed from the courtroom, bringing me back to the present. I could feel the walls closing in, the sharpness of his gaze piercing through the carefully constructed layers of my armor.

"I'm not running from anything, Reid," I said, forcing a smile that didn't quite reach my eyes. "But it seems you're more interested in my story than your own."

His expression faltered for just a moment, and that fleeting hint of pain flared again before he masked it with a practiced smile. "Touché," he echoed, but the lightness of his tone was gone, replaced by an undertone of something heavier.

Just then, the bailiff called for order, and the cacophony of murmured conversations settled into a hush. I felt the shift in energy as everyone turned their attention back to the courtroom, but I couldn't shake the lingering tension between us. There was something about Reid—a depth to his character that tugged at my curiosity, an enigma wrapped in a tailored suit.

As we both took a step back, the air thick with unsaid words, I felt a jolt of realization. This wasn't just about the cases anymore. It was about our histories, our choices, and the shadows lurking beneath the surface, threatening to pull us both under if we weren't careful.

"Let's get back to work," he said finally, the mask firmly back in place. "I'm sure your clients are waiting for you."

As I turned away, I could feel his gaze on my back, an electric pulse that lingered long after I had distanced myself. I steeled myself for what lay ahead, the courtroom doors opening with a loud creak, a stark reminder that the battle was far from over.

The following day, the air outside the courthouse felt electric, as if the atmosphere itself were charged with the unresolved tensions of yesterday. I arrived early, hoping to gather my thoughts before the proceedings began. As I crossed the threshold into the familiar stone structure, I could hear the echoes of footsteps and hushed whispers, the bustling rhythm of the legal world surrounding me like a living organism.

I settled into a quiet corner of the lobby, the cool marble beneath me a welcome contrast to the heat rising in my chest. The weight of Reid's words hung over me like a dark cloud, taunting me with their implications. Why did I choose family law? The question looped through my mind, relentless as a tide. Was it truly about justice for others, or was it a way to shield myself from my own tumultuous past?

As I pondered, the distant clang of a gavel cut through the reverie. The court was calling to order, the soft murmurs of conversations fading into a sharp focus. I stood and made my way toward the courtroom, adjusting my blazer with a determined flick of my wrist. If Reid thought he could rattle me, he was in for a surprise. I was here to represent my client, and I intended to do it with all the ferocity I could muster.

Inside, the courtroom was a tableau of earnest faces and tense silence, all eyes on the judge seated high on the bench, a modern-day monarch presiding over a realm of disputes. I took my seat, glancing across the room to where Reid sat, his expression unreadable as he reviewed his notes. He looked composed, perhaps even serene, but I could still sense the simmering energy between us, a current that pulsed just beneath the surface.

The case unfolded with the expected drama, witnesses called, evidence presented, and each side's arguments crafted with precision. My opponent's relentless pursuit of victory was evident, his tactics sharp and calculated. Yet as the hours dragged on, I found my attention wandering. It was difficult not to observe the small nuances of Reid's demeanor—how he leaned back in his chair when he was particularly pleased with a point, or the way his brow furrowed slightly when he was deep in thought.

During a particularly heated exchange, I noticed him glance my way, his gaze piercing and intense. It was as if he were daring me to join the fray, to leap into the fracas and turn the tide in a way only I could. I fought the urge to smile at the challenge, keeping my focus on my client's needs.

"Ms. Harrington, would you care to respond?" the judge asked, pulling me from my reverie.

"Your Honor," I began, my voice steady as I rose to present my rebuttal. As I spoke, I felt Reid's gaze remain fixed on me, an anchor tethering my resolve. Each argument I laid out was a brick, reinforcing the wall I was building around my past.

Yet as the day wore on, the courtroom drama faded into the background, replaced by the uninvited thoughts of Reid that flitted through my mind like an errant butterfly. What were the secrets he kept hidden behind that cool façade? Each time I caught a glimpse of his more vulnerable side, it intrigued me further.

Finally, as the day came to a close and the gavel echoed its final call, I breathed a sigh of relief. My client's case had progressed well, but I couldn't shake the sense of unfinished business with Reid. The case was merely a battleground; the real war raged in the territory of our interactions, marked by unspoken words and shared glances.

Once outside the courthouse, the sun painted everything in hues of gold, the late afternoon light spilling over the sidewalk as if inviting me to linger. I paused, unsure of where to go next, when a familiar voice called out.

"Ava!"

I turned to see Reid striding toward me, his features framed by the soft glow of the setting sun. There was a resolve in his step that hadn't been there before, a purposeful energy that made my heart quicken.

"Reid," I said, attempting to keep my tone neutral, even though my pulse raced.

"Can we talk?" He asked, his tone low and earnest, a hint of something vulnerable lurking just beneath the surface.

I weighed the options in my mind. Was this a continuation of our sparring match, or something deeper? Curiosity gnawed at me, and despite every instinct that screamed to maintain my distance, I found myself nodding.

"Sure," I replied, and we walked together toward a nearby café, the world around us fading into a blur of chatter and clinking cups.

Once settled at a small table outside, I could feel the tension curling around us, a palpable energy that hinted at the revelations to come. He leaned forward, elbows resting on the table, his blue eyes searching mine.

"I wanted to clarify something," he began, his voice low but intense. "About our last conversation. I didn't mean to pry."

"It's fine," I said, though my stomach twisted. "I'm used to it."

"Used to what? People wanting to dig into your life?"

"Something like that." I forced a smile, trying to deflect. "What about you? You seemed rather interested for someone who claims not to believe in lines."

Reid's gaze sharpened, the laughter fading. "It's complicated. People see me as a relentless shark, but there's more to it. Everyone has their reasons."

The honesty in his words pulled me in, and for a moment, the café's noise faded into the background, leaving just the two of us suspended in this delicate moment of vulnerability.

"Maybe I'm just a little tired of being perceived as just one thing," he continued, his voice dropping to a whisper. "You think I relish the idea of being the villain?"

"Who said you were the villain?" I challenged, leaning back in my chair, intrigued by the sudden shift in our conversation.

His lips quirked into a small smile, one that held a hint of challenge. "You don't think so? That's quite the compliment."

Before I could respond, the waitress approached, breaking the spell between us. We placed our orders, the clatter of cups and the aroma of freshly brewed coffee returning me to reality. But as I watched Reid, his expression shifting from playful to contemplative, I realized we were delving into a territory I hadn't expected—one filled with uncharted paths and the promise of unexpected truths.

The coffee arrived, steam curling into the air like wisps of our unspoken thoughts. Reid wrapped his hands around the warm cup, his fingers long and elegant, each movement betraying a tension beneath his calm exterior. The café around us thrummed with life—laughter mingled with the sharp sounds of espresso machines, the air rich with the scent of roasted beans. Yet in our little bubble, an electric silence hung, charged with the possibilities of what was to come.

"I didn't mean to pry," he said again, his gaze piercing mine. "But you have to admit, there's something compelling about the stories we tell ourselves."

"Is that what you think I'm doing? Telling myself a story?" I raised an eyebrow, feigning nonchalance even as a flutter of unease danced in my stomach. "Sounds like something a psychologist would say. I'm not here for a therapy session, Reid."

"Just an observation," he replied, a playful smirk dancing on his lips. "But let's face it, our lives are a collection of narratives. Yours, especially, seems—" He paused, searching for the right word. "Rich."

"Rich? Is that a compliment or a thinly veiled insult?" I couldn't help but laugh, the sound breaking the tension between us, a bridge forged in wry humor.

"Take it as you will," he said, leaning back in his chair, confidence radiating from him like sunlight through clouds. "But there's something intriguing about someone who chooses to navigate the complexities of family law. It suggests depth, perhaps even a touch of heartbreak."

A chill raced down my spine. Did he know? I'd spent years burying those wounds, convincing myself they were mere scars, not open wounds. "Or maybe it just means I'm good at reading people. Everyone has their troubles, Reid. Yours just seem to come wrapped in a shiny bow."

His laughter rang out, a rich sound that turned a few heads nearby. "Touché. But that bow hides something, doesn't it? You don't become a shark without a story worth hiding."

As I took a sip of my coffee, the bitterness mirrored my thoughts. "Is that your strategy? Provoke until someone reveals their secrets? Is this all part of your grand plan to get under my skin?"

He raised an eyebrow, feigning innocence. "And if it is?"

"Then I'd say you've succeeded." I smiled, but there was an edge to my tone that hinted at the vulnerability I felt. "Yet I still know nothing about you."

The playful banter shifted, becoming more serious. "That's the point, Ava. Some things are better left buried. But we can't deny the shadows that cling to us. They make us who we are."

His words echoed in my mind like a haunting melody. The shadows were everywhere, creeping into my thoughts, twisting memories I thought I had tucked away. "What if we're not defined by those shadows? What if we choose to step into the light instead?"

"Easy to say, harder to do." His eyes softened for a fleeting moment, and for an instant, I saw a man wrestling with his own darkness. It intrigued me, ignited a spark of empathy I couldn't afford.

Before I could respond, a sudden commotion erupted from the entrance. The café doors swung open, letting in a gust of cool air that sent a shiver through me. A woman stormed in, her heels clicking angrily against the floor as she scanned the room with fierce determination. She wore a designer outfit, her hair slicked back into a tight bun, and I recognized her instantly—Nina Matthews, a powerful attorney known for her no-nonsense approach and ruthless tactics. She was a legend in the legal community, and the air shifted, charged with her presence.

"Nina," Reid greeted her, a hint of caution creeping into his voice. "What brings you here?"

"Cut the pleasantries, Reid. I need to talk to you. Now." Her tone left no room for debate.

I felt an uncomfortable twist in my stomach as I observed their exchange. Reid straightened, all traces of our earlier conversation fading away. "Can it wait until later? I'm in the middle of something—"

"Not a chance." Nina's glare was fierce, her resolve unwavering. "This can't wait."

"What's going on?" I interjected, unable to hold back my curiosity. The tension between the two of them was palpable, thick with unspoken stakes.

Nina turned to me, her expression softening just slightly. "Ava, this concerns you too. We need to discuss what's happening with the Matthews case."

A sinking feeling lodged in my chest. "The Matthews case? But—"

Reid cut in, his voice steady but laced with urgency. "You don't need to involve her, Nina. This is between us."

"Don't be naïve," she snapped, her eyes narrowing. "This is bigger than either of you realize. I can't let it fall into the wrong hands."

"What do you mean?" I leaned in, my interest piqued despite my reservations.

Nina's gaze darted around the café, as if the very walls had ears. "You're both caught in the middle of something that could change everything for us in this industry. If we don't act quickly, it won't just be our reputations at stake."

My heart raced as the implications of her words sank in. "What kind of change?"

"It involves a whistleblower," Reid interjected, his expression now grim. "Someone is prepared to expose the corruption that runs deeper than any of us can imagine. And they're targeting us."

"Targeting you?" I felt a chill creep down my spine. "Why us? We're just lawyers trying to do our jobs."

Nina leaned closer, her voice a low whisper. "That's exactly the point. They're coming for the top players in the game. If they succeed, everything we've built could come crashing down."

An unsettling silence fell over the table, the weight of her words pressing heavily on my chest. The air buzzed with uncertainty, a sudden urgency transforming the mundane café into a battlefield of hidden agendas and veiled threats.

"What do we do?" I asked, my pulse quickening.

"We fight back," Reid said, determination flickering in his eyes. "But we need to be smart about it. This isn't just about our cases anymore. It's about survival."

Just as the gravity of his words settled, the door swung open again, a new figure stepping into the café. My heart stopped as I recognized the man: Peter, a rival attorney with a reputation for manipulation. His presence felt like a dark omen, a shadow that loomed larger than the very walls around us.

Before I could process the implications, Reid stiffened beside me. "No," he breathed, his voice a mere whisper, laced with a dread that sent chills racing down my spine.

The tension snapped, and in that moment, I realized that everything was about to change. The shadows we had tried to navigate were now closing in, and the light we sought seemed further away than ever.

Chapter 5: The Woman in the Red Dress

I had nearly managed to block him from my mind by the time we both ended up at a gala hosted by one of our mutual clients. The venue was grand, a lavish ballroom bathed in soft, golden light that danced across the crystal chandeliers like shimmering stars in a velvet sky. The air hummed with laughter, the clinking of champagne glasses, and the rustling of silk and satin as elegantly dressed guests twirled and spun beneath the opulent ceiling. The rich scent of roses intermingled with hints of citrus from the extravagant cocktails being served at the bar, each drink a work of art in itself, garnished with delicate flowers and fragrant herbs.

As I moved through the crowd, exchanging pleasantries and forced smiles, my thoughts were a tangled mess. I had nearly forgotten how his laughter could slice through the ambient noise, how it echoed in my mind like a haunting melody. But then I saw him—leaning against a marble pillar, dressed in a tailored suit that hugged his broad shoulders, a wry smile playing on his lips as he entertained a group of our mutual clients. The sight was unsettling; he looked different outside the suffocating confines of our office, almost human, and the flicker of recognition ignited a heat in my cheeks that I could not ignore.

He caught my eye, and for a moment, time slowed. The laughter around us faded into a dull roar, and it was just him and me in that crowded room. There was an undeniable electricity in the air, a tension I couldn't afford to acknowledge. I quickly turned back to the conversation, trying to distract myself with tales of office misadventures and the latest gossip about our clients, but the laughter felt hollow as the space between us crackled with unspoken words.

Before I knew it, he was beside me, effortlessly weaving through the throng of guests as if he were born to command the room. "You look stunning tonight," he said, his voice a rich baritone that sent shivers down my spine. I could see the playful glint in his eye, a mixture of mischief and something deeper that made me want to believe in all the silly romantic notions I had buried.

"Thanks," I replied, attempting to sound nonchalant, but the word caught in my throat, heavy with the weight of unexpressed feelings. I glanced down at my dress, a flowing crimson number that swirled around my knees, its fabric soft and cool against my skin. It was a daring choice for me—bold, confident, the sort of garment that promised to turn heads. And there I stood, the very embodiment of the woman I always wished to be, yet still tethered to the cautious version of myself.

He extended his hand, and before I could formulate a protest, I found myself swept into a dance. The music was slow and sultry, wrapping around us like a warm embrace, and as we swayed, I felt the world blur at the edges. His hand rested on the small of my back, firm yet gentle, and I couldn't ignore the heat radiating from his touch, making me acutely aware of the gap between us.

"Is this where I say something witty and charming to make you laugh?" he asked, his breath warm against my ear as he leaned in closer. "Or would you prefer a heartfelt confession about how I miss our morning coffee debates?"

"Definitely the latter," I shot back, unable to suppress the smile that tugged at my lips. "Those debates were riveting. Who could forget your hot take on staplers?"

His laughter rang out, and I felt a flicker of joy fluttering in my chest. "Ah, the stapler wars of '23. You have to admit, my argument was compelling. You just didn't want to concede the point."

"Concede? I prefer to think of it as holding my ground, thank you very much."

Our playful banter continued, weaving a delicate thread of camaraderie amidst the tension simmering beneath the surface. I could almost forget the weight of our professional relationship, the unspoken boundaries that had kept us apart. But with every turn, I felt that warmth creeping back in, the allure of the man I had been trying to forget.

As the song reached its crescendo, the air between us thickened, charged with the thrill of possibility. I could see it in his eyes—the intrigue, the challenge. But just as I felt myself teetering on the edge of something new, he leaned in closer, his voice low and steady. "You know, we could talk about this, whatever this is. We could figure it out."

My heart raced, caught in a whirlwind of emotions. I had built walls to protect myself from him, from the complications that could arise, but here he was, tearing them down with each sincere word. "Or we could just enjoy the dance," I suggested, my voice laced with a nervous edge.

"Always the diplomat," he teased, pulling me closer.

The moment hung in the air, a fragile balance between what was and what could be, before the music began to fade. I felt the need to pull away, to retreat to the safety of my carefully constructed boundaries, but I lingered for a heartbeat longer, unwilling to break the spell that had ensnared us. I closed my eyes, allowing myself to be swept away in the rhythm of the moment, but deep down, I knew that as the song ended, I would have to confront the truth that lay just beneath the surface—one that threatened to unravel the very fabric of my carefully curated life.

His hand on my back felt both familiar and foreign, like a favorite song playing unexpectedly on a radio you thought was broken. I wanted to lean into the moment, let the warmth of his presence drown out the logical part of my mind warning me to maintain my distance. The soft fabric of my dress glided against his suit, and for a heartbeat, I lost myself in the cadence of the music and the pulse of the crowd, each twirl drawing us closer together in a way I had never anticipated.

"Tell me you're not just here for the hors d'oeuvres," he said, a teasing smile dancing across his lips. "Because I'm pretty sure I saw you eyeing the mini quiches with a touch too much desire."

"Guilty as charged," I replied, biting back a laugh. "But let's be honest, it's not my fault. They practically glow like beacons of hope in a sea of canapés."

He laughed, a rich, velvety sound that resonated deep within me, and the moment hung between us, suspended like the last note of a song. "If you're that passionate about food, we should definitely get dinner together sometime. I could give you an exhaustive rundown on the best places to indulge."

My heart skipped at the suggestion, a playful twist in the conversation that felt dangerous yet thrilling. "You mean the best places that serve kale, right? I'm on a health kick, and by 'health kick,' I mean I'm trying to eat more than just ice cream and potato chips."

"Nothing wrong with a little self-care through ice cream," he shot back, an eyebrow raised. "But I can see how your taste for kale might not pair well with our company lunches."

A mischievous grin spread across my face. "Our company lunches are a battlefield of bad decisions. I think we should consider making it a rule: no one can order anything that resembles a salad unless they are willing to admit it in front of the entire team."

His eyes twinkled with laughter. "Now that's a rule I could get behind. But you have to promise to show up, looking as stunning as you do tonight."

I felt a flutter of something light and hopeful. "I might need to start an evening dress fund. My closet currently resembles a shrine to practical footwear and power suits."

DUAL FLAME

The dance slowed, the last strains of the song fading, but I was reluctant to let go of his presence. The world around us resumed its frenetic pace, guests swirling by in sequined dresses and tailored suits, but in that moment, it felt like we were in a bubble, untouched by the chaos outside.

"Can I ask you something?" he ventured, his expression shifting from playful to serious, and my stomach tightened.

"Depends on what it is," I said, feigning lightness even as my heart raced.

"Why do you keep me at arm's length?" His voice was low, genuine, and it sent a shiver down my spine. "You're brilliant, and I've seen glimpses of who you are beyond the office. You can't possibly believe that the rest of us don't see it."

My breath caught in my throat, and I cursed the way my heart betrayed me. I could feel the walls I'd meticulously built around my feelings threatening to crumble under the weight of his words. "Maybe I just prefer to keep my work life and personal life separate."

"Or maybe you're scared," he countered, leaning in closer, his gaze locking onto mine with an intensity that sent a jolt of electricity through me. "You don't need to be. I promise, it's not that terrifying."

"Maybe it is," I shot back, my voice sharper than intended, and a flash of vulnerability crossed his face, making me regret the words as soon as they left my mouth.

"Then let's make it less terrifying together," he said softly, and I could see the flicker of sincerity in his eyes. It was disarming, the way he seemed to peel back my defenses effortlessly, layer by layer, revealing the rawness beneath.

"I'm not sure it works like that," I replied, stepping back slightly, needing to create some space, some distance. "There's a lot more at play here than just a dance or a few clever remarks. This isn't just about us."

"What's it about, then?" he pressed, unfazed by my retreat. "Is it about work? Because we both know we can handle that. Or is it something else?"

The truth was, it was something else—something deeper and scarier than I was willing to admit. The idea of vulnerability felt like standing on the edge of a cliff, teetering between the exhilarating rush of freefalling and the gut-wrenching fear of plummeting into uncertainty. "You're charming and infuriating in equal measure," I muttered, half-heartedly trying to deflect his probing.

He grinned, that familiar, wicked spark lighting up his features. "I prefer to think of myself as an adventure wrapped in a mystery. But I'll admit, I'm not going anywhere."

His confidence was both intoxicating and alarming. I could feel the tension thickening in the air, a mix of desire and apprehension that weighed heavily upon my shoulders. The gala continued around us, but I was caught in a whirlwind of thoughts. I wanted to be swept away, to embrace the risk of falling into whatever this was, but the stakes felt too high, too real.

"I should go find some of those mini quiches," I blurted, desperate to escape the intensity of the moment. "They're probably wondering why their number one fan has gone missing."

"Mini quiches are a fine excuse," he replied, stepping back but keeping his gaze steady on mine. "But I'm not done with you yet. You can't hide behind hors d'oeuvres forever."

I forced a laugh, trying to mask the racing of my heart. "Challenge accepted. Just try to keep up, Mr. Adventure." With that, I turned and made my way through the crowd, my pulse pounding in my ears as I searched for the familiar buffet table, desperate for the comfort of food to ground me in reality. But even as I reached for a quiche, I couldn't shake the feeling that this dance was only the beginning of something I wasn't ready to face, a flicker of a flame threatening to ignite a fire I had long kept under wraps.

The mini quiches were as delightful as I remembered, but the thrill of the dance lingered like an unwelcome guest at a party. I savored each bite, trying to drown out the relentless chatter in my mind, a cacophony of doubts and desires. My fingers clutched the tiny plate as if it were a lifeline, while the laughter and music swirled around me, each note pulling me deeper into the chaos of my thoughts.

As I stood near the buffet table, I could feel him watching me from across the room, that undeniable pull drawing my gaze back to where he stood with a small group, animatedly recounting a story that had everyone leaning in, hanging on his every word. I wanted to hate how easily he commanded attention, how he transformed into the center of gravity wherever he went, but instead, I found myself mesmerized. A small part of me longed to be the one he focused on, to be the target of that charming smile rather than an observer.

"You know, if you keep staring at him like that, you might burn a hole in his perfectly tailored suit," came a teasing voice from beside me. It was Claire, my colleague and confidante, a whirlwind of energy wrapped in a sparkly blue dress that seemed to twinkle with every movement. She had a knack for popping up at just the right moment, usually with a quip ready to go.

I shot her a mock glare. "I'm not staring. I'm simply... observing."

"Observing? Is that what you call it?" She winked, lifting her glass in a mock toast. "You're practically broadcasting your interest like a neon sign."

"Oh please," I scoffed, though my cheeks felt uncomfortably warm. "There's no interest. I just... have a healthy curiosity about how he manages to charm everyone in the room."

"Right, because that's what it's called when your heart races at the mere sight of him." She leaned closer, a conspiratorial grin spreading across her face. "What did you two even talk about during the dance? You looked like you were sharing secrets."

"We were discussing kale," I shot back, half-serious. "Very riveting conversation."

"Ah, yes. The seductive allure of leafy greens. Quite the aphrodisiac," she quipped, raising her eyebrow with a flourish. "But seriously, you need to give him a chance. You're both adults; you can handle whatever comes next."

Before I could respond, the music shifted to a faster beat, pulling the crowd back into the rhythm of celebration. Claire nudged me playfully, urging me to join the throng of dancers. "Come on! Let loose! Show him that the woman in red can rock a dance floor."

I hesitated, my instincts still clinging to caution, but the urge to escape the tension between us was powerful. I set my plate down and followed her onto the floor, my body moving to the music while trying to ignore the heat of his gaze. The energy surged through the crowd, each body moving in sync with the beat, and I found myself smiling and laughing as the rhythm took over.

Just as I started to enjoy the moment, I felt a presence beside me. It was him again, his hair slightly disheveled, a playful glint in his eye. "What's this? You're actually dancing? I thought you were too busy judging my moves from the sidelines."

"Clearly, my judgment was misplaced," I replied, matching his playful tone. "I didn't realize you had such moves hidden beneath that polished exterior."

He grinned, the kind of smile that made my heart flutter and my resolve waver. "I could show you some more if you'd like. But I must warn you, I can be dangerously entertaining."

"Dangerously entertaining? Sounds like a challenge," I said, tilting my head as I tried to sound casual. But inside, I was acutely aware of the stakes, the delicate balance between fun and vulnerability.

He took my hand, guiding me deeper into the crowd as we fell into a rhythm together, laughter spilling from our lips like the champagne we had consumed. Each spin brought us closer, every move blurring the line between friendship and something more electrifying.

"Are you always this fun at galas, or is it just the kale-fueled excitement?" he teased, his breath warm against my ear, sending shivers cascading down my spine.

"I save my wild side for special occasions," I shot back, reveling in the playful banter, but the truth hung like a cloud over us. Each moment danced on the edge of something that could either spark a flame or burn me to ashes.

As the song began to wind down, he leaned in, his voice dipping low. "You know, I've never been great at playing it safe. And yet, here I am, trying to navigate this tightrope of your mysterious nature."

"Don't flatter yourself," I replied, attempting to sound nonchalant. "You just happen to be very persuasive."

"Is that what I am?" he asked, his expression growing serious. "Or maybe you just like me a little more than you're willing to admit?"

The music faded, leaving an echo of intimacy between us, and I found myself hesitating, caught in a moment that felt both exhilarating and perilous. "Maybe I do," I admitted, my heart racing with the thrill of honesty. "But it's complicated."

"Complicated is my middle name," he replied, an earnestness creeping into his tone that made my chest tighten. "Tell me what you need from me. I'm not here to complicate your life; I want to help untangle it."

Before I could respond, a sudden commotion erupted nearby, snapping us back to reality. The crowd around us shifted, and I saw a figure pushing through the throng, a wild-eyed woman clutching her phone, her face pale with urgency.

"Someone call 911!" she screamed, panic lacing her voice as the music ground to a halt. "There's been an accident outside!"

My stomach dropped, and my heart raced for an entirely different reason. The warmth of the moment shattered like glass, replaced by a sharp tension that crackled in the air. I exchanged a quick glance with him, the lightness of our earlier banter extinguished, and in that instant, the gala became a world of uncertainty and fear.

"Stay here," he instructed, but I could see the determination in his eyes as he pushed forward into the crowd. I wanted to follow him, to ensure he was safe, but the instinct to help the unfolding situation anchored me in place.

As I turned to assess the chaos, I felt a sharp tug at my arm, and a voice hissed in my ear, drawing me back from the brink of the chaos. "You need to get out of here now!"

I spun around, my heart racing as I met the eyes of a man I didn't recognize, his expression dark and urgent. "What do you mean?" I stammered, a knot forming in my stomach. "What's happening?"

"Just trust me," he insisted, his grip tightening as he pulled me away from the gathering crowd. "There's no time to explain!"

Panic surged as I caught a glimpse of the chaos behind me, the dance floor turning into a whirlwind of confusion. I glanced back, searching for him, but the sea of bodies obscured my view. The gala that had felt like a fairy tale moments before was now spiraling into something I couldn't comprehend. I was caught between two worlds—one where laughter reigned and another on the brink of something dark and dangerous, my heart torn between the familiar warmth and the looming unknown.

Chapter 6: Rumors and Realizations

The courthouse hummed with the low drone of voices, a symphony of legal jargon and hushed gossip swirling around like autumn leaves in a brisk wind. I had grown accustomed to the clatter of heels on the marble floors and the occasional rustle of crisp documents, but now, in the wake of those insidious rumors, the atmosphere felt charged, electric. Every time I brushed past Reid, his smirk ignited an urge to roll my eyes or perhaps, just perhaps, fling a legal pad in his direction. Yet, I resisted. There was something oddly compelling about him, like a magnet I couldn't quite ignore, even as my mind battled against my heart's treacherous inclinations.

As I settled into my usual spot at the small café across the street from the courthouse, the aroma of freshly brewed coffee wrapped around me like a warm embrace. I savored the rich, dark liquid, letting it mingle with the familiar tension that had begun to coil in my stomach. It was there, in that cramped yet cozy sanctuary, that I found a sense of normalcy amidst the chaos swirling around my professional life. The barista, a wiry man with a penchant for quirky jokes, flashed me a grin as he served my order.

"Still avoiding the headlines, huh?" he quipped, sliding my steaming cup across the counter.

"Headlines? More like soap opera scripts," I replied with a laugh, my voice laced with a touch of sarcasm. "What's next? A dramatic confrontation in the middle of the courtroom?"

"Wouldn't put it past you," he shot back, his eyes sparkling with mischief.

I chuckled, a genuine laugh escaping my lips. In moments like these, the weight of the rumors felt lighter, almost laughable. But once I stepped back into the world of the courthouse, reality would come crashing back, a tide of speculation and half-truths. The irony was that Reid and I were both too stubborn to give the gossip any credence, yet here we were, caught in a tangled web of assumptions and wild imaginations.

Later that afternoon, while reviewing case files in my office, I caught a glimpse of Reid's silhouette through the frosted glass of the door. He paused, knocking lightly before entering, his casual confidence filling the small space. My heart raced—not out of excitement, but from a cocktail of irritation and curiosity.

"Fancy seeing you here," he drawled, leaning against the doorframe with that infuriatingly charming grin. "I thought you might be too busy dodging my admirers."

"Please," I retorted, crossing my arms. "If they're anything like you, I'll take my chances with solitude."

His laughter was deep and rich, echoing in the otherwise quiet room. "I have to admit, it's kind of nice having a rival who doesn't fawn over me."

I huffed, shaking my head, though I couldn't suppress the small smile that tugged at the corners of my lips. "Well, consider me a breath of fresh air."

"More like a gust of wind," he replied, stepping further into the room, his presence filling the space with a warm intensity that was hard to ignore. "But I appreciate it. So, what's the verdict on the rumors? I hear they're making the rounds like wildfire."

I rolled my eyes. "What do you want me to say? That we're planning a romantic getaway? Please. You and I? It's like mixing oil and water."

"Yet here we are, mixing it up anyway," he countered, his expression turning serious for a moment. "But you have to admit, the banter is kind of... fun."

"Fun? That's one word for it." I leaned back in my chair, studying him. There was something disarming about the way he navigated the conversation, his confidence palpable. "But you thrive on drama, don't you?"

"Maybe," he conceded with a smirk. "But I think you're underestimating how much I enjoy the challenge you bring. Most people don't push back."

"Or maybe they're just smart enough to avoid you," I shot back, laughter mingling with the tension.

"Smart or scared? There's a fine line, you know."

He leaned closer, a playful glint in his eye, and I could feel the heat radiating between us. It was intoxicating, yet terrifying. The way his gaze lingered made it hard to concentrate, as if he were peeling back my defenses with each word.

"Isn't it interesting?" he said, changing the subject ever so slightly. "How we started as rivals, and now... I don't know, maybe we're evolving?"

"Evolving?" I echoed, raising an eyebrow. "More like a slow, painful crawl."

"Crawls can be enlightening," he mused, his voice low and teasing. "After all, they say that knowledge is power."

I laughed, but there was an undercurrent of something deeper, something that made my heart flutter uneasily. He was right; with each encounter, each shared laugh and glimmer of vulnerability, the distance between us was narrowing. The rivalry had shifted, transformed into something with more texture, a complicated fabric woven with threads of challenge, attraction, and the undeniable chemistry that crackled in the air.

"Let's keep it professional, shall we?" I finally said, attempting to reclaim some semblance of composure.

"Professional? How dull." He tilted his head, an amused smile playing at the corners of his mouth. "Besides, who says we can't mix business with pleasure?"

I felt my cheeks flush, an unwelcome warmth spreading through me. "I'm pretty sure that's a recipe for disaster."

"Maybe," he said, pushing off the doorframe, a lightness to his step. "Or maybe it's the spark we didn't know we needed."

As he walked out, I sat back, my heart racing, mind swirling with possibilities I hadn't allowed myself to entertain. Was it truly just rivalry? Or was there something more lurking beneath the surface, waiting to be acknowledged? The air was thick with unspoken words and potential revelations, a thrilling uncertainty that had me both on edge and utterly captivated.

The following week felt like a series of finely tuned strings vibrating with unspoken tension, each encounter with Reid sparking a new resonance that was hard to ignore. It became increasingly clear that our exchanges had transformed from mere rivalry to something more nuanced, a dance we were both unwillingly performing. The courthouse buzzed with the hum of gossip, the air thick with speculation, and I found myself gritting my teeth every time someone cast a sidelong glance at Reid and me.

I perched at my desk one morning, a stack of files towering beside me, the pages filled with legalese that had lost their meaning in the face of what was unfolding. The sunlight streamed through the tall windows, illuminating motes of dust that floated lazily in the air. I glanced up, catching Reid across the room. He was leaning against a wall, talking animatedly with a fellow attorney, laughter bubbling up from their conversation. It irritated me how easy he made it look, as if he were the sun itself, effortlessly warming everything around him.

"Hey, you with us?" My colleague Jenna's voice pulled me back from my thoughts. She waved a hand in front of my face, concern etched in her features. "You've been staring at Reid like he's a piece of art you want to critique."

"Very funny," I shot back, rolling my eyes, but even I could hear the defensiveness in my tone. "I was simply... contemplating the implications of case law. You know, the usual."

"Right. Because that's what you do when you stare at someone like that," she teased, her eyes sparkling with mischief. "Let's face it, the rumors aren't just whispers anymore; they're practically a full-blown news bulletin. You two are the latest courthouse sensation."

I huffed, turning back to my files, but Jenna's words hung in the air like an unwelcome perfume, cloying and intoxicating. "It's just ridiculous," I muttered, trying to focus. "There's nothing happening between us."

"Maybe not yet," she said, her tone light but her eyes sharp. "But you can't deny there's something simmering beneath the surface. I've seen the way you both light up when you argue. It's like watching fireworks on a dark night."

Fireworks. The word flared in my mind, sparking a whirlwind of images: flaring tempers, heated debates, and an undeniable chemistry that had begun to tangle my thoughts. I wanted to deny it, to shake off the notion like a stubborn cold, but the truth lingered just out of reach, like a ghost in the back of my mind.

That afternoon, as I was reviewing a particularly dense case file, Reid appeared at my door once more, this time holding two steaming cups of coffee, the rich aroma wafting through the air like an invitation I couldn't refuse. He offered one to me, a playful glint in his eye.

"Thought you might need a pick-me-up. Heard you were slaying dragons in here," he said, a cocky grin stretching across his face.

"More like trying to decipher a puzzle designed by a madman," I replied, accepting the cup. "But thank you for the caffeine."

"Anytime," he said, leaning against the doorframe, the casual posture doing nothing to calm the fluttering in my stomach. "You know, I've been thinking. We could take this rivalry to the next level."

"Oh? How so?" I couldn't help but bite, my curiosity piqued.

He leaned forward slightly, lowering his voice as if sharing a secret. "We could hold a mock trial, see who can present their case better. Winner gets to pick dinner."

"Dinner?" I echoed, half-laughing, half-wondering if he was serious. "Are you really suggesting we turn our professional lives into a game? What's next? A bake-off?"

"Why not?" he countered, his tone playful. "Imagine the chaos. Plus, I make a killer chocolate soufflé."

I laughed, shaking my head. "I'll stick to my takeout, thank you very much. I don't want to end up with a soufflé that flops. Besides, I'd probably win, and then you'd have to eat your pride."

"Is that a challenge I hear?" His voice dipped, a spark igniting in his eyes.

"Maybe," I replied, crossing my arms defiantly. "But I prefer my victories to be grounded in reality, not in sugary confections."

"Challenge accepted," he declared, a triumphant smile spreading across his face as he pushed himself off the door and turned to leave. "We'll see who comes out on top. Just don't cry when you lose."

The door clicked shut behind him, and I sat back in my chair, bemused by the unexpected twist our relationship had taken. A mock trial? It felt ridiculous, yet thrilling. This was more than just a game; it was a line drawn in the sand, a signal that neither of us was willing to back down.

Later that week, the courthouse was abuzz with the impending verdict on a high-profile case. The air was electric, filled with anticipation and whispers. I couldn't shake the feeling of being on the precipice of something monumental, and Reid's challenge loomed over me like a banner in the wind.

As I walked into the courtroom, the tension coiled tightly around me, the spectators murmuring in excitement. I caught sight of Reid, his demeanor shifting from playful rival to focused attorney, every ounce of his attention dedicated to the case. For a moment, I was struck by the intensity of his presence, the way he commanded the room with an effortless confidence that made the hairs on the back of my neck stand on end.

As the judge entered, the atmosphere became solemn, the stakes palpable. My focus sharpened, thoughts racing through my mind as I prepared to deliver my arguments. But even amidst the gravity of the situation, Reid's earlier words echoed, a lingering tease weaving through my thoughts.

I took a deep breath, grounding myself in the moment, reminding myself that this was my arena. I was here to fight, to make my mark, and while the rumor mill churned and speculation whirled, I would not be swayed. But as I began to speak, I couldn't help but steal a glance at Reid, whose unwavering gaze met mine. And in that brief moment, I realized the game we were playing was far more intricate than I had anticipated—a balance of rivalry and something else entirely, a line that could easily be blurred, leaving us both hanging in the balance.

The courtroom buzzed with the weight of anticipation, a tangible energy that crackled through the air like static before a storm. I perched at my desk, a flurry of papers strewn around me, my mind dancing between the complexities of the case at hand and the chaos that Reid had stirred up in my heart. As the judge settled into her seat, the gavel poised to strike, I took a moment to collect my thoughts, steeling myself for what lay ahead. I could feel Reid's presence even before I turned to look, an anchor in the turbulent sea of emotions that threatened to pull me under.

His eyes, sharp and unwavering, met mine across the room, and for an instant, the noise around us faded into a dull hum. The courtroom felt like a theater, each participant playing their part, but it was our private exchange that made my heart race. The light from the ornate windows caught the edges of his jaw, highlighting the determined set of his expression. There was an unspoken challenge in the air, a thread that connected us despite the world swirling around us.

As the proceedings began, I focused on my arguments, my voice steady and clear as I presented my case. The words flowed smoothly, honed by the late nights of preparation and the fire ignited by my determination to win. I glanced at Reid intermittently, catching the slight nod of approval as I hit a particularly compelling point. Each time, it sent an unexpected thrill coursing through me, making it harder to ignore the connection that was blossoming amidst our rivalry.

When it was his turn to speak, I couldn't help but lean forward, captivated. Reid had a way of weaving narratives that brought the facts to life, wrapping them in vivid imagery that demanded attention. He danced around the courtroom, his charisma infectious, and despite the fact that we were opposing counsel, I found myself rooting for him in a way I hadn't anticipated. His passion was palpable, the kind that set off sparks in the air and made my heart flutter against my will.

"Now, if I may interject," he began, a playful glint in his eye that was all too familiar. "My esteemed opponent might be too focused on the minutiae to recognize the bigger picture. It's like arguing whether the cherry on top of a sundae should be red or green while ignoring the fact that the ice cream is melting."

A ripple of laughter spread through the courtroom, and I bit back a smile, well aware of the audience we had cultivated. "And if I may counter," I shot back, leaning into the banter, "a melting sundae is hardly worth discussing unless you're prepared to savor every last drop. Perhaps we should focus on the substance instead of the garnish, Reid."

He raised an eyebrow, clearly impressed. "Touché. But if we're going to dive into the depths of this case, let's not forget the toppings that add flavor."

As he spoke, the tension between us shifted. It was as if the walls we had both erected were starting to crumble, leaving room for something more nuanced to emerge. I could sense the curiosity in his gaze, an invitation for me to explore the depth of our complicated relationship beyond the courtroom's confines. Yet, the stakes of our professional lives loomed large, and with each quip exchanged, I felt a mixture of exhilaration and trepidation.

The trial continued, but it felt less like a battle and more like a collaborative dance, with our words intertwining in a way that blurred the lines of competition. Each point countered, each jest shared, only deepened the connection between us, and I found myself wondering if there was more to this rivalry than mere ambition. A part of me thrilled at the prospect, while another part screamed for caution, warning me of the chaos that could ensue if I allowed myself to care too much.

When the day's proceedings finally drew to a close, I felt an overwhelming sense of exhaustion mingled with exhilaration. Reid approached me as we exited the courtroom, his expression a mix of satisfaction and challenge. "You're a formidable opponent, I'll give you that," he said, a genuine compliment hidden beneath the veneer of our rivalry.

"Likewise," I replied, my heart racing at the proximity of his presence. The air between us was thick with unspoken possibilities, a palpable tension that left me momentarily breathless. "But don't think I'll go easy on you next time."

"Oh, I wouldn't dream of it," he responded, a wicked grin spreading across his face. "I thrive on the challenge. It's what makes this whole thing so exhilarating."

Just then, the phone in my pocket buzzed insistently, breaking the spell that had momentarily enveloped us. I fished it out, glancing at the screen, my heart sinking as I read the message.

We need to talk. Now. —Mark

Mark was my boss, and the tone of his message sent alarm bells ringing in my head. I looked up at Reid, who was watching me with an intensity that made my stomach twist.

"Everything okay?" he asked, concern etched in his features.

"Yeah, I just—" I paused, trying to gather my thoughts. "I need to take care of something. It's... work-related."

Reid's brow furrowed slightly, but he nodded. "Of course. You should handle it."

As I turned to walk away, I felt his gaze on me, a weighty reminder of the tension that had grown between us. I hurried through the bustling courthouse, the walls closing in around me as I replayed Mark's message in my mind. The urgency was unmistakable, but I couldn't shake the feeling that something more was brewing beneath the surface—not just in my work life, but in the tangled web of emotions that had sprung up around Reid and me.

The moment I stepped into Mark's office, the atmosphere shifted dramatically. He leaned back in his chair, arms crossed, a storm brewing behind his eyes. "We need to discuss your performance in the trial today."

"Did I do something wrong?" I asked, a knot forming in my stomach.

Mark waved a hand dismissively. "No, it's not about that. It's about Reid."

The mention of his name sent my heart racing, a flash of unease pooling in my gut. "What about him?"

"He's playing a dangerous game," Mark warned, leaning forward, his expression serious. "And you're caught in the middle of it."

"What do you mean?" My voice was steady, though I felt the panic clawing at my insides.

"He's not just your opponent. There are bigger implications here, and you need to be careful. You have no idea what kind of hold he has on this case—or on you."

I felt the world tilt on its axis, the pieces of the puzzle shifting chaotically in my mind. "What are you saying?"

Just then, the door swung open, and a figure stepped into the office—Reid, his expression a mix of confusion and concern. "I was looking for you—"

The air thickened with unspoken words, tension flaring as Mark's gaze darted between us, a knowing look settling in. And in that instant, everything shifted. What had begun as a playful rivalry was now entangled in a web of suspicion, and as Reid's eyes met mine, I realized I stood at the precipice of something much larger than I had anticipated.

In that charged moment, with the weight of Mark's warning hanging in the air and Reid's presence casting shadows on my thoughts, I was left with one unsettling question: How much of this rivalry was a game, and how much was real?

Chapter 7: A Night of Thunder

The thunderstorm was a tempestuous symphony, a cacophony of nature's fury drumming against the courthouse windows. It roared and raged, filling the cavernous halls with echoes of distant chaos. I leaned against the cool stone, the faint scent of rain-soaked earth creeping in through the cracks, a reminder that I was trapped—no chance of escaping this deluge. My paperwork lay scattered around me, a testament to a day spent buried in the minutiae of legal jargon, but the real chaos was unfolding outside.

I had anticipated a quiet evening, maybe even a drink at my favorite bar to celebrate a small victory in court. Instead, I found myself surrounded by the dull hum of fluorescent lights and the anticipation of what was to come: a restless night spent mulling over the case I was too invested in. I should have been focused, but with each rumble of thunder, my mind wandered to the vast storm brewing not just outside but within me.

And then, as if conjured by the storm itself, he appeared. Reid Stanton, my frequent sparring partner in the courtroom, strode into the entrance hall like a force of nature. His dark hair, tousled by the wind, framed a face that was both infuriating and magnetic. His sharp jawline and stormy gray eyes glinted with mischief as he approached, his demeanor a mix of confidence and warmth. The tension that had simmered between us during our countless legal battles surged to the forefront, transforming the air into a charged current.

"Looks like you're stuck," he said, his voice deep and gravelly, cutting through the storm like a knife.

I hesitated, my instincts urging caution. Reid was nothing if not unpredictable—an enigmatic blend of charm and ruthlessness. "I suppose I am. I don't suppose you're offering to give me a ride?"

"Unless you'd rather wait here for the storm to pass," he replied, a teasing lilt in his tone.

The tempest outside howled in response, rattling the windows as if to emphasize his point. The world beyond was a blur of rain and darkness, threatening to swallow the very air I breathed. With a resigned sigh, I nodded, my resolve crumbling in the face of reality. I followed him out, the gust of wind and rain sweeping over me, and I scrambled into his car, grateful for the brief shelter.

As we pulled away from the courthouse, I couldn't help but notice how his hands gripped the steering wheel, strong and confident. The rhythmic patter of raindrops against the roof created a surreal atmosphere, each beat matching the quickening pace of my heart. I stole glances at him, marveling at the way his brow furrowed slightly in concentration, his lips occasionally curling into a faint smile as he navigated the slick streets.

"I didn't think I'd ever see you outside the courtroom," he said, breaking the silence, his voice low and inviting.

"Well, I don't make a habit of waiting out thunderstorms in legal offices," I shot back, my tone lighter than I intended. The corners of his mouth twitched as he turned to look at me, the fleeting warmth between us palpable.

"Touché," he replied, amusement dancing in his eyes.

With the storm raging outside, we slipped into a comfortable rhythm, our banter punctuated by the occasional rumble of thunder. Reid shared snippets of his life, tales of growing up in a small town, where storms were not just weather phenomena but events that pulled communities together. I found myself captivated, not just by his words but by the passion with which he spoke.

"So, are you always this charming, or is it just the rain?" I teased, trying to deflect the way his stories made me feel—like I was catching glimpses of a hidden side, a part of him I hadn't seen before.

"Oh, it's definitely the rain," he said, laughter breaking the tension. "I think I'll start charging for rides during storms. Everyone loves a little adventure, right?"

The roads wound through the city, and the rain seemed to wash away the barriers we had built over the years, dissolving the formalities of our previous encounters. Each shared story revealed layers, peeling back the facades we wore in court. I found myself leaning closer, drawn to him in ways that made me question everything I had ever thought about my professional boundaries.

As we reached a traffic light, I felt a sudden rush of uncertainty. The glow from the streetlight flickered in the rain, casting a halo around his silhouette. "Reid," I said, my voice trembling slightly. "Do you ever think about how far we've come? From rivals in the courtroom to... this?"

He turned to me, his gaze steady, and for a moment, the world outside faded into the background. "I do. It's funny, isn't it? Life has a way of throwing unexpected curveballs."

Before I could respond, the light turned green, and he pressed the accelerator, propelling us forward into the night. But the words hung between us, a tangible thread of connection pulling tighter with each mile. I couldn't deny that the tension simmering in the car felt electric, charged with an energy that promised more than just a friendly ride home.

As we approached my apartment building, the rain began to relent, the tempest giving way to a gentle patter, like nature itself sighing in relief. Reid parked and turned to me, the intensity in his gaze sparking a fire within me.

"Do you want to come in for a cup of coffee? It seems a shame to end the night like this," I suggested, half hoping he would accept.

"Coffee sounds perfect," he replied, and just like that, my heart raced with anticipation. Little did I know, that night would alter everything I thought I knew about rivalry, camaraderie, and perhaps even the uncharted waters of attraction. The thunder had not yet ceased, but a different kind of storm was brewing between us, one that promised to be even more tumultuous than the weather outside.

The scent of wet asphalt filled the air as I stepped into my dimly lit apartment, trailing behind Reid like a curious shadow. The warmth from the overhead lights created a cozy cocoon, contrasting sharply with the storm still thrumming against the windows. I tossed my damp jacket over the back of a chair, trying to shake off the lingering chill of the downpour, but my thoughts remained entangled in the moment we had just shared.

"Coffee, right?" I said, heading toward the kitchen with a casualness I didn't quite feel. My fingers danced over the cabinet handles, searching for a semblance of normalcy amid the whirlwind of emotions swirling inside me. I could hear Reid's footsteps behind me, the soft patter of his shoes a reminder of his presence—a comforting weight amidst the chaos of the storm outside.

"Please tell me you have something stronger than instant," he quipped, a playful glint in his eyes as he leaned against the counter, arms crossed, exuding an effortless charm.

"I might have a bottle of wine somewhere," I replied, turning to face him with a smirk. "But it depends on whether you want to make a sophisticated impression or just get drunk."

"Why not both?" he shot back, grinning, and I felt my heart race in response. The electricity crackled between us, and I couldn't shake the feeling that we were skirting the edges of something far more profound than the pleasantries of a casual drink.

I dug through the cabinets until I unearthed a half-empty bottle of red, the label faded but the promise intact. "A classic choice," I said, pouring us each a glass, my movements a touch more deliberate than necessary. I offered one to him, our fingers brushing briefly, and the moment sent a jolt of awareness straight through me.

Reid took a sip, his gaze never leaving mine. "This is good," he said, his tone sincere. "Better than expected from a woman who spends all her time at the courthouse."

"Hey now, don't judge my coffee choices," I retorted, holding my glass defensively. "I like to keep things interesting."

"I can see that," he replied, his voice low, inviting. "You've certainly turned my expectations upside down tonight."

We settled onto the couch, the storm still growling outside, a perfect backdrop for what felt like a scene ripped from a romance novel. Reid reclined comfortably, and I tucked my legs beneath me, caught in a balance between our shared history and the unexplored territory ahead. The tension hung like a thick fog, wrapping around us as we exchanged glances that lingered a heartbeat too long.

"Tell me about that case you were working on today," he said, tilting his head slightly, a genuine interest in his eyes. "You seemed passionate in court."

I hesitated, the weight of my work creeping back in. "It's just... complicated. It's about more than just the law; it's about people's lives, their futures. It makes everything feel much heavier."

"Life has a way of doing that, doesn't it?" he mused, taking another sip of wine. "Makes you feel like you're always juggling ten balls at once."

"Exactly! And it's infuriating sometimes," I replied, the wine warming my cheeks and loosening my tongue. "But I guess it's why I love it, too. Every case is a puzzle, a new challenge."

"Is that what you love about it?" he asked, leaning forward, his curiosity igniting the space between us. "The challenge?"

"Partly. But it's also the people," I admitted, my voice softening. "Helping them find justice, a resolution. It's... fulfilling."

He nodded, absorbing my words. "I get that. Sometimes, I think my job is more about managing the chaos than winning cases. You learn a lot about people when you see how they react under pressure."

"Is that your way of saying you're a people person?" I teased, a smirk dancing on my lips.

"Only when it suits me," he replied with a laugh. "But really, there's a certain thrill in watching someone's facade crack, seeing the raw truth beneath it. It's... intoxicating."

His admission sent a shiver through me, the sincerity of his words disarming. There was a hidden depth to Reid that I hadn't expected, layers waiting to be explored. Just then, a particularly loud clap of thunder rattled the windows, making us both jump.

"Okay, I'll admit it—this storm is a little unsettling," I confessed, chuckling nervously.

Reid leaned back, a devilish grin spreading across his face. "Are you scared of a little thunder, Counselor? I thought you were tougher than that."

"Not scared, just... aware. Nature has a way of reminding us of our place, doesn't it?" I shot back, enjoying the playful back-and-forth.

His laughter was rich and warm, filling the room with a sense of ease. "True. But you should also know, the storm is the perfect backdrop for a confession."

"Oh really?" I raised an eyebrow, intrigued. "What kind of confession?"

He shifted, leaning closer, his expression suddenly serious. "The kind that requires a drink in hand. I've spent so much time in this legal battlefield, I forgot how to enjoy myself. How to let go. But tonight, with you, it feels different. I want to know more about you."

The sincerity of his gaze sent butterflies spiraling in my stomach. This was uncharted territory, a delicate dance that could lead us to either disaster or something beautiful. "What is it you want to know?" I asked, my heart pounding as I braced myself for whatever came next.

"Everything," he replied, his voice low and earnest. "But I'll start with this: why do you fight so hard?"

My breath caught in my throat as I realized the implications of his question. It wasn't just about the cases; it was about everything I had built, every battle I had chosen. I paused, contemplating how to articulate the tangled emotions I felt, the years of struggle and determination that fueled my passion.

"Because I believe in what I do," I finally answered, my voice steadier than I felt. "Because when it feels like the world is crashing down, I want to be the one who helps someone rebuild. And maybe—just maybe—I'm fighting for myself, too. To prove that I can make a difference."

Reid's gaze was unwavering, and in that moment, the storm outside faded into the background. What lingered was the promise of something more, a connection that stretched beyond the confines of rivalry and respect. The boundaries we had set in our professional lives began to blur, and I felt the pull of curiosity, of potential—of the unknown that awaited us both.

Just as I opened my mouth to speak again, the lights flickered overhead, plunging the room into a brief darkness, our laughter abruptly swallowed by the thunder's roar. It was a reminder that the storm was far from over, both outside and within this new chapter of our lives. Yet, amidst the uncertainty, I felt an undeniable thrill—a sense that this night might just change everything.

The lights flickered back on, casting a warm glow over the room and breaking the momentary spell that had bound us. Reid leaned back, a smirk playing at the corners of his mouth as he gestured dramatically toward the now-illuminated surroundings. "Well, that was one way to keep the mood alive. What's next? A candlelit dinner?"

I couldn't help but laugh, the tension easing as I swirled the wine in my glass, watching the deep red liquid catch the light. "If only I had a full dining set and a six-course meal prepared. You might have to settle for takeout."

"Takeout and wine? Now that's a combo I can get behind," he said, his eyes sparkling with mischief. "But if we're indulging in that, I demand a side of your most dramatic courtroom stories."

"Ah, so you want the juiciest gossip instead of the culinary experience," I replied, raising an eyebrow. "I can oblige, but I warn you, my tales might be a bit scandalous."

"Perfect. Scandal is my middle name," he joked, leaning in as if he were about to hear the most thrilling secret.

I took a deep breath, gathering my thoughts. "Alright, picture this: it was my first major trial. I was green, fresh out of law school, and I thought I could charm the judge and jury with sheer enthusiasm. Spoiler alert: I couldn't."

Reid laughed, a rich sound that made my stomach flutter. "Go on, I'm all ears."

"I was representing a client accused of fraud. The evidence was stacked against us, but I believed in his innocence. So, during closing arguments, I decided to throw in a personal story to tug at the jury's heartstrings. I stood there, sweat dripping down my back, recounting how my grandmother taught me the value of honesty while trying to hold back my nerves."

"And how did that go?" he asked, clearly entertained.

"Let's just say it didn't have the intended effect. I tripped over my words, and halfway through, the defense attorney snickered loudly, drawing the jury's attention away. I ended up turning a serious moment into a comedic performance. The judge had to stifle his laughter, and I could see the jury's expressions shift from sympathy to pure amusement."

"That sounds like the stuff of legend," he said, shaking his head with an amused grin. "But did you win?"

"Of course not. I lost the case, but I gained something much more valuable: the realization that authenticity matters more than theatrics. From then on, I focused on being genuine, not just entertaining."

He nodded, his expression thoughtful. "You're resilient, I'll give you that. I admire how you turned a disaster into a lesson. It takes guts to put yourself out there like that."

"Thanks," I replied, feeling a warmth creep into my cheeks. "But I can't take all the credit. I've had some pretty great mentors guiding me along the way."

"Your grandmother sounds like a force of nature," he said, raising his glass in a toast. "To strong women and the chaos they inspire."

"To strong women and their reckless grandchildren," I added, clinking my glass against his, a playful spark in our eyes.

As we sipped our wine, the storm outside began to subside, the furious claps of thunder fading into a gentle patter. The atmosphere inside felt different, charged with a shared understanding that was both exciting and terrifying. Reid's gaze lingered on me, and for a moment, the world outside seemed to vanish, leaving just the two of us suspended in this intimate space.

"What about you?" I asked, suddenly curious about the man across from me. "What's your story? What drove you to law?"

Reid took a deep breath, his expression shifting from playful to contemplative. "Honestly? It was my family. My parents went through a messy divorce when I was a kid. I watched as each of them fought tooth and nail for what they thought was right, often without thinking about the consequences for us. It made me realize how easily justice can become a battlefield."

His words hung in the air, heavy with a weight I hadn't anticipated. "That's... tough. I can't imagine how that shaped your perspective."

"It did, in a way. I wanted to be the one who made sense of the chaos, who fought for the people caught in the crossfire." He paused, a shadow passing over his features. "But it also taught me that sometimes, there's more at stake than winning."

"Like what?" I asked, intrigued.

"Like relationships, for one. Winning a case means little if it costs you the people you care about," he said, his gaze unwavering. "And for all my victories, I've lost a few too. Sometimes you have to let things go."

The honesty in his words struck a chord, resonating deep within me. It felt like an unspoken truth we both understood but rarely acknowledged. In that moment, I felt the walls I had built around myself begin to tremble. "And what have you lost, Reid?" I asked, leaning forward, my curiosity piqued.

He hesitated, the humor that usually danced in his eyes dimming slightly. "A friend. A few of them, actually. It's easy to lose yourself in this world, and when you do, you risk losing those who matter most."

The rain had turned into a soft drizzle, casting a muted glow through the windows. I wanted to reach out, to pull him back from whatever memory threatened to drown him. "You're not that person anymore, though. You've evolved," I reassured him, my voice gentle.

"Have I?" He smirked, but there was a hint of vulnerability beneath the surface. "Maybe I've just learned to hide it better."

"Or maybe you're just learning to let someone in," I said softly, and I could see a flicker of recognition cross his face. The air thickened around us, charged with the unspoken, a bridge forming between our separate worlds.

Just then, a loud bang echoed outside, a crash of thunder louder than before, shaking the very foundation of the building. I jumped, my heart racing, and instinctively reached for Reid's hand, gripping it tightly as the storm roared back to life.

"What was that?" I exclaimed, my pulse quickening as the lights flickered ominously again.

Reid's expression shifted, his brow furrowing. "I don't know, but it didn't sound like just thunder."

The tension in the air morphed into something sharper, a sense of foreboding creeping into the edges of my mind. The phone rang, jarring the moment and interrupting the brewing storm of emotions between us. Reid's phone, sitting on the table, vibrated violently, the screen flashing a name that sent a shiver down my spine.

"Who is it?" I asked, curiosity blending with an inexplicable sense of dread.

He hesitated, his fingers hovering over the screen as if he were weighing his options. "It's my brother," he finally admitted, his voice low.

"Should you answer?" I asked, my heart racing for reasons I couldn't quite grasp.

"It's probably just about the case," he said, but there was an edge to his tone, a hint of something unspoken.

Before I could respond, another loud crash reverberated through the night, shaking the walls and sending a tremor through my chest. Reid's gaze shot to the window, worry etched on his features. "Stay here," he instructed, rising to his feet with an urgency that left no room for argument.

"Reid—" I started, but he was already moving toward the door, tension coiling in the air around us.

The rain began to fall harder, the world outside morphing into a shadowy blur as I watched him, a sense of unease knotting in my stomach. Whatever lay beyond that door felt like a revelation, an impending storm that had nothing to do with the weather.

Just then, the phone rang again, and Reid paused, caught between the pull of duty and something deeper. "I have to see what's going on," he said, glancing back at me, uncertainty flickering in his eyes. "But I'll be right back."

As he opened the door, the force of the storm rushed in, mingling with the chaos of our conversation. I felt a chill wash over me—not from the cold, but from the sudden fear of what might happen next. "Reid, wait—"

But the door slammed shut behind him, leaving me alone in the dim light, the echoes of his departure resonating in the silence. Outside, the storm raged on, and I could only hope that whatever awaited him would lead him back to me. The world felt precarious, and with every heartbeat, I sensed the tension mounting, leaving me teetering on the edge of uncertainty, both for him and for what our night had become.

Chapter 8: The Chase Begins

The courtroom buzzed with energy, a charged atmosphere of hushed whispers and sharp glances that rippled through the air like a live wire. I could feel the weight of scrutiny on my shoulders, the curious stares from colleagues and onlookers alike. They didn't know the half of it; I barely did myself. But one thing was clear: standing there, amid the chaos of legal jargon and clinking coffee cups, was Ethan. The man who ignited every flicker of defiance in my heart, and the one I had sworn to forget.

He stood with his arms crossed, a fortress of confidence, radiating an intensity that demanded attention. His crisp navy suit clung perfectly to his frame, making him appear both formidable and unapproachable. Yet it was the way he surveyed the room that captivated me. Those piercing green eyes swept over the crowd, each gaze slicing through the ambient noise with laser precision. In that moment, it felt as though he could see straight through the carefully constructed barriers I'd spent years erecting.

I tried to focus on my case, but my mind wandered like a curious child, tugging at my thoughts until I surrendered to the inevitable pull of his presence. It was maddening, the way he sparked an electrical current in the air around him. I could practically hear the crackle of our unspoken connection amid the drone of legal discourse. Just one look—one fleeting moment of eye contact—and the world outside faded away, replaced by the undeniable truth that we were locked in a game neither of us had chosen.

A sudden thump of a gavel broke the reverie, pulling me back to the present. The judge, a balding man with a penchant for theatrics, called for order. I shifted in my seat, my fingers grazing the cool surface of the table, hoping the wooden veneer could absorb my anxiety. The prosecution was outlining their case, words tumbling out in a monotonous rhythm that threatened to lull me into a stupor.

Yet, my pulse quickened every time I dared glance in Ethan's direction. Each interaction felt like a fresh challenge, as though we were racing against time, the stakes rising higher with each passing moment.

It wasn't until the break that I found myself cornered, trapped in a world of legal briefs and whispered allegations, when Ethan approached me. The air thickened with an unsaid tension, the sort that thrummed with energy, coaxing my heart into a frenetic dance.

"Nice performance back there," he said, his tone deceptively casual. There was a spark of mischief in his eyes, one that suggested he had savored every moment of my struggle to maintain composure.

I raised an eyebrow, feigning indifference. "You mean the part where I nearly lost my case to your theatrics?"

He chuckled, a low sound that reverberated in my chest. "Oh, please. Your counter was impressive. I wouldn't have expected anything less from you."

The compliment hung in the air between us, warm and inviting, yet also unsettling. It was the sort of exchange that could easily tip into something more, a dangerous line we'd both danced around for too long.

"Flattery won't win you any points," I shot back, trying to keep my voice steady despite the way my stomach fluttered.

"Maybe not. But it's fun to watch you squirm." He leaned closer, the scent of his cologne—fresh with a hint of cedar—filling my senses, grounding me in the moment while simultaneously sending me spiraling into distraction. "You know you can't escape this, right?"

"Escape what?" I retorted, though my voice wavered slightly.

"The truth. The chase. Us."

There it was, laid bare in front of us like an unmade bed, each thread of conversation weaving us tighter into an intricate tapestry of tension and unresolved emotions. I had built walls, fortifications to keep the chaos of my life at bay, but he was chipping away at them, piece by tantalizing piece.

"Us?" I echoed, feigning innocence even as a blush crept into my cheeks. "You're delusional if you think this is anything but a professional rivalry."

"Is that what you tell yourself?" His gaze bored into mine, challenging me to delve deeper, to confront the undeniable spark that ignited whenever we were close.

I opened my mouth to respond, but the words escaped me. The truth was tangled and messy, a web of emotions I couldn't afford to untangle. Ethan had a way of drawing me in, and each encounter left me more vulnerable, more intrigued. I could feel the game shifting beneath us, the stakes heightening with every playful jab, every sly smile exchanged across the crowded courtroom.

Suddenly, a loud crash interrupted our moment, drawing our attention to the hallway outside. A commotion erupted, and the door burst open, revealing a group of reporters clamoring for sound bites, cameras flashing like lightning. In the chaos, I felt Ethan's hand brush against mine, a fleeting connection that ignited a warmth in my chest.

"Seems like our moment's been interrupted," he murmured, though his voice held a playful lilt, as if the madness outside was merely an afterthought.

"Or perhaps it's the perfect excuse to retreat," I replied, trying to mask the thrill his touch ignited.

But he held my gaze, a silent challenge lingering in the air between us. The chase was on, an unrelenting pursuit through shadows and secrets, and with every heartbeat, I felt the boundaries of my carefully curated life blur into a horizon filled with uncertainty and reckless desire.

As the courtroom buzzed with renewed energy, I knew one thing for certain: whatever this was between us, it would not be easily ignored. And as I watched him slip away, a sly smile on his lips, I realized that in this dangerous game of chase, I was already in too deep—and I wasn't sure I wanted to escape.

The air in the break room was heavy with the scent of burnt coffee and stale pastries, a far cry from the electric tension of the courtroom just moments before. I leaned against the counter, watching the steam rise from the coffee pot as if it held the answers to questions I had yet to articulate. My heart still raced, not from the caffeine but from the undeniable truth that lingered between Ethan and me. With every stolen glance, every shared moment, we were weaving a story that neither of us had fully embraced but both were unable to escape.

As I poured myself a cup, the chipped mug trembling in my hands, I caught sight of my reflection in the metallic surface of the coffee pot. My hair, usually neatly pinned back, had rebelled into loose tendrils that framed my face, and my cheeks were still flushed from our encounter. I couldn't help but wonder if anyone else could see the chaos inside me, the whirlwind of emotions swirling just beneath the surface.

"Are you going to drink that, or are you planning to take a bath in it?" a familiar voice interrupted, pulling me from my reverie. It was Mia, my colleague and self-appointed confidante, her dark hair pulled into a messy bun that somehow made her look effortlessly chic. She plucked a donut from the box on the table, eyeing me with a mixture of concern and curiosity.

"Just trying to make sense of everything," I replied, attempting to infuse my tone with nonchalance.

"Ah, the classic 'I'm fine' dance," she said, rolling her eyes playfully. "You look like you just stepped out of a rom-com. Hair askew, heart racing—what gives?"

I snorted, but the truth was, Mia was onto something. The disarray of my appearance was the least of my worries. "It's nothing. Just another day in court."

"Sure, if by 'nothing' you mean the tall, brooding attorney you can't stop staring at," she shot back, her eyebrow arched with mischief. "I saw you two during the recess. The tension was thicker than the cream in this coffee."

My cheeks burned hotter than the coffee pot, and I took a hasty sip, hoping it would cool me down. "Ethan is just... frustratingly good at what he does."

"Frustratingly good? You mean devastatingly handsome, infuriatingly charming, and completely unforgettably captivating?" Mia added, a teasing grin spreading across her face. "You're in trouble, my friend. Like, run-for-the-hills kind of trouble."

"Please," I scoffed, though deep down, I could feel the weight of her words. "It's not like that."

"Oh, it absolutely is," she insisted, her eyes sparkling with delight. "You're practically glowing. Just admit it—you're caught up in a whirlwind romance that you don't want to acknowledge."

"Romance? This is a rivalry, and it's professional," I protested, but even I could hear the uncertainty lacing my voice.

"Professional? That's rich." She leaned closer, lowering her voice conspiratorially. "Every time he's in the room, you practically forget how to speak."

"I do not," I replied defensively, though the blush creeping up my neck betrayed me.

Mia laughed, shaking her head. "Okay, fine. Let's call it what it is—delicious, tantalizing, and completely bonkers. Just be careful, alright? This isn't just about you anymore. The stakes are high."

I nodded, grateful for her concern, but the truth was, I wasn't entirely sure I wanted to be careful. The thrill of the chase, the excitement of flirting with danger—it all felt exhilarating in a way

I hadn't anticipated. Just as I was contemplating my next move in this dangerous game, the door swung open, and in walked Ethan, his presence causing the room to shift, the air thickening with an electric charge.

"Still contemplating the meaning of life in the break room?" he asked, a smirk dancing on his lips as he approached the counter.

"Just trying to avoid you," I shot back, not missing a beat, a spark of adrenaline rushing through me.

"Oh, come on," he said, feigning hurt. "You know I'm the highlight of your day."

Mia smirked at me, clearly enjoying the banter unfolding before her eyes. "I'll leave you two to your... meaningful conversation." With a wink, she slipped out, leaving us in a bubble of palpable tension.

"Where's the fire?" I asked, attempting to sound nonchalant as I took a deliberate sip from my coffee.

"Just checking in on my favorite adversary," he replied, leaning against the counter with a casual grace that belied the tension coiling in my stomach. "Didn't want you to forget that the chase is still on."

"Chase? This isn't a race. It's a courtroom, and we both have jobs to do." My attempt at professionalism wavered under his gaze, a flicker of something more brewing beneath the surface.

"True, but it makes for a more interesting narrative, don't you think?" He stepped closer, the space between us shrinking, his voice dropping to a conspiratorial whisper. "You know we can't avoid each other forever. What's your strategy?"

"Strategy?" I echoed, caught off guard. "What do you mean?"

"Your approach to this... rivalry. Are you planning to keep dodging me, or are we going to address this undeniable chemistry between us?"

His words hung in the air, an invitation wrapped in challenge, and I could feel my pulse quicken. It would be so easy to give in, to let the façade drop and embrace the thrill of what lay between us. But the stakes were higher than ever.

"What if I told you that I prefer to keep things professional?" I countered, my voice steadier than I felt.

"Then I'd say you're lying to yourself," he replied smoothly, a confident smile tugging at his lips. "And if you think this is just a game, you're mistaken. I have my eyes set on winning, and I don't play to lose."

I swallowed hard, caught in the storm of emotions swirling between us. The chase had taken a turn, an unexpected twist that made my head spin. I could feel the world around us fading, the bustling office and its myriad distractions disappearing as we stood locked in this moment of possibility.

"I don't know if I want to play your game," I managed to say, though even I could hear the uncertainty in my tone.

"Then let's change the rules," he suggested, his expression shifting from playful to serious. "Let's redefine what this chase means. After all, every chase leads somewhere."

I opened my mouth to retort, but no words came. The room felt impossibly small, the distance between us charged with unspoken possibilities. The chase had begun, but where it would lead was anyone's guess. With every heartbeat, I felt the delicate balance between desire and duty tipping, and for the first time, I wondered if I was brave enough to leap into the unknown.

The tension between us crackled like static in the air, a thrilling pulse that left my heart racing and my breath hitching in my throat. I fought the urge to step closer, to bridge the gap that felt simultaneously exhilarating and terrifying. Instead, I forced myself to feign nonchalance, leaning back against the counter as if I had all the time in the world to play this game.

"Change the rules? Is that your strategy? Because I'm pretty sure we both know how that would end," I said, forcing a smirk that I hoped masked the uncertainty swirling inside me.

"Oh, I think you'd be pleasantly surprised," he replied, tilting his head in that infuriatingly charming way of his. "Imagine if we joined forces instead of opposing each other. We'd be unstoppable."

The thought was ludicrous and enticing all at once. Teaming up with Ethan felt like throwing gasoline on a fire. It would be exhilarating, sure, but also reckless. I could almost see the sparks flying as our combined energies clashed, igniting something wild and unpredictable.

"Join forces? With you?" I laughed lightly, but the sound was laced with apprehension. "I'm not sure whether that sounds like a winning strategy or a recipe for disaster."

"Disaster? You keep using that word," he mused, his expression shifting from playful to something more earnest. "Maybe it's time to redefine what disaster means for you."

I blinked, taken aback by the sincerity in his gaze. He was right, of course. I had spent so long building walls, barricading myself behind a shield of rationality and professionalism. But what had that earned me? Loneliness wrapped in a neat little bow, an empty schedule filled with legal briefs rather than meaningful connections. It was easier to dismiss the connection between us as mere rivalry, a harmless spark.

"Look, I appreciate your enthusiasm, but I'm not looking for a partner—especially not a partner who's my biggest competition," I replied, trying to maintain a façade of strength even as his words began to seep into my consciousness.

"Are you sure?" he challenged, stepping even closer. I could feel the warmth radiating from him, a magnetic pull that blurred the lines of reason. "Because the way I see it, we're not so different. We both want to win."

"Winning isn't everything, you know," I shot back, though the moment the words left my mouth, I wondered if I really believed them.

"Tell that to the judges." He smiled, a glimmer of mischief in his eyes. "But let's be real—if we're talking about winning, it's going to take more than just legal arguments. It'll require teamwork. Chemistry."

With that, he leaned in slightly, and the air thickened around us. Every nerve in my body tingled, urging me to lean into the moment, to give in to the wild, uncharted territory of what we could be. But I resisted, painfully aware of the precarious edge we were teetering on.

Just then, a loud commotion outside the break room interrupted our moment, a cacophony of shouts and rushing footsteps echoing through the hall. My heart leaped in my chest as the door swung open again, revealing a swarm of panicked interns and anxious attorneys spilling into the room.

"Have you heard? There's been a security breach!" one of the interns gasped, her face pale as she caught her breath. "We need to evacuate the building immediately!"

The announcement shattered the tension between Ethan and me, drawing our attention to the urgency in the air. My instincts kicked in; I couldn't afford to panic. "What do you mean a security breach? Is everyone okay?"

"Apparently, someone set off an alarm in the basement," another colleague chimed in, his brow furrowed with concern. "They said it might be a false alarm, but we can't take any chances."

Ethan and I exchanged a charged look, the unspoken words lingering between us. The moment we'd shared was abruptly overshadowed by the chaos erupting around us, yet I felt a flicker of adrenaline surging through my veins. Maybe this was a blessing in disguise—a distraction from the emotional whirlwind I had been battling.

DUAL FLAME

"Let's move," Ethan said, his tone shifting to that of a leader, the spark of determination igniting in his eyes. "We need to regroup outside."

I nodded, adrenaline racing as we followed the throng of people making their way toward the exit. The hallways were alive with urgency, a frantic energy buzzing like electricity. As we reached the staircase, I caught sight of Ethan, his jaw set with resolve. The chaos around us seemed to fade, and suddenly it was just the two of us, pushing through the throng toward the door.

"Just so you know, if we make it out of this, I'm going to hold you to that promise of teamwork," he said, his voice steady as we ascended the stairs.

"I'm not sure that's a promise I'm willing to make," I replied, but the way my heart raced told a different story.

We burst through the door into the blinding sunlight, the fresh air filling my lungs as I shielded my eyes against the brightness. Outside, the scene was both hectic and surreal. A crowd had gathered, everyone trying to piece together what was happening, their faces a mosaic of confusion and fear. Emergency vehicles blared in the distance, their sirens piercing the air, creating a backdrop of chaos that felt disorienting.

"What do you think happened?" I asked, glancing at Ethan, who was scanning the crowd, his focus sharp and intense.

"Not sure yet, but we can't just stand here," he replied, determination etched across his features. "Let's find out what we're dealing with."

As we moved deeper into the throng, I could feel the tension coiling in the pit of my stomach. Whatever had set this chaos in motion was no mere false alarm; there was an undercurrent of something more serious lurking beneath the surface.

Just then, a sharp voice cut through the confusion, drawing our attention. "Everyone needs to stay calm! We'll have more information shortly!" A security officer shouted, his tone firm yet reassuring, though his eyes darted nervously.

Suddenly, a loud bang echoed from inside the building, sending a ripple of panic through the crowd. People screamed, scattering in all directions, and I instinctively grabbed Ethan's arm, the heat of his skin grounding me in the chaos.

"Stay close," he urged, his grip firm around my wrist, but his eyes were scanning the area, looking for any signs of danger.

And then I saw it—through the chaos, a shadow darted past the entrance of the building. My heart raced as I locked eyes with Ethan, an unspoken understanding passing between us. Whatever was happening, we couldn't let fear dictate our actions.

"Let's check it out," I said, feeling a rush of adrenaline course through me. There was no turning back now; the chase had taken on a life of its own.

As we moved toward the entrance, the shadows deepened, and I felt the unmistakable thrill of uncertainty mingle with the fear in the air. We were stepping into uncharted territory, where danger lurked just beyond the doorway, and I had no idea what awaited us.

But one thing was clear: the chase was far from over. And whatever awaited us on the other side would change everything.

Chapter 9: Beneath the Surface

The morning light filtered through the blinds of my office, casting thin stripes across the cluttered desk, a chaotic landscape of case files and half-empty coffee cups. I was knee-deep in paperwork, but my thoughts were a jumbled mess, spiraling back to Reid. His voice, laced with vulnerability and guarded edges, replayed in my mind like a haunting melody. He had offered glimpses into his world, pieces of a puzzle that felt infinitely incomplete, a labyrinth of emotions I had no compass to navigate.

As I flipped through the pages of the case files, the familiar scent of ink and paper mingled with the faint aroma of the jasmine plant I kept in the corner—a meager attempt to bring life into my otherwise sterile environment. The plant, a survivor against all odds, thrived in that space, reminding me that beauty could exist even in the confines of my unyielding work. But today, my senses felt heightened, the air thick with unspoken tension. I was itching to peel back layers, to explore the secrets buried within the minds of my clients, especially those like Reid, who wore their masks with such precision.

With a sharp intake of breath, I picked up the next file, its contents slipping from the usual mundane matters to something more tantalizing. A divorce case, complete with a heavily redacted background. The name—Katherine Devereaux—echoed in my head, rich with potential stories waiting to be unraveled. My fingers danced over the pages, absorbing the details that felt painstakingly curated. Katherine was not just any client; she had connections that radiated influence, her past obscured like the mysterious mist that often blanketed the city in early morning hours.

The clock ticked on the wall, its steady rhythm a reminder that time was slipping through my fingers like sand. I grabbed my phone, the smooth glass surface cold against my skin. The temptation to call Reid surged within me. I wanted to ask about Katherine, to prod him about his past connections, but a thread of hesitation tugged at my resolve. What if this was the rabbit hole I had been warned against? What if digging deeper only led to trouble, to layers of regret that could choke me in their grasp?

Still, the allure of the unknown was a siren song I couldn't ignore. I scrolled through my contacts, my thumb hovering over Reid's name. The brief connection we'd shared felt electric, the sparks still fizzing in the air between us. I could almost hear his laughter, a low rumble that settled warmth deep in my chest. And just like that, I felt myself surrendering to the pull. I pressed the call button, my heart racing as the phone rang.

When his voice finally broke through, smooth and deep, a sense of urgency bubbled to the surface. "Hey, is everything okay?" he asked, a hint of concern threading through his tone.

"More or less," I replied, trying to sound casual while my pulse quickened. "I was just reviewing some case files, and I stumbled across Katherine Devereaux's—"

"Katherine?" His interruption was immediate, his tone sharpening. "Why are you looking into her?"

"Curiosity, I suppose," I said, adopting a lightness I didn't quite feel. "She's not your typical divorcee, and her file is... intriguing."

A brief silence followed, and I could almost envision him running a hand through his hair, a telltale sign of his growing unease. "Intriguing how?"

"There are a lot of redactions," I explained, determined to tread carefully. "It feels like there's a story buried beneath the surface. And knowing you, I figured you might have some insights."

He sighed, the sound weighted with a blend of frustration and something else I couldn't quite place. "Look, her case is complicated. It's better if you don't get involved."

"Better for whom?" I challenged, heat rising to my cheeks. "I'm not some bystander here. My job is to uncover the truth, and something tells me there's more to Katherine's story. What aren't you telling me?"

"Some truths are better left undiscovered," he replied, his voice flat, but I could sense the tension coiling beneath his calm exterior.

"You're not just talking about her case, are you?" I pressed, feeling the thrill of the chase igniting within me. "You're speaking from experience, Reid. What happened with you and Katherine?"

A beat passed, silence stretching like a taut wire between us. "This isn't about me," he said finally, but the words felt hollow. I could hear the unspoken layers, the things he had yet to share, and I was determined to peel them back like the layers of an onion, each one revealing a little more of the truth.

"Reid," I coaxed, my tone softening. "I know there's more beneath the surface. You don't have to hide from me."

The silence grew thick, wrapping around us like a heavy fog. I held my breath, waiting, willing him to share even a sliver of his reality, hoping that perhaps this time, he would take the leap.

"You don't understand," he finally said, a hint of vulnerability creeping into his voice. "Katherine's life is more intertwined with mine than you know. It's messy, and it can't end well for anyone involved."

"Messy often leads to clarity," I shot back, feeling bold. "What if this is your chance to face whatever you've been running from?"

"Some things are better left buried, Ava," he warned, his voice low, heavy with foreboding.

I wanted to argue, to break through the barriers he had carefully erected around his heart, but I could sense the storm brewing within him. The tension danced in the air, a palpable force that had the potential to unravel us both. So I took a step back, willing myself to breathe, to let the silence settle as I processed the layers of what we were both trying to protect.

The morning sun settled into its rightful place, casting a warm glow across my office as I tried to ignore the prickling sensation of unease that had wrapped itself around my chest like a python. My phone lay silent, mocking my impatience. Reid's last words echoed in my mind, weaving an intricate tapestry of curiosity and concern. He had always been an enigma, but this case felt like a tempest brewing just beneath the surface, each unturned stone potentially leading to deeper currents that could drag us both under.

I returned to the file on Katherine Devereaux, my fingers tracing the edges of the pages as if they held the key to unraveling the puzzle. There was something alluring about her story, one that seemed to swirl in shadows. The pages were barely touched, indicating either a lack of interest from previous counsel or an acute awareness of what might happen if her past came to light. I could almost hear the whispers of office gossip surrounding her, like a cloud of smoke—at once intoxicating and suffocating.

Suddenly, my thoughts were interrupted by a knock on the door. I looked up to find Sarah, my assistant, peeking in with her trademarked blend of enthusiasm and anxiety. "Ava, you have a visitor," she said, her eyes wide as if she were announcing a royal arrival.

"Who?" I asked, momentarily distracted from the tangled web of my thoughts.

"It's Reid. He said he needed to talk to you about Katherine."

A jolt of surprise shot through me, quickly followed by a flutter of excitement. I motioned for her to let him in, a wave of anticipation washing over me. The moment he stepped through the door, the atmosphere shifted, charged with unspoken energy. Reid looked as handsome as ever, his tailored suit accentuating the angles of his face, but today there was a gravity in his expression that I had never seen before.

"Ava," he greeted, his voice smooth but layered with tension. "Can we talk?"

"Of course," I replied, gesturing toward the chair opposite my desk. "You can start by telling me why you were so tight-lipped about Katherine."

He sat, his posture rigid as he ran a hand through his hair, the familiar gesture pulling at my heartstrings. "It's not that simple. Katherine isn't just a case; she's... complicated."

"Complicated how?" I asked, leaning forward, eager to pry open the door he had cracked ajar. "Did you date her? Were you involved?"

His gaze flickered, a flash of something that looked like regret mixed with surprise. "I knew her—briefly. But it's not just our past that complicates things. There's a lot more at stake."

"What do you mean?"

He took a deep breath, his eyes searching mine as if he were weighing the consequences of his next words. "Katherine's divorce isn't just a personal matter; it involves a lot of money and influence. Her husband has connections that run deep, and if she's hiding something, it could get ugly."

"Are you saying she's dangerous?" I asked, incredulity lacing my tone.

"No," he replied, shaking his head. "But the people surrounding her are. I don't want you to get dragged into this mess, Ava. You deserve better."

The unexpected concern wrapped around me like a warm blanket, but it also irked me. "I appreciate your concern, Reid, but I can handle myself. And besides, we both know I'm already knee-deep in this."

"Exactly. And that's what worries me." He leaned in closer, his voice dropping to a conspiratorial whisper. "There are things she's not telling you. Secrets that could unravel everything."

"Then help me uncover them," I urged, frustration seeping into my voice. "You've got insights I don't. You can't just drop breadcrumbs and expect me to walk away."

He sighed, running his hands over his face, and for a fleeting moment, I glimpsed the vulnerability hidden beneath his confident exterior. "Ava, you don't know what you're asking for. Some truths can hurt people. It might not just be Katherine who gets hurt—it could be you, too."

The weight of his words settled heavily between us, a chasm of unsaid fears and untapped potential. My pulse quickened at the prospect of delving deeper, but the reality of his warnings pressed against my ribs like a steel band. "So, what's your plan? To let her navigate this alone? She deserves someone fighting for her."

Reid's eyes hardened, and I could see him struggling against the tide of my determination. "You really think you can save her? What if saving her means putting yourself in danger? You could lose everything."

"Maybe I already have," I shot back, my frustration boiling over. "Maybe I'm tired of sitting on the sidelines, watching lives unravel because no one is brave enough to stand up."

He opened his mouth to argue but paused, his expression shifting as he considered my words. "You're stubborn," he finally said, a faint smile breaking through the tension.

"And you're infuriating," I retorted, unable to suppress a laugh. "But we're not getting anywhere with this back-and-forth. So let's put our stubbornness to good use."

Reid leaned back in his chair, a reluctant acceptance softening his features. "Okay, but I need you to promise me something."

"What's that?"

"Promise me that you won't do anything reckless. If we dig deeper into Katherine's life, it's going to get messy, and I won't let you take unnecessary risks."

His earnestness was disarming, yet I couldn't help but feel the thrill of defiance bubbling within me. "Deal. But we do this together."

He nodded slowly, the gravity of our unspoken alliance settling in the space between us. Just then, a sudden buzz interrupted the moment—a text notification chimed from my phone, cutting through the tension like a knife. I glanced at the screen and felt my heart drop.

It was a message from Katherine, and the words sent a chill down my spine: I need to talk. It's urgent. Meet me at the café on Fifth in thirty minutes.

Reid's gaze snapped to mine, and the urgency of the situation hit us both like a wave. "We need to go," he said, rising to his feet.

"Now?" I asked, my mind racing.

"Yes. Now."

The thrill of the chase ignited my spirit, but as I grabbed my bag and headed for the door, a single thought anchored itself in my mind. Beneath the surface of every life lay hidden currents, and the deeper we swam, the more perilous the journey would become. But I had no intention of turning back now.

The café was a whirlwind of energy, its cozy interior filled with the clatter of cups and the soft hum of conversation. As I stepped inside, the rich aroma of freshly ground coffee mingled with the sweet scent of pastries, creating an almost intoxicating ambiance that wrapped around me like a warm embrace. I scanned the room, my heart thudding with a mix of excitement and trepidation. Reid followed closely behind, his presence a steady anchor in the chaotic sea of patrons.

Katherine sat in the far corner, her back straight and poised, but I could sense an undercurrent of anxiety emanating from her. She glanced up, her expression shifting as she spotted us, a flicker of relief mingling with something darker in her eyes. I felt a twinge of empathy, recognizing the weight of her situation. After all, we were about to dive into the depths of her troubled life.

Reid's posture became even more guarded as we approached, his instincts on high alert. "Stay close," he murmured, his voice low but laced with urgency. I nodded, absorbing the tension that hung between us, like the thick humidity before a storm.

"Thank you for coming," Katherine said, her voice steady despite the storm brewing behind her blue eyes. "I'm glad you both could make it."

"What's going on?" I asked, taking the seat opposite her, while Reid lingered beside me, a protective presence. "You said it was urgent."

She hesitated, glancing around the café as if gauging who might be eavesdropping on our conversation. "I've received some... threats," she finally confessed, her voice barely above a whisper. "I thought it was just a prank at first, but it's escalated."

A chill ran down my spine. "Threats? From whom?" I leaned in closer, my instincts kicking into overdrive. Reid remained silent, but I could feel his tension radiating next to me.

"From my soon-to-be ex-husband," Katherine replied, her gaze flickering to the window as though expecting him to appear at any moment. "He's not the type to let go easily. And the more I push for the divorce, the more aggressive he becomes."

"Have you reported this?" Reid asked, his tone even but edged with concern.

Katherine shook her head, her lips pressed tightly together. "I can't. Not yet. I don't want to give him any more power over me than he already has. If I go to the police, it'll become a public spectacle, and I can't afford that."

"Then what do you need from us?" I pressed, feeling the urgency in the air thickening like smoke.

"I need you to help me find out what he's hiding," she said, her eyes locking onto mine with a fierce intensity. "There are things in our marriage that he doesn't want anyone to know, and if I can get my hands on them, I can turn the tables."

"What kind of things?" Reid asked, his interest piqued.

"Financial discrepancies," she explained, her voice steadying. "I suspect he's been involved in some shady dealings. If I can prove that, it could shift the entire power dynamic."

"Why haven't you looked into it yourself?" I asked, curiosity mingling with concern.

"Because he has eyes everywhere. I can't risk him knowing that I'm onto him," she replied, biting her lip. "That's where you two come in. I need a discrete investigation."

Reid exchanged a glance with me, the weight of the situation pressing heavily on us. "This isn't going to be simple," he warned. "If he's involved in anything illegal, it could get dangerous."

"I understand," Katherine said, her voice firm. "But I'm running out of options. I need to take control of my life again."

The air hummed with tension as I weighed her words. I could see the determination in her eyes, the way she fought against the current threatening to pull her under. "Okay, we'll help you," I said finally, feeling a swell of resolve. "But we need to do this carefully. No reckless moves."

"Thank you," she breathed, relief flooding her features. "I don't know what I would do without you."

As we settled into a discussion about logistics, I felt a sense of purpose solidifying within me. Each word exchanged felt like a stepping stone, paving the way toward unearthing the truths that lay hidden. But beneath that resolve, a nagging worry lurked at the edges of my mind. Was I delving into something I wasn't prepared for? Was Reid right to be concerned?

Just as I was about to voice my thoughts, the door to the café swung open, and a gust of wind swept through, momentarily silencing our conversation. My gaze flicked toward the entrance, and I felt the blood drain from my face. A tall figure entered, his posture exuding a predatory confidence that made my stomach drop. It was Katherine's husband, Mark.

"Is that him?" I whispered, barely able to catch my breath.

Katherine's face paled as she glanced over her shoulder. "I—I didn't expect him to show up here."

Reid's body tensed beside me, his protective instincts kicking in. "Stay calm," he murmured, his eyes narrowing as he assessed the situation.

Mark strolled toward our table, a charming smile plastered on his face that felt more like a threat than an invitation. "Katherine," he said, his voice smooth but dripping with condescension. "Fancy seeing you here."

"What are you doing here, Mark?" she asked, her tone edged with defiance, but I could sense her apprehension.

"Just out for a coffee," he replied, his gaze flicking between the three of us. "You didn't think you could hide from me, did you? I'm always watching."

The air thickened with tension, every moment stretching out like an eternity. I felt Reid's body shift closer to mine, a silent promise that he would protect me. "We were just leaving," I said, forcing my voice to remain steady, but the unease churned in my stomach.

"Oh, no need to rush off," Mark said, his smile widening as he leaned against the table, his eyes darkening. "I wouldn't want to interrupt your little chat. After all, secrets have a way of coming to light."

Katherine's breath hitched, and I felt the gravity of the situation close in around us. There was something dangerously poised in Mark's demeanor, a sense that he had the upper hand.

Before I could react, he leaned in closer, his voice dropping to a whisper meant only for Katherine. "You think you can just walk away from me? You have no idea what I'm capable of."

The intensity of his words hung in the air, electric and charged with a threat that sent a shiver down my spine. I glanced at Reid, who was watching the scene unfold with a grim determination. My heart raced, the stakes suddenly higher than I'd anticipated.

And just as the tension reached its peak, my phone buzzed again, the screen lighting up with a message that sent my world crashing down. We need to talk. Now. It's about Katherine.

The message was from an unknown number, but the implications were clear. Something was about to change, and the undercurrents swirling beneath the surface were more turbulent than I had ever imagined. The world around me faded into a blur as the weight of the moment settled in, and I realized with a sinking dread that we were all in deeper than we had bargained for.

Chapter 10: Dark Corners

The dim lights flickered above me, casting elongated shadows that danced along the cold, tiled floor of the courthouse. Each step echoed like a heartbeat in the stifling silence, the air thick with an electric anticipation. My heart raced, fueled by equal parts fear and curiosity. I had promised myself I wouldn't let Reid's enigmatic presence worm its way into my thoughts, yet here I was, chasing ghosts down these deserted hallways. The soft hum of fluorescent bulbs was the only accompaniment to my silent quest, as I instinctively drew closer to the source of the footsteps, my senses heightened.

Reid's silhouette emerged from the darkness, tall and imposing, his posture radiating a confidence that both intrigued and unnerved me. The sharp lines of his jaw were accentuated in the muted light, and there was something about the way he held himself—like a predator sizing up his prey—that made the hair on the back of my neck stand on end. His eyes, those deep pools of mystery, locked onto mine, and in that moment, I was both mesmerized and terrified, trapped in a gaze that felt like a collision of worlds.

"What are you doing here?" he asked, his voice low and gravelly, echoing softly in the silence. There was no warmth in his tone, only a challenge, as if I had trespassed into a realm I had no right to enter.

"I could ask you the same thing," I shot back, my bravado surprising even myself. I had expected his presence to send me running, yet there I stood, unwilling to back down. "It's late, Reid. Shouldn't you be filing your secret documents or whatever it is you do in the dark?"

His lips twitched at the corners, a flicker of amusement crossing his face before it vanished behind a carefully constructed mask of indifference. "And what makes you think I have secrets worth hiding?"

The question hung in the air, charged with an unspoken tension. I took a step closer, emboldened by the faintest glimmer of something more than just rivalry between us. "Because you're here, in the dark, when no one else is. People who have nothing to hide don't sneak around like this."

A moment of silence stretched between us, heavy with the weight of unsaid words and unasked questions. Reid's gaze shifted, the intensity softening for just a heartbeat, revealing a flicker of something deeper—regret, perhaps, or longing. But just as quickly, it vanished, replaced by a hard edge that reminded me of the walls he had built around himself.

"I could say the same about you," he replied, his voice taking on a sharper edge. "You shouldn't be here either. This isn't a playground for the curious."

"I didn't realize curiosity was a crime," I replied, crossing my arms defiantly. The air between us crackled, charged with a mix of frustration and a palpable tension that made the very air seem thick. "If anything, it's a virtue in this line of work. Or do you not like being challenged, Mr. Reid?"

He stepped closer, closing the distance, his breath warm against my skin. "Challenge can be dangerous, especially when you're poking around in the dark. You never know what you might uncover."

A shiver ran down my spine at the implication. What exactly was he hiding? The thought sent my mind spiraling, conjuring up all sorts of scenarios that could explain his clandestine behavior. The secrets buried beneath the polished veneer of the courthouse were like landmines waiting for someone to stumble across them.

Before I could respond, a sudden noise broke the fragile moment—a door creaked open down the hall, and the sound of voices floated through the air. My heart raced, instincts kicking in as I glanced over my shoulder.

"We should go," I urged, the adrenaline pumping through my veins, urging me to flee.

Reid's expression shifted, a flicker of something—concern?—flashing in his eyes. "You're right. Let's not get caught." He stepped back, his demeanor suddenly all business, the previous tension dissipating like smoke in the wind.

We moved in tandem, slipping down the corridor, our footsteps quiet as we navigated the maze of hallways. I could feel Reid's presence beside me, both a comfort and a reminder of the chasm that lay between us—a chasm filled with unspoken words and unresolved tension.

As we reached the end of the hallway, the voices grew louder, spilling into the corridor like a torrent. I glanced up at Reid, our eyes locking for a brief moment, a silent understanding passing between us. Whatever secrets he carried were not meant for the light, not yet.

We ducked into a shadowed alcove, pressing ourselves against the cool stone wall as footsteps approached. My heart thundered in my chest, the thrill of the chase mingling with a growing sense of danger. Reid's shoulder brushed against mine, and I could feel the warmth radiating from him, a stark contrast to the chill in the air.

The voices drew closer, hushed but urgent, fragments of conversation piercing the silence. "...didn't see him at the meeting... the files are missing... we can't let this get out."

I exchanged a glance with Reid, confusion swirling in my mind. Missing files? A meeting? The pieces felt like they were teetering on the edge of a much larger puzzle, and suddenly, I was standing at the precipice of something far more dangerous than I had anticipated.

"Do you know what they're talking about?" I whispered, my voice barely audible.

He shook his head, his expression darkening. "Whatever it is, it's not good. We need to get out of here."

In that moment, the gravity of our situation pressed down on me like a weight I couldn't shake. I had stumbled into something far bigger than I had ever imagined, and as Reid led the way back through the shadows, I couldn't help but wonder what other secrets lay waiting in the dark corners of the world we inhabited.

The footsteps drew closer, each sound reverberating in the quiet, and for a split second, I considered retreating back into the sanctuary of familiarity. But something in me, that wild part fueled by a heady mix of intrigue and defiance, refused to let me back down. I squared my shoulders, preparing for the confrontation that seemed inevitable. As the shadow materialized, I recognized Reid—not just the man I had been circling like a moth around a flame, but a puzzle waiting to be solved.

"What exactly are you hoping to find?" he asked, an amused smirk curling his lips, lighting up his otherwise stern expression. The playfulness of his tone contrasted sharply with the tension of the moment, and I felt a mix of irritation and excitement.

"Maybe I'm just here to uncover your secrets," I shot back, leaning into the challenge. "Or maybe I'm the one with secrets worth hiding." I realized the words tumbled out more confidently than I intended.

"Secrets?" He leaned in closer, his voice dropping to a conspiratorial whisper that sent shivers up my spine. "In this place, everyone has secrets. Some just guard them better than others." His gaze, piercing and unwavering, searched mine, as if trying to determine if I was a friend or foe in this twisted game we were playing.

"Seems like the only thing hiding in the dark here is you," I retorted, my heart racing. "What do you think you're doing, lurking around the courthouse like a villain in a cheap novel?"

He chuckled, a sound both rich and unexpected. "And you're the heroine charging into the fray without a plan. You do know that might not end well for you, right?" There was an edge of sincerity in his words, a hint of concern cloaked beneath the playful banter.

I scoffed lightly, the tension easing just a fraction. "I thrive on danger. It's what keeps things interesting. You might want to try it sometime."

"Maybe I'm just not ready to jump into the deep end with a mystery wrapped in a riddle," he replied, his expression suddenly serious. "You have no idea what's at stake here."

I felt the weight of his words settle around us like a thick fog, momentarily displacing the bravado that had driven me to seek him out in the first place. "Try me," I challenged, refusing to let the fear creep in. "I'm here. Clearly, I'm not the one afraid of what lurks in the shadows."

For a heartbeat, he hesitated, and I could see the internal battle playing out behind his carefully curated mask. "You really don't want to know. There are some corners of this place that are better left unexplored."

"Or maybe some corners just need a light shined on them." I crossed my arms defiantly, feeling bolder by the second. "Besides, you can't keep me out forever. You may want to try, but I have a knack for digging up the truth."

"Digging up the truth can sometimes lead to more than you bargained for," he warned, stepping back slightly, his demeanor shifting from playful to ominous. "You need to trust me on this. The truth is messy, and once you start unraveling it, it's hard to put back together."

"Is that why you're avoiding it?" I shot back, my irritation flaring again. "Because it's messy? You can't just bury your head in the sand and pretend everything is fine."

Reid's eyes narrowed, the playful spark extinguished. "It's not that simple, and you know it. Some things can't be fixed. Not without collateral damage."

The sharpness in his voice cut through me. A chilling realization washed over me: this was more than just a battle of wits. This was a warning cloaked in concern, and the stakes were much higher than I'd anticipated.

"Are you saying I'm collateral damage?" I asked, incredulity creeping into my tone.

"Not just you. Anyone who gets too close."

My breath caught as the weight of his words settled around us. The air felt thick with unsaid truths, and for a moment, I could almost see the tension coiling like a spring between us, ready to snap. The shadows loomed large, casting uncertainty in every direction.

"I'm not afraid of a little danger, Reid," I said, though my voice wavered slightly. "I can handle it."

He took a step closer again, the distance between us shrinking, charged with an unnameable energy. "You think you can handle it, but you have no idea what you're inviting in. The darkness can be seductive. It can wrap around you until you can't find your way back."

"You keep talking about darkness like it's some kind of monster," I said, my voice barely above a whisper. "What are you really afraid of?"

His gaze softened momentarily, vulnerability flickering beneath the bravado. "I'm afraid of losing people I care about," he confessed, the honesty of his admission hanging heavy between us. "And I'm afraid you might end up one of them."

The gravity of his words sunk into my chest like a stone. Here was Reid, the enigmatic figure who had been nothing but an obstacle, revealing a glimpse of his humanity. I felt a rush of empathy, a warmth blooming in the chilly corridor. "Then let me in," I urged, stepping forward, the urge to close the gap between us almost overwhelming. "You don't have to carry this alone."

For a moment, he seemed to weigh my words, the conflict evident on his face. Just as I thought he might relent, the moment shattered like glass as another set of footsteps echoed through the hall, jolting us back into reality.

"Reid!" a voice called out, harsh and authoritative, slicing through the tension. My heart raced as I recognized the speaker—Detective Mason, the last person I wanted to see in this moment.

"Let's move," Reid commanded, grabbing my wrist with an urgency that sent my pulse racing. He tugged me into a nearby storage room, the darkness enveloping us as the door clicked shut behind us, leaving us cloistered in shadows.

The air inside was thick with the scent of old paper and dust, the remnants of forgotten cases lingering like specters. My heart thudded loudly in my ears as I pressed against the wall, adrenaline coursing through my veins. Reid stood close beside me, his body tense, the unspoken connection between us pulsing like a live wire.

"What are we doing?" I whispered, barely able to contain the rush of emotions swirling inside me.

"Waiting," he replied, his voice low, barely audible over the thumping of my heart. "And hoping we're not discovered."

As the footsteps outside faded, I felt a sense of urgency settle in the pit of my stomach. We were playing a dangerous game, and with each heartbeat, the stakes only seemed to grow. The world outside continued to spin, unaware of the secrets lurking just beyond the doors, and somehow, I found myself caught in the crosshairs of Reid's hidden battles and my own burgeoning curiosity.

The small storage room felt like a universe contained within four unyielding walls, cloaked in darkness and uncertainty. My heart raced as I pressed myself against the cool concrete, feeling the tension pulse between Reid and me like a living thing. The muffled sounds of the bustling courthouse outside faded into a distant hum, replaced by the electric charge in the air around us.

"What now?" I whispered, my voice barely breaking the silence, laced with the urgency of our precarious situation. The shadows seemed to swallow my words, yet Reid remained steadfast, his eyes flicking to the door as if willing it to remain closed.

"Just... wait," he murmured, his voice low and steady. It was both a command and a reassurance, yet the unyielding cadence suggested that waiting was not a luxury we could afford for long. I could see the tension in his jaw, the way his hands clenched into fists by his sides.

"What are we waiting for?" I pressed, curiosity mingling with impatience. "Is it your conscience, or are we waiting for Detective Mason to decide we're hiding in here?"

"Neither," he replied, a faint smirk breaking through the seriousness, albeit briefly. "Though I admit, my conscience is a bit crowded these days."

I couldn't help but roll my eyes. "A crowded conscience? Is that what you call a moral dilemma? Because from where I'm standing, it looks more like a moral quagmire."

Reid chuckled softly, his tension easing ever so slightly. "You know, it's refreshing to meet someone who can throw words around like they're confetti."

I raised an eyebrow, pushing against the urge to smile. "Confetti? You make it sound festive."

"Nothing about this situation is festive," he said, his tone dropping again as he leaned closer, his breath brushing against my ear. "And yet here we are, hiding from the very people who could expose the truth."

The proximity sent a flutter through me, something dangerously akin to thrill. I should have felt trapped, claustrophobic, yet there was something intoxicating about our predicament—the blend of fear, adrenaline, and the tantalizing hint of his presence.

Just as the moment stretched and expanded, the sound of footsteps approached again, stopping abruptly outside the door. My breath caught in my throat as I exchanged a wide-eyed glance with Reid. "What now?" I whispered urgently, my mind racing.

"Be quiet," he hissed, his expression serious again.

I bit my lip, struggling to still my racing heart, but the sense of impending danger heightened my awareness. The footsteps shifted, a low murmur of conversation seeping through the door.

"—had to have gone this way," a familiar voice broke through the silence. It was Detective Mason. "Check the storage rooms."

"Great," I muttered under my breath, a wave of panic sweeping through me. "We're trapped like mice in a cheese factory."

Reid's expression darkened, the playful banter slipping away, replaced by a resolute determination. "We can't let them find us. If they do, we'll never uncover the truth."

"What truth?" I pressed, suddenly realizing that the stakes had grown higher than I'd anticipated. "What exactly are we up against, Reid?"

He hesitated, clearly weighing the consequences of revealing more. "If they discover what we've been investigating, it could implicate more people than just us. It's bigger than the courtroom shenanigans we see every day."

"So what? You're just going to keep me in the dark?" I challenged, the frustration bubbling to the surface. "I can't help if I don't know what I'm helping with."

"Trust me, you don't want to get involved in this," he insisted, his eyes flashing with intensity. "You have no idea how deep this goes."

"Then enlighten me, Reid!" I shot back, feeling both helpless and indignant. "Because right now, I feel like I'm playing a game with no rules and no idea of the consequences."

His gaze softened for just a moment, the vulnerability in his eyes nearly disarming. "I care about you, okay? I don't want you dragged into something that could endanger your life. The people we're dealing with don't play fair."

Before I could respond, the door rattled as Detective Mason's voice rang out again, sharp and commanding. "I know you're in there, Reid. Come out with your hands up!"

Panic surged through me, and Reid's expression hardened into focus. "We have to move."

"Move where? They'll catch us!" I whispered, desperation creeping into my voice.

He took a breath, as if preparing for a leap into the unknown. "Through the back door. I know a way out."

Without waiting for my response, he grabbed my hand, the warmth of his grip anchoring me as he pulled me toward the rear of the storage room. My heart pounded in rhythm with our hurried steps, an exhilarating mix of fear and determination flooding my veins.

"Okay, lead the way," I said, my voice steadier than I felt.

We ducked behind a shelf piled high with dusty legal files, the faint scent of mildew clinging to the air as Reid maneuvered to the back wall. My pulse quickened as I pressed against him, acutely aware of the proximity, of the heat radiating off his body as he fished for a hidden latch.

"I just need a second," he murmured, his voice a low murmur against the backdrop of the encroaching footsteps. "If I can just find the—ah!"

A soft click echoed in the silence, and my breath caught as he pulled a hidden door open, revealing a narrow passageway that seemed to stretch into the shadows.

"After you," Reid said, a teasing lilt in his voice, but the urgency belied the jest.

I hesitated for just a moment, the darkness ahead feeling ominous and foreboding. "You first," I shot back, feigning bravery while my insides churned with uncertainty.

"Fine," he sighed, stepping into the unknown, and I followed closely, the door closing behind us with a soft thud that seemed to echo in the silence.

The passageway was barely illuminated, a flickering bulb hanging precariously from the ceiling, casting erratic shadows that danced along the walls. The air was thick and stale, the sensation of confinement closing in around us.

"Is this really the way out?" I asked, trying to keep the tremor out of my voice.

"Trust me," he said, his tone reassuring yet resolute. "I've done this before."

"Of course you have," I muttered, rolling my eyes, but the banter was short-lived as we moved deeper into the passage.

Every sound seemed amplified—the creaking of the floorboards, the distant hum of voices echoing from above. Anxiety coiled in my stomach, and with each step, the realization that we were unraveling something dangerous loomed larger.

Just as I began to feel a semblance of safety, a loud crash erupted from behind us, reverberating through the corridor, followed by a chorus of shouts. My heart lurched at the sound, the certainty that they were onto us igniting a fresh wave of panic.

"Run!" Reid barked, urgency threading through his voice as he pulled me forward.

We raced down the darkened passage, every footfall echoing like a drum in the stillness, until we reached a door at the far end. Reid yanked it open, and we stumbled into what felt like a storage area filled with old furniture and boxes stacked high, the smell of dust and neglect assaulting my senses.

"We can't stop now," he said, urgency etched into his features as he scanned the room. "There has to be another way out."

I barely had time to register my surroundings when Reid's hand shot out, and he gestured toward a window partially hidden behind a stack of crates. "That might be our best bet."

"Are you serious?" I gaped at the small opening, the thought of climbing through it daunting.

"Do you have a better idea?" His eyes bore into mine, the intensity of his gaze igniting something fierce within me.

"No," I admitted, biting my lip as I realized the truth in his words.

"Then let's move," he urged, urgency palpable in his tone.

I nodded, a sense of determination washing over me as we approached the window, adrenaline fueling my resolve. We climbed atop the crates, my heart racing not just from fear, but from the reckless thrill of the unknown. As I glanced at Reid, the stakes seemed clearer than ever.

With one last look back at the darkened room, I prepared to scramble through the window, but before I could leap, a loud thud echoed behind us—the unmistakable sound of footsteps rushing into the room.

"Reid!" I gasped, the realization crashing over me.

His eyes widened in alarm as we both turned, and my heart sank at the sight of Detective Mason leading a team of officers, their flashlights cutting through the darkness like spears of light.

"There they are!" Mason shouted, and I felt the grip of panic seize me.

In that fleeting moment, as the officers surged toward us, I felt time slow. Reid's hand tightened around mine, the world fading away except for the space between us—the darkness, the danger, and the unspoken bond that tethered us together.

"We have to jump!" he shouted, his voice fierce and insistent.

Without thinking, I nodded, fear and adrenaline melding

Chapter 11: Closer Than You Think

The morning sun slanted through the slatted blinds, casting lines across the cluttered desk that had become a makeshift war room in my tiny apartment. Papers and files spilled over the edges like an avalanche of information, each a potential thread to pull in unraveling the intricate tapestry of Reid's world. I rubbed my eyes, still heavy with sleep, while the lingering taste of coffee clung to my tongue like a bitter reminder of the long night I had spent dissecting every detail, every rumor. The walls around me felt like they were closing in, echoing the tension that hummed in the air.

The weight of his warning lingered, cold and tangible. Reid had approached me with a look that could freeze fire, his words sharp and laced with something I couldn't quite pin down—was it fear or merely a threat? My instinct screamed at me to retreat, to pull back into the comforting shadows of my research, but my resolve only strengthened. There was something beneath the surface of his words that drew me closer, a magnetic pull I couldn't resist. I leaned into it, brushing aside the growing unease that skittered across my skin like a chill.

Each word I had unearthed felt like a stepping stone leading deeper into the labyrinth of his life. I had always been good at reading people, picking apart their motivations as easily as I dissected their statements. Reid was no exception, though he was a puzzle with missing pieces, an enigma wrapped in tailored suits and that infuriating smirk. The more I probed, the more the shape of his reality came into focus—a world riddled with shadows, and I had stumbled into the darkest corner.

As evening descended, I made my way to the firm, the dim lights inside flickering like the last gasps of daylight. The air was thick with the scent of old leather and polished wood, a place steeped in power and ambition. I could almost hear the whispers of secrets swirling around me, enticing yet dangerous. My heart raced with anticipation and dread, the thrill of the chase coursing through my veins. I was a moth drawn to the flame, and the heat was intoxicating.

Navigating through the office was a careful dance; I had learned the art of invisibility well. People moved around me like shadows, their conversations blending into an indistinguishable murmur. I ducked into the records room, a sanctuary of chaos where files lay stacked like forgotten dreams. The fluorescent lights hummed above, creating an eerie ambiance that made my skin prickle. I rifled through the folders, searching for anything that might connect Reid to the rumors swirling in the air like a thick fog—deals made in back rooms, whispers of corruption that clung to the walls like a second skin.

Hours slipped by as I sifted through documents, absorbing every detail, piecing together a narrative that was increasingly sinister. With each passing moment, I felt the weight of unseen eyes watching me, lurking just beyond the threshold of my focus. The tension thickened, coiling in my stomach as I pushed deeper, tracing names and dates that began to form a shadowy web of deceit. The more I learned, the more I uncovered hidden threads binding Reid to those whose whispers echoed with treachery.

I stumbled upon a file that made my heart race—a collection of emails between Reid and a client with dubious ties. Words leapt off the page, laden with implications. My fingers trembled as I absorbed the implications, the startling realization that I was on the brink of something monumental. Yet, the thrill of discovery was tempered by the gnawing fear that I was overstepping, that I was delving too deep into waters far too murky. The very air felt charged, electric, as if the universe itself was warning me to turn back.

But I was past the point of no return. There was something so compelling about Reid, a magnetic force that kept me bound to him despite the darkness that surrounded his life. I could almost hear his voice in my head, low and warning, cautioning me against getting too close. Yet, I craved the truth, that elusive knowledge that danced just out of reach, taunting me. What was he hiding? What secrets had he buried beneath layers of charm and bravado?

I was jolted from my thoughts by the sound of footsteps echoing in the corridor. Panic surged through me as I ducked behind a towering stack of files, my heart thundering in my chest. The door swung open, and a figure stepped inside. My breath hitched as I recognized him—Reid. He moved with an effortless grace, his presence commanding and yet somehow disarming. There was a tension in the air, a palpable charge that felt both exhilarating and dangerous.

"Looking for something?" His voice sliced through the silence, smooth yet laced with a challenge that sent a shiver down my spine. I held my breath, caught between the urge to run and the desire to stand my ground. The irony wasn't lost on me; I was the hunter, yet here I was, feeling like the prey caught in a snare of my own making.

"Just organizing a few things," I managed, my voice steadier than I felt. He arched an eyebrow, skepticism etched across his features. The moment hung between us, electric and loaded with unspoken truths. I could see the flicker of interest in his eyes, a dangerous spark that ignited a rush of adrenaline through my veins. This was more than just a confrontation; it was a dance on the precipice, a tantalizing brink that left me breathless with possibility.

And as the shadows deepened around us, I realized I was closer to the truth than I had ever imagined—and yet, the closer I got to unraveling Reid's secrets, the more I felt the boundaries of our relationship begin to shift. Each revelation was a thread pulling me into the intricate tapestry of his life, a pull I could neither deny nor escape.

The dim light of the office flickered as I stood rooted in place, the tension coiling tighter around us like a serpent preparing to strike.

Reid's presence was a force of nature, overwhelming and magnetic, yet beneath that charm lay an undercurrent of danger that sent a thrill of adrenaline coursing through my veins. "Are you going to ask me to leave, or are we just going to stand here and stare at each other like two deer caught in the headlights?" I shot back, surprising myself with the casual bravado lacing my tone.

A faint smirk tugged at the corners of his mouth, transforming his steely gaze into something almost playful. "You seem quite at home in the shadows. I wouldn't want to disrupt your little game." His words were layered, rich with challenge and something else, something that made my heart race even as my mind screamed at me to stay focused.

"I'm not playing," I replied, crossing my arms, adopting a defensive stance. "I'm searching for answers, and you're in my way." My heart pounded, fueled by the simmering undercurrent of our dynamic, which felt like an intricate dance of attraction and animosity. He was not just an adversary; he was a riddle I couldn't solve, a puzzle that pulled me deeper into its tangled web.

His expression shifted, a flicker of seriousness breaking through the levity. "Careful, Evie. Some riddles have consequences." The weight of his words settled heavily between us, a stark reminder that the world I was probing was fraught with peril. Yet, that realization only stoked my resolve.

"I thrive on consequences," I quipped, attempting to mask the tremor in my voice with bravado. "In fact, I might even say they're my favorite part of this whole adventure." The banter felt alive, a spark igniting the air around us, despite the shadows lurking just outside the flickering glow of the office lights.

Reid stepped closer, the intensity of his gaze unwavering. "Adventure can lead you down paths you didn't intend to take. Are you sure you want to follow me?" His words danced dangerously on the edge of flirtation and warning, and I fought the urge to lean into his proximity, to bridge that final gap between us.

"Honestly? I don't even know what I want anymore," I confessed, the honesty spilling out before I could rein it in. "But I do know that whatever you're hiding won't stay buried forever." The truth of my determination hung in the air, a challenge wrapped in vulnerability.

Before he could respond, the shrill ring of my phone sliced through the tension, pulling me back to reality. I fished it out of my pocket, glancing at the caller ID, my stomach dropping as I recognized the name—Hannah, my best friend and confidante, the one person I hadn't had the heart to drag into this chaos. I hesitated, torn between the gravity of the moment with Reid and the grounding presence of Hannah.

"Go ahead and answer it," Reid said, a hint of amusement flickering in his eyes. "I promise I won't bite."

Rolling my eyes, I swiped to answer, forcing a smile to mask my apprehension. "Hannah, hey! What's up?"

"Evie! I've been trying to reach you. You won't believe what I just heard!" Her voice crackled with excitement, pulling me momentarily away from the charged atmosphere surrounding Reid.

"Something good, I hope?" I asked, glancing up at him, only to find him leaning against the doorframe, arms crossed, an amused smile playing on his lips.

"Let's just say there's more going on at Reid's firm than just a little office drama," she said, her tone conspiratorial. "I caught a rumor about some big players involved in a scandal. They're talking shady deals, Evie. You need to dig deeper."

My heart raced at the implication, the thrill of the chase igniting anew. "I'm already knee-deep in it," I replied, casting a glance at Reid, whose expression had shifted to a mask of cool calculation. "But thank you for the heads-up."

"Just promise me you'll be careful, okay? I don't want to see you get hurt," she insisted, her voice laced with genuine concern.

"I will, I promise. I'll call you later." I hung up, my thoughts racing. I needed to move quickly, to gather whatever fragments of information I could before the walls closed in around me.

"Well, that was enlightening," Reid remarked, pushing off the doorframe and stepping closer, his voice low and steady. "What's this about a scandal?"

"None of your business," I shot back, a teasing glint in my eye as I maneuvered past him, intent on reclaiming my power.

"Everything that happens in this place is my business, Evie." His tone was serious now, underscoring the weight of his words. "You don't know what you're dealing with. There are things you might uncover that would put you in real danger."

"Danger is my middle name," I retorted, heart pounding, the thrill of the game pulsing through my veins. "Or at least it should be, considering how often I seem to find it lately."

Reid's eyes narrowed, studying me as if he were trying to dissect my very soul. "You think you're prepared for this? The truth isn't always as glamorous as you might imagine."

"I don't want glamor," I snapped, my voice steadying as determination swelled within me. "I want the truth, and I want it now."

A flicker of respect crossed his features, a glimmer of something akin to admiration that made my pulse race faster. But it vanished almost as quickly as it had appeared, replaced by the hard mask of resolve. "Fine, but you need to promise me one thing. If you dig deeper, you need to be ready to walk away when it gets too deep."

"Like you'd ever let me do that," I challenged, the playful banter returning, sparking back the tension between us.

"Maybe you're right," he replied, his voice suddenly low and intense. "But you're the one who's walking this tightrope, Evie. Just remember that."

With those final words, he turned, his back to me, a silent sentinel guarding secrets I was only beginning to unravel. The promise of danger loomed like a dark cloud overhead, but the thrill of the chase, the adrenaline rushing through my veins, was a heady mixture I couldn't resist. I was standing at the edge of something monumental, and despite the warnings, I was ready to leap.

I watched Reid retreat into the shadows, his silhouette disappearing down the corridor, leaving a palpable void in the air behind him. The lingering scent of his cologne clung to the space where we'd just stood, an intoxicating mix of cedarwood and something distinctly him—warm and inviting, yet layered with an edge of danger that sent my mind reeling. I shook my head, trying to dispel the memory of his smirk, the challenge in his eyes. It was a potent reminder that I was playing a game with high stakes, and I needed to stay sharp, even as my heart felt dangerously distracted.

The office hummed with activity as I returned to the records room, but the chaos around me faded into a background murmur. My focus narrowed, fueled by a new urgency. I needed to uncover the truth behind Reid's façade, to expose the connections hidden beneath the surface. I dove back into the files, sifting through documents like a relentless detective piecing together a mystery that felt both thrilling and perilous.

A sudden thought struck me—Hannah's warning about the scandal echoed in my mind, each word resonating like a bell tolling in the quiet corners of my thoughts. I couldn't shake the feeling that I was being watched, as if the very walls were listening, ready to swallow my secrets whole. But the thrill of the chase drowned out the anxiety; it was a sweet song that urged me forward, deeper into the labyrinth.

I reached for a particularly worn file, its edges frayed from years of handling. Inside, I found an exchange of emails between Reid and a partner from another firm—a partner who had recently made headlines for a series of questionable deals. My heart raced as I scanned the contents. There it was, a thread woven into the tapestry of deceit, connecting Reid to someone who had been implicated in the very rumors I sought to unravel.

"Bingo," I whispered to myself, triumph flooding my veins. I copied the information, my fingers trembling with excitement as I carefully placed the papers back where I found them. Each revelation brought me closer to the truth, but I knew the path ahead was riddled with hidden traps. I had to be cautious; I couldn't let my excitement blind me to the dangers lurking in the shadows.

Just as I was about to leave the records room, the door swung open with a soft creak, startling me. My heart lurched as I turned, ready to confront whatever threat had just entered. Instead, I found myself staring at Reid again, his expression unreadable as he stepped inside, closing the door with a quiet click behind him.

"Still digging?" he asked, his voice smooth but edged with an unmistakable tension.

"Are you following me now?" I shot back, crossing my arms defensively. "I thought you were all about keeping your distance."

"Keeping my distance isn't the same as ignoring the danger," he replied, the sincerity in his voice disarming. "You don't understand what's at stake here, Evie."

"I might not understand your world completely," I countered, "but I know enough to recognize a smokescreen when I see one. You're not fooling me."

Reid stepped closer, invading my space in a way that made my breath hitch. "And you think you can take it on all by yourself? You're playing with fire, and fire burns." The intensity in his gaze made it hard to remember why I had been so resolute just moments ago.

"Maybe I like a little heat," I shot back, trying to maintain my bravado, though my heart betrayed me, racing beneath the weight of his scrutiny. "Or maybe I just like uncovering the truth, no matter how hot it gets."

A flicker of something—admiration, perhaps?—crossed his face before he masked it behind his usual cool demeanor. "This isn't a game, Evie. I can't let you get hurt." His concern felt genuine, and for a moment, the walls I had built around my heart wavered.

"What about you?" I challenged, pushing past the unsettling feeling that he cared in some way I didn't want to acknowledge. "What are you hiding, Reid? What's so important that you're willing to let me walk into danger alone?"

For a heartbeat, we were locked in a stalemate, the air thick with unsaid words and unacknowledged feelings. He hesitated, just long enough for me to see a glimpse of vulnerability beneath his armor. But then it was gone, replaced by the familiar shield of arrogance.

"I'm not the one in danger here," he replied, his voice steady. "You have no idea who you're dealing with. There are people involved who won't hesitate to eliminate anyone who gets too close to the truth."

A chill ran down my spine at his words, but the fire within me flared brighter. "Then I guess I'll just have to be careful, won't I?"

"Careful isn't enough," he insisted, moving closer, his presence engulfing me in a mix of warmth and tension. "I need you to promise me that if things get dangerous, you'll walk away."

"I'm not walking away from this. Not now." My voice was steady, but inside, uncertainty gnawed at me like a persistent itch. What if he was right? What if I was too deep in, too entangled in a web I couldn't escape?

Reid's jaw tightened, the frustration evident in the way he ran a hand through his hair. "You're infuriating, you know that? You could have a safe path out, yet you choose to dive headfirst into chaos."

I laughed, a sharp sound that echoed in the confined space. "You make it sound so easy. Just turn around and pretend this doesn't matter? I can't do that. I need to know what's really happening."

His expression softened for a brief moment, a flicker of understanding that sent my heart racing. But it vanished as quickly as it appeared. "Then you're more reckless than I thought."

"Recklessness has its merits." The tension between us crackled, electricity sparking in the charged silence. "Sometimes you have to be a little reckless to get the truth."

"Sometimes it leads to disaster," he countered, stepping back, the space between us filled with unspoken words and unresolved feelings.

Before I could respond, a loud bang echoed from outside the office, jolting us both. The sound was followed by shouts, the clamor of voices rising in panic. I exchanged a look with Reid, a shared understanding igniting between us.

"Stay here," he commanded, his voice low and urgent.

"Like I'd let you go out there alone," I shot back, adrenaline flooding my veins. "What was that?"

But he didn't respond, his expression hardening as he moved toward the door. I followed closely, heart pounding, the realization settling over me like a heavy shroud. Whatever was happening outside was linked to the secrets I had been uncovering, the danger closing in around us like a tightening noose.

As he cracked the door open, chaos spilled into the room. A figure rushed past, a blur of motion that sent my heart racing, and in that instant, I knew that the stakes had just escalated to a terrifying new level. Reid turned to me, his eyes fierce with determination, but behind them lurked a fear that sent a jolt through my core.

"Get back," he hissed, urgency coating his words. But I couldn't move, rooted to the spot as the sounds of commotion escalated into a cacophony of chaos.

Then, just as quickly as it had begun, everything went silent. A deafening stillness enveloped us, pregnant with tension, and I felt a chill creep up my spine. Reid's expression shifted from concern to something darker as he stepped fully into the hallway, pulling me with him.

"What is happening?" I asked, my voice a whisper against the eerie quiet.

But before he could respond, a figure emerged from the shadows, face obscured but unmistakably threatening. In that moment, the world around us snapped into sharp focus, and I knew that whatever truth I sought, it was now more elusive than ever, shrouded in layers of danger I had only just begun to uncover.

Chapter 12: An Unexpected Alliance

The dim glow of my desk lamp cast flickering shadows across the cluttered papers that littered my workspace, a chaotic reflection of my racing thoughts. The quiet hum of the city outside my window was a comforting backdrop, but it did little to ease the tension coiling in my stomach. The usual clatter of heels and bustling voices in the hallway was absent, leaving an eerie silence in its wake. It was in this hushed atmosphere that I found myself wrestling with the truth I was beginning to uncover—an intricate web of deceit that threatened to ensnare not just my career but my very life.

As the clock struck ten, the office door swung open with a decisive creak, and in walked Reid, a figure cloaked in shadows. I hardly recognized him; his usual air of effortless confidence was replaced by an intensity that made my heart race for reasons I didn't want to dissect just yet. His shirt was rumpled, tie askew, and the typically charming smile had been replaced by a look of grim determination. There was a storm brewing in those hazel eyes, and it made my own pulse quicken.

"I found something," he stated flatly, his voice low and urgent as he stepped further into the office. "We need to talk."

I glanced at the papers sprawled across my desk, moments of vulnerability laid bare in the margins—notes from our previous encounters, the intricate dance of our rivalry penned in ink. I had never imagined that I'd be sharing my space, my secrets, with Reid, the man who had been both my nemesis and my reluctant ally. "What do you mean, 'something'?" I leaned back in my chair, crossing my arms defensively. "And why should I trust you?"

He ran a hand through his tousled hair, frustration flickering across his features. "Because if we don't figure this out, we're both going to lose everything."

I paused, weighing his words. There was a raw honesty in his voice that cut through the skepticism I had built up over months of rivalry. "Go on."

Reid stepped closer, lowering his voice further. "I intercepted communications between some of our clients. It's worse than we thought. There's a network—money laundering, blackmail, the works. And it involves people in positions of power."

My stomach knotted as the implications sank in. This wasn't just about our professional reputations anymore; it was about something much larger and more insidious. "Who?" I asked, dread creeping into my tone. "Who's involved?"

"I don't have all the details yet," he replied, pacing back and forth in front of my desk. "But if we don't join forces, we'll be picked off one by one. I need your expertise to navigate this. You're the only one who knows how to dig through the corporate layers without raising alarms."

A million thoughts raced through my mind—most of them screaming for me to reject his proposition. Working together felt like stepping into a minefield, and yet the gravity of the situation loomed larger than my misgivings. "And what's in it for you, Reid?"

His gaze met mine, intense and unyielding. "Survival," he said simply, but there was more to it. Beneath the urgency lay a flicker of vulnerability that startled me.

I sighed, the weight of his request pressing down on me. "Okay. But if we're going to do this, it has to be on my terms."

Reid's lips curved into a smirk that didn't quite reach his eyes. "I wouldn't have it any other way."

As we settled into an uneasy alliance, the boundaries of our interactions shifted, marked by whispered secrets and frantic late-night brainstorming sessions that blurred the lines of professionalism. Each meeting was a delicate dance, the air thick with unsaid words and unresolved tensions. We moved closer to each other, physically and emotionally, a magnetic pull I both craved and feared.

On one such night, the rain tapped insistently against the window, each drop a reminder of the stakes at play. We sat across from each other, the table strewn with reports and files that painted a chilling picture of the corruption that snaked through the city's veins. Reid leaned back in his chair, fingers steepled beneath his chin, and I found myself drawn to the way his brow furrowed in concentration.

"I can't believe we're in this mess," I murmured, glancing at him, feeling a strange kinship forming amidst the chaos.

"Life's funny that way," he replied, his tone teasing but laced with sincerity. "You spend years trying to outsmart each other, and then—bam—you're on the same side."

"Funny? I'd call it tragic," I shot back, unable to suppress a smile. "Next, we'll be sharing our deepest secrets and bonding over late-night pizza."

"Don't tempt me," he laughed, the sound warm and surprisingly disarming. "Though I prefer tacos."

Our laughter mingled in the air, breaking the tension, and for a moment, the weight of our situation faded into the background. The unexpected ease between us grew, but it was shadowed by the reality of our mission.

"Do you really think we can take them down?" I asked, the lightness fading as the seriousness of our task settled over me once more.

"Together, I think we stand a chance," he replied, his eyes reflecting a mixture of determination and something else—something that sent a shiver down my spine.

The partnership we forged felt as fragile as glass, yet with every whispered exchange and every risk we took, it became clearer that we were entwined in a way neither of us anticipated. I found myself questioning everything I thought I knew about Reid and about myself. The dance of rivalry had transformed into something more complicated, something that left me longing for answers to questions I didn't know how to ask.

The next few days unfolded in a blur, a whirlwind of late nights and stolen moments where Reid and I found ourselves working side by side, navigating the murky waters of deception. Our once-predictable meetings had morphed into something exhilarating, tinged with an unspoken understanding that danced just out of reach. With every shared laugh, every strategic brainstorm, the façade of rivalry faded, revealing the complexity beneath.

One afternoon, with the sun filtering through the blinds and casting striped shadows across my desk, I shuffled through a pile of documents, scanning for anything that could provide insight into the tangled web we were trying to unravel. Reid leaned against the doorframe, arms crossed, a bemused expression on his face. "You know, you'd be far more intimidating if you didn't look like you were about to fall asleep on that pile of paperwork."

I shot him a glare, though I couldn't help the smile creeping onto my lips. "I was concentrating, thank you very much. Not all of us have the luxury of effortlessly leaning against a door and looking like a cover model."

"Ah, but that's the secret to my charm," he replied, pushing off the door and stepping closer, a playful glint in his eyes. "You should try it sometime. Less stress, more allure."

"Less stress? Allure? Is that what you call it when you do absolutely nothing productive?" I retorted, pretending to flip through the documents with feigned interest.

"Productivity is overrated. Sometimes it's about cultivating a captivating presence," he said, mock-seriously.

Just then, my phone buzzed, jolting me from our banter. The screen lit up with a message from an unknown number. My heart raced as I read it: I know what you're doing. Stop now, or there will be consequences. A cold shiver ran down my spine. I quickly glanced at Reid, whose expression shifted from amusement to concern.

"Everything okay?" he asked, stepping closer.

I turned my phone away, forcing a laugh that came out more brittle than I intended. "Just a spam message. You know how it is."

"Spam, huh?" Reid's eyes narrowed, clearly not buying my act. "Let me see."

"Really, it's nothing," I insisted, waving him off. But his intensity made me reconsider. I could feel the pulse of tension in the air, thickening like the humidity before a storm. I took a breath, the lightness of our earlier conversation evaporating as I handed him my phone.

He read the message, his brow furrowing deeper with each word. "This isn't good. Someone knows we're digging. We have to be more careful."

"I didn't think anyone would notice," I admitted, anxiety twisting in my gut. "We're just two people looking for the truth. How could they possibly know?"

Reid straightened, his demeanor shifting from playful to serious in an instant. "You'd be surprised how quickly whispers turn into shouts in our world. We need to tighten our circle. No more late-night meet-ups at my place, no more public discussions. Let's communicate through encrypted messages from now on."

The gravity of the situation hit me. This wasn't just a game anymore. We were playing with fire, and the threat was no longer abstract. "Reid, I—"

"I don't want to hear any 'buts' right now," he interrupted, his voice firm yet laced with an undercurrent of worry. "We're in this together, and I'm not about to let anything happen to you."

Something about the protectiveness in his tone struck a chord deep within me, causing a swirl of emotions I wasn't prepared to face. "Fine. I'll do whatever it takes to keep us safe."

As the day wore on, we shifted our focus to the files before us, a tapestry of names and numbers weaving together the sordid tales of betrayal and greed. Hours melted away as we pieced together connections, uncovering layers of deceit that made my skin crawl. With every discovery, I felt the stakes rise higher, the walls closing in.

As the sun dipped below the skyline, painting the room in hues of orange and purple, I leaned back, exhaustion creeping into my bones. "We're never going to make sense of all this," I sighed, rubbing my temples.

"Don't throw in the towel just yet," Reid replied, his voice laced with determination. "We'll crack this. Together."

"Together," I echoed, the word hanging in the air, heavy with meaning.

He shot me a sidelong glance, a teasing smile tugging at the corners of his mouth. "And hey, if we fail, at least we'll go down in flames—two stars that burned too brightly."

I couldn't help but laugh, even as a sliver of anxiety twisted in my gut. "True, but I'd prefer to survive this mess, if it's all the same to you."

"Survival is the plan," he said, leaning back in his chair with that casual confidence that had always irked and intrigued me in equal measure.

With the night deepening around us, a sudden beep from my phone drew my attention. I frowned at the screen, my stomach twisting again. Another message from that unknown number. *This is your last warning. Leave it alone, or you'll regret it.*

I glanced at Reid, who had already caught sight of the message. "What do we do?" I asked, my voice barely above a whisper.

"Now we take it seriously," he said, his tone steady but urgent. "No more half-measures. We need to find out who's behind this and put a stop to it."

"Easier said than done," I muttered, my heart racing with the reality of what lay ahead. The atmosphere thickened with uncertainty, but an undeniable spark of determination ignited within me.

"Let's not waste time," Reid replied, rising to his feet. "We'll need to dig deeper. If we can trace the source of these messages, we might find out just how tangled this web is."

I nodded, adrenaline coursing through my veins. The prospect of uncovering the truth both thrilled and terrified me, but one thing was certain: this was no longer just about survival; it was about exposing the darkness lurking in the corners of our world. Together, we would shine a light on the secrets hiding in the shadows, even if it meant confronting the very people who thought they were untouchable.

As we gathered our things, a sense of purpose settled over us, and I felt a flicker of hope in the midst of chaos. Whatever lay ahead, we would face it together, side by side, navigating the storm of deceit with our newfound alliance. Little did I know, this was just the beginning of an unpredictable journey that would challenge everything I believed about trust, loyalty, and the line between friend and foe.

In the days that followed our uneasy alliance, the atmosphere around us crackled with an electric tension. Each moment we spent unraveling the sinister threads that bound our clients to a dark underbelly of corruption only deepened our connection, weaving a tapestry of shared experiences and silent glances that spoke volumes. Reid and I transformed our small conference room into a command center, walls plastered with whiteboards filled with names, connections, and inked arrows that led into the murky depths of deceit.

One late evening, as I sipped on yet another cup of bitter coffee, I glanced up from the notes spread across the table. Reid was leaning over a document, the light from the desk lamp illuminating his profile. He looked so intent, brow furrowed in concentration, that it made my heart skip. "You know, if you keep frowning like that, you might scare small children," I teased, trying to lighten the heavy mood that had settled between us.

He shot me a sideways glance, his expression softening into a smile. "And if you keep drinking that sludge you call coffee, you might scare even the bravest souls. Seriously, how do you survive on this?"

"It's called caffeine and sheer determination," I quipped back, raising my cup as if in toast. "And it's doing wonders for my will to fight this war."

"Fair enough," he chuckled, shaking his head. "But if we're going to keep doing this, I suggest you add some actual food to your diet. I don't want to be responsible for your eventual collapse due to coffee overdose."

"Noted," I replied, a playful spark igniting between us. The banter felt familiar, a breath of fresh air amid the turmoil surrounding us.

Suddenly, my phone buzzed on the table, the sound slicing through the comfortable atmosphere. I glanced at the screen, my heart plummeting as I saw another message from the unknown number. *You're digging too deep. Stop before it's too late.*

I felt the blood drain from my face. "Reid," I said, my voice barely above a whisper, "it's happening again."

He straightened, the playful demeanor vanishing as he leaned closer, studying my expression. "What does it say?"

I read the message aloud, my fingers trembling as I passed the phone to him. "This isn't a joke anymore, is it?"

"No," he replied, his voice laced with concern as he read the words. "We need to figure out who's behind this, and fast."

I took a deep breath, my mind racing. "It feels like they're watching our every move. What if we're being tracked?"

"Then we need to switch things up," Reid suggested, determination flaring in his eyes. "We can't stay here. Let's meet at the café down the street tomorrow morning. It'll be easier to blend in, and we can plan our next steps without feeling like we're under a microscope."

I nodded, the tension in my shoulders easing slightly at the thought of a public space. "Good idea. But we have to be careful about what we discuss."

"Agreed," he said, his tone turning serious. "And I mean it about the food. You're not leaving that café until you've eaten something other than your infamous coffee."

"Maybe I'll treat you to a pastry, but only if you stop looking so grim," I countered, trying to lighten the mood again.

As we finished up for the night, I felt a strange mix of exhilaration and dread. Each step deeper into this twisted world drew us closer, binding us together in ways I hadn't anticipated. Yet, the shadows loomed larger than ever, threatening to swallow us whole.

The next morning dawned crisp and clear, a stark contrast to the storm brewing in my mind. I arrived at the café early, the sweet scent of freshly baked goods filling the air. I chose a small table by the window, hoping the sunshine would offer a semblance of warmth amid the brewing chaos. I'd barely settled in with my order—an almond croissant and a steaming cup of tea—when Reid burst through the door, winded but undeniably charming, with that ever-present spark in his eyes.

"I thought I was late!" he exclaimed, sliding into the seat across from me. "You haven't eaten yet, have you?"

"Just the pastry and some tea. I thought you'd want me alert for our clandestine meeting," I replied, teasing him while enjoying the way his presence lit up the room.

He reached for the croissant and took a bite, a satisfied look crossing his face. "Not bad. But it's missing something."

"Like what? A side of sass?" I shot back, laughter bubbling between us.

His grin widened. "Maybe some cream cheese. Next time, I'll bring the bagels."

But our light banter was abruptly cut short as a figure entered the café—a man in a tailored suit, eyes scanning the room like a hawk. My heart raced as I recognized him; he was someone I had seen in the files, a name tied to the web of deceit we were untangling.

"Reid," I whispered, leaning closer, "I think we have company."

Reid's gaze snapped to the entrance, his demeanor shifting instantly. "Stay calm," he murmured, as we both tried to appear nonchalant. "Let's not draw attention."

The man's eyes settled on us, a predatory glint in his gaze. I felt a wave of nausea wash over me. "What do we do?" I whispered, panic creeping into my voice.

Reid's mind was racing, and I could see the gears turning behind those hazel eyes. "We need to act like we belong here. Just keep talking. Whatever you do, don't look directly at him."

I nodded, trying to focus on the warm croissant in front of me rather than the impending sense of doom. "So, about that bagel situation," I said, forcing a smile. "I think we could go on a quest to find the best bagels in town."

"Definitely. It's vital to our survival," Reid replied, his voice steady despite the tension thrumming between us.

But the man was moving toward our table, and I felt like a deer caught in headlights. "Excuse me," he said, a smooth but unnerving smile playing at the corners of his lips. "Mind if I join you?"

The world around me dimmed as his presence enveloped us. This was the moment I had dreaded—a point of no return. Reid glanced at me, and in that fleeting look, I felt the weight of our fragile alliance, the bond that had grown between us, teetering on the edge of chaos.

"Of course," Reid replied, his voice deceptively calm as he gestured toward an empty chair. "We could use another opinion on our bagel strategy."

I wanted to scream, to bolt from the café, but the man's icy gaze pinned me in place. "You two have been quite busy lately," he remarked, a dangerous edge to his tone. "I hope you're not getting in over your heads."

Reid's smile was cool, collected, but I could sense the tension radiating off him like a heatwave. "Just the usual coffee and pastries. What brings you here?"

"Curiosity, mostly," the man replied, leaning forward slightly. "And I must say, I find your little venture quite... interesting."

My heart raced as I exchanged a glance with Reid, silently communicating the urgency of the moment.

"We're just enjoying a quiet morning," I managed to say, my voice steady despite the turmoil within me. "Nothing to worry about."

The man's smile widened, but it didn't reach his eyes. "Ah, but quiet can be deceiving."

With a single glance, I could see that our world was unraveling at the seams, and the storm of consequences loomed just ahead. As I sat across from Reid, the tension palpable, I realized that our fight for the truth was only just beginning. The stakes had risen, and the darkness that had threatened to engulf us was now inching closer, revealing itself in the form of an enemy sitting at our table.

The man's next words hung in the air like a noose tightening around our necks. "I believe you both have something that belongs to me."

As panic coursed through my veins, I knew one thing for certain: we were no longer just searching for the truth; we were fighting for our very lives.

Chapter 13: The Breaking Point

The hum of fluorescent lights buzzed overhead as I perched on the edge of the leather chair in Ethan's office, the air thick with the aroma of stale coffee and tension that could be sliced with a knife. The walls were lined with bookshelves, each brimming with tomes that had likely witnessed as many sleepless nights as we had. I drummed my fingers against my thigh, counting the days since we first stumbled into this mess—a case that felt more like a spiral into madness than the straightforward justice we had envisioned.

"Did you really think it would end there?" Ethan's voice broke through my thoughts, a low growl that sent a shiver racing down my spine. He leaned back in his chair, arms crossed, and those intense eyes bore into mine, each glance carrying the weight of unspoken frustrations. The blueprints of the case sprawled across the desk like a chaotic map to a treasure that we might never find. The scent of ink mingled with the tension, creating an atmosphere both familiar and fraught with impending disaster.

"I wanted to believe it could," I shot back, allowing my irritation to rise like a tide. I stood, pacing the room, feeling the walls closing in as I replayed our latest findings—the evidence stacked against a corruption scandal that spread through the very heart of the city, poisoning everything it touched. "But this is bigger than us, Ethan. We're chasing shadows."

"Chasing shadows?" He stood suddenly, the chair scraping harshly against the floor. "What do you think we've been doing for the past three months? We've uncovered links to the mayor's office, dirty money flowing like a river through the veins of this city. And now you want to give up?"

I paused, the weight of his words settling in. He was right; we had unearthed connections that ran deeper than mere cases of malpractice. Yet, I felt a creeping unease gnawing at the edges of my resolve. Every twist and turn revealed a new layer of deceit, and I could sense the danger coiling closer around us like a predator stalking its prey.

"The more we find, the more dangerous it becomes," I murmured, the shadows in the corners of the room seeming to thicken with each passing second. "Do you think they'll stop? They won't let us walk away from this."

Ethan moved closer, the air crackling between us, and for a moment, all I could hear was the quickening of my heart. "Then we won't walk away. We'll finish this, together." The intensity in his voice made my stomach flutter, a confusing mix of admiration and apprehension. I took a step back, my body instinctively trying to create distance, but he reached out, fingers brushing against my wrist, grounding me in a way that felt both comforting and perilous.

"Ethan..." My breath hitched as I searched his face, his expression a tempest of determination and something else—something more intimate that made my chest tighten.

"Just... trust me."

His plea lingered in the air like the scent of rain just before a storm, heavy with unspoken emotions. Trust was a fragile thing, and ours had been built on the foundation of shared experiences and whispered secrets in dimly lit rooms. It was a bond forged in the fires of adversity, but now it teetered on the edge of something far more personal.

And then, without warning, he closed the distance between us, drawing me into his orbit. His lips found mine in a rush, a collision of passion and uncertainty that ignited every nerve in my body. It was intoxicating and terrifying all at once, a jolt of electricity that shot through me and shattered the carefully constructed barriers I had erected. I leaned into the kiss, lost in the warmth of his body, the chaos outside momentarily forgotten.

But the moment slipped away like sand through my fingers. Reality crashed back in with a rush, cold and unforgiving. I pulled back, breathless, my heart racing in protest. "What was that?"

Ethan stepped back as if burned, the realization of what had just transpired dawning on us both. "I... I don't know," he admitted, raking a hand through his tousled hair, frustration etching deeper lines into his face. "It was a mistake. We shouldn't have... I shouldn't have done that."

The air crackled with confusion and regret, and I could feel the space between us widen, not just physically but emotionally. "Yeah, it was," I said, the bitterness of those words twisting in my throat. "But maybe it was also inevitable."

He ran a hand across his face, his eyes darting to the floor as if he could physically push away the implications of our actions. "This case is consuming us. It's blurring the lines between personal and professional."

"It's more than that," I shot back, unable to suppress the heat of my anger. "You're right; this case is consuming us. But it's not just the investigation. It's us."

Silence fell, heavy and oppressive, wrapping around us like a shroud. The enormity of our situation loomed over me, a dark cloud that threatened to engulf everything we had fought for. I felt a wave of nausea wash over me as the implications of our shared moment settled in. What if this kiss—this lapse in judgment—was a sign of something deeper, something that could lead us down a path from which there would be no return?

As I stood there, the weight of our choices bearing down on me, I couldn't shake the feeling that we were at a crossroads. This kiss, however fleeting, had altered the course of our partnership. The investigation that had once felt like a clear path was now obscured by a fog of emotions we had barely begun to understand.

In that charged silence, the walls of the office felt both confining and liberating. I wanted to unravel this knot of feelings, to explore the possibilities that lay ahead, but I was equally terrified of what those possibilities might mean for us. My heart raced as I caught his gaze, searching for answers in the depths of his blue eyes, but all I saw was a reflection of my own uncertainty.

The silence that followed our kiss was palpable, a weighty pause in the air that seemed to vibrate with unspoken thoughts. I could feel my heart drumming against my ribcage, a frantic rhythm that mirrored the chaos of my mind. The office, once a sanctuary of investigation, now felt like a cage, trapping us in the aftermath of our impulsive entanglement. I stepped away, feeling the loss of warmth like a chill settling over my skin.

"Maybe we should take a step back," I suggested, my voice steadier than I felt. I crossed my arms tightly, trying to ward off the chill of reality seeping in. "We need to focus on the case, not... whatever this is."

Ethan raked a hand through his hair, his frustration palpable. "You think I wanted that to happen? I mean, sure, you're impossible to resist—" He paused, the corner of his mouth quirking up slightly. "But this is about more than us. We've got a job to do, and if we don't figure this out, we're in deep trouble."

"Right," I nodded, swallowing hard. "Trouble. Like, being followed by dark SUVs kind of trouble." The image of black tinted windows and menacing figures lurking in the shadows flashed through my mind, and I shuddered.

"Exactly." He stepped back, the space between us suddenly feeling like a chasm. "If we don't keep our heads in the game, we could end up like the others who tried to take down this corruption. You saw the reports; people disappearing, evidence going missing..." His voice trailed off, but the implication hung heavily in the air.

"Yeah, I get it." I inhaled deeply, trying to shake off the anxious fog clinging to me. "But we also can't pretend we don't feel something."

A beat passed before he replied, his expression softening. "I don't want to ignore it. I just don't want it to jeopardize everything we've built."

"Right, the whole saving-the-city-from-a-corruption-ring thing." I forced a laugh, trying to lighten the atmosphere, but it felt like laughter wrapped in a shroud of tension. "You know, sometimes I wish we could just hit pause on everything."

"Wouldn't that be nice?" Ethan mused, a flicker of a smile breaking through the seriousness. "But I fear the universe doesn't have a pause button, just an awkward fast-forward."

Our banter hung in the air, a delicate thread of camaraderie woven through the heaviness, but reality swiftly pulled me back. I took a seat, the leather creaking beneath me, and gestured to the mess on the desk, redirecting the focus. "So, what's next? The surveillance footage from the last meeting?"

He nodded, his professional demeanor returning like an old friend. "We need to analyze it closely. There's bound to be something we missed." He reached for his laptop, fingers flying over the keys as he pulled up the footage, and for a moment, the tension eased, replaced by a shared determination.

The grainy video flickered to life, revealing a dimly lit room filled with figures I recognized from our investigations—powerful people wrapped in a web of deceit. My stomach churned as I watched them, the laughter and casual exchanges cloaked in an air of foreboding. "It's sickening," I muttered, watching as they passed envelopes back and forth, the weight of corruption visible in their gestures.

Ethan leaned closer, his shoulder brushing mine, the proximity igniting an awareness I desperately tried to ignore. "They think they're untouchable," he said, his voice low and fierce. "But we're going to prove them wrong."

My heart raced again, but this time it wasn't just the closeness; it was the thrill of the hunt. "How do we get to them?" I asked, eyes glued to the screen. "There must be a way in."

Ethan paused, his eyes narrowing as he contemplated the faces before us. "If we can track down the source of the funding, we might find a way to expose them. Someone must be overseeing the operation."

"Sounds like a plan." I felt invigorated by the prospect of action, the adrenaline washing over the earlier confusion. "I'll start digging into financial records. We can follow the money trail."

"Good." He turned to me, the intensity in his gaze both daunting and exhilarating. "But let's be careful. We're already treading a fine line, and I don't want to lose you in this."

His words, earnest and layered, sent a warmth blooming in my chest, quickly quelled by the reminder of our current predicament. "You're not going to lose me," I assured him, forcing a smile that felt a little too bright. "I can take care of myself. Just remember to look both ways when you cross the street, will you?"

"I'll try to remember," he replied, his lips twitching in amusement. "Especially when it's your side of the street."

The banter between us felt natural again, a reprieve from the heaviness that had lingered moments before. But beneath the surface, the tension simmered, a reminder of the kiss that still clung to the air, unaddressed yet undeniable.

As we continued to review the footage, my mind wandered. What would happen when this case was finally closed? Would we go back to being just colleagues, or had we crossed an irrevocable threshold? The thought hung over me like a shadow, persistent and troubling.

DUAL FLAME

With every passing moment, the investigation unfurled before us like a scroll filled with secrets waiting to be revealed. Each clue pulled us deeper into the murky waters of corruption, the stakes rising higher with every revelation. I could feel the thrill of the chase igniting my spirit, but the shadows of doubt loomed larger, ready to envelop me at any moment.

Hours slipped away as we analyzed footage and connected dots, our minds synchronized in a dance of strategy and resolve. The unease of our earlier confrontation faded into the background, replaced by the exhilaration of our mission. But as I glanced at Ethan, intent on the screen, I knew our uncharted territory was a path fraught with both danger and desire. The investigation promised to challenge us in ways we couldn't yet comprehend, and the lines we walked would only blur further as we ventured deeper into the darkness together.

The hours of sifting through the murky waters of deception faded into the background as we delved deeper into the case. Each piece of evidence felt like a clue in a twisted game, and the stakes kept climbing higher. I leaned closer to the laptop screen, eyes scanning the flickering footage of those high-powered meetings, where secrets were exchanged beneath the guise of joviality, laughter masking the sinister undercurrents flowing through our city.

"Look at how they interact," Ethan said, his voice barely above a whisper. "It's all so rehearsed. They think they're untouchable, sitting in their fortress of greed."

I caught a glint of anger in his eyes, a fiery resolve that made my heart race. "It's disgusting," I replied, my stomach churning as I watched one of the figures casually slip a briefcase under the table. "They're stealing from the people who trust them. They'll ruin lives just to pad their pockets."

"Which is why we can't let this slide." Ethan's gaze shifted from the screen to my face, the intensity of his focus making it hard to breathe. "We need to be smarter. We can't let emotions cloud our judgment."

His words struck a chord, reverberating through the clutter of my thoughts. As much as I wanted to ignore the feelings simmering beneath the surface, I knew he was right. But then again, emotions were the fuel driving this investigation, and I could feel my heart wrestling against the chains of reason.

"Agreed," I said, forcing a smile, though it felt like a mask. "But if we're going to outsmart them, we need to think outside the box. These people don't play by the rules. They rewrite them to fit their agenda."

He chuckled softly, the tension easing just a fraction. "Welcome to the club. But let's not forget who we are. We've got some rules of our own. We're not alone in this, and we're not just some pawns on their chessboard."

As we continued to examine the footage, a pattern began to emerge. The players were shifting, and the stakes felt personal. I could sense the urgency escalating, and with it, the anxiety gnawing at my insides.

Just as I leaned forward to get a better view, my phone buzzed insistently on the desk. I snatched it up, and the message from a blocked number made my heart plummet.

"Stop digging. You're in over your head."

"What's wrong?" Ethan asked, noticing my sudden stillness.

"Just a... nuisance." I quickly dismissed the message, but the implications sent a shiver down my spine. "Let's keep going. I think I spotted something in the last meeting we missed."

We turned our attention back to the screen, but I could feel the weight of those words pressing down on me, an ominous shadow whispering warnings I didn't want to heed. As we paused the footage, I couldn't shake the feeling that we were being watched.

The world outside the office felt darker, more threatening, and my instincts screamed at me to be cautious.

"Look at this," I said, pointing at a particularly animated discussion between two figures. "Their body language says everything. There's something happening here that they're not discussing openly."

Ethan leaned in, scrutinizing the details. "Yeah, they're nervous. This could be a chink in their armor. We need to find out what they're really hiding."

"Exactly. We just need to connect the dots." I clicked to expand the footage, my heart racing as I scoured every moment. "If we can find the connection between this meeting and the financial records—"

A sudden crash from the hallway startled us, the sound echoing through the office like a gunshot. We exchanged alarmed glances, adrenaline flooding my veins.

"What was that?" Ethan's voice dropped to a tense whisper.

"I don't know, but it didn't sound good." I stood, instinctively moving toward the door, heart pounding with urgency. "We need to check it out."

"Wait!" he grabbed my arm, his grip firm yet urgent. "We should stay here. It might be better to—"

"Do nothing?" I interrupted, pulling free from his grasp. "You know that's not in my nature."

I stepped into the hallway, the flickering lights casting long shadows that danced along the walls. The office building was eerily quiet now, a stark contrast to the bustling day we'd had. Each footstep felt amplified, the echoing sound a reminder that we were stepping deeper into unknown territory.

The noise came again, a loud thud followed by shuffling footsteps, and instinct kicked in. I rushed down the hall, my heart hammering, the dim light revealing glimpses of chaos. Papers lay scattered across the floor like fallen leaves, and my stomach twisted at the sight.

"Ethan, stay close," I called over my shoulder, glancing back to see him hovering in the doorway, uncertainty etched across his features.

The thuds grew louder, and I edged closer to the source, a door at the far end of the hallway that was slightly ajar. I peered inside, my breath hitching as I caught sight of two shadowy figures rifling through boxes, their movements swift and deliberate.

"Are they—" Ethan whispered, anxiety lacing his voice.

"Shh." I held a finger to my lips, my eyes widening as I tried to make sense of the scene. "I think they're looking for something."

"Or someone," he added quietly, stepping closer.

A sudden crash interrupted our whispers as a box toppled to the floor, sending files spilling across the ground. "We need to back away," I said, adrenaline coursing through me. "This is not safe."

But just as I turned to retreat, a voice rang out, clear and menacing. "You shouldn't have come here."

I froze, the blood draining from my face as a figure emerged from the shadows, eyes glinting with a cold, predatory intent. My instincts screamed at me to run, but there was nowhere to go. The walls seemed to close in, and for a split second, everything hung in the balance.

"What do you want?" I managed to stammer, the question sounding feeble in the heavy air.

"Simple," the figure said, stepping closer, a sinister smile playing on their lips. "To ensure you don't find what you're looking for."

Panic clawed at my throat as I took a step back, but before I could react, Ethan stepped forward, an unexpected shield between me and the impending threat. "You need to leave her out of this," he asserted, voice steady despite the trembling tension.

"Ah, the gallant knight. How quaint." The figure chuckled, but the sound was devoid of humor, echoing through the hallway like a death knell.

My heart raced as I felt the gravity of the moment shift, the air thickening with an impending sense of doom. I reached for Ethan's hand, the warmth grounding me, but I could feel the tremors of fear creeping in.

"Let's go," I whispered urgently, desperation spilling into my tone.

But before we could retreat, the lights flickered again, plunging the hallway into darkness. The world around us erupted into chaos as the ominous figure lunged forward, and my heart stopped. In that moment, as shadows closed in and reality blurred, I knew we were standing at the precipice of something far more dangerous than we could have ever anticipated. The fight for our lives had just begun.

Chapter 14: The Betrayal

Reid moved through the office like a shadow, his presence both commanding and isolating. The light from the window illuminated his sharp jawline, but it couldn't pierce the fog that had descended around him. I watched him from my desk, a sea of papers and unfinished projects scattered around me, as he brushed past, barely acknowledging my presence. The laughter we had shared the night before felt like a distant echo, a fading song that had lost its melody.

"Reid," I called out, my voice soft yet tinged with urgency. He didn't turn, his attention focused on the computer screen, the steady click of keys punctuating the silence between us. It was like trying to penetrate a fortress, and the more I pushed, the more he fortified his defenses. "Can we talk?"

He glanced at me, but his eyes were like ice—cold and impenetrable. "I'm busy," he replied curtly, dismissing me with a wave of his hand as if I were nothing more than an annoying fly buzzing around his head. The bite of his words felt like a slap, and I recoiled, the warmth of our connection now a painful memory.

As the hours dragged on, I fought to concentrate on my work. I poured over documents, piecing together evidence, my mind a tumult of confusion and frustration. Reid's sudden withdrawal left a gnawing emptiness inside me, a chasm I couldn't ignore. Had I misread everything? The way he had looked at me, the way he had laughed, the secrets he had whispered late into the night—they all swirled in a tempest of doubt.

That evening, driven by an unshakable need to understand, I ventured into Reid's office, the air thick with an unsettling tension. I knew it was a breach of trust, but curiosity clawed at me like a persistent cat, urging me to dig deeper. I shuffled through his papers, the scent of ink and aged paper mingling in a way that felt both intimate and invasive. Then, my fingers brushed against something slick and smooth beneath a stack of files—a manila folder, worn at the edges, as if it had been handled too many times, the secrets inside begging to be uncovered.

With trembling hands, I opened the folder. My heart raced, each beat echoing the dread pooling in my stomach. Inside lay documents that twisted my insides, each page revealing a narrative I had never imagined. It was a web of deceit and manipulation, a list of transactions that linked Reid to the very corruption we had vowed to expose. My breath caught in my throat as the implications crashed over me like a tidal wave, each revelation more shocking than the last. I had trusted him. I had let my guard down, woven my heart into a tapestry of vulnerability, and now it all felt like a cruel joke.

The room around me spun, the walls closing in as reality hit with the force of a freight train. How could he do this? I had shared my fears, my dreams—everything that made me who I was, and he had turned it into fodder for his schemes. The betrayal stung like a wasp, sharp and relentless, and I fought back tears that threatened to spill over, blurring the damning words on the page.

I closed the folder with a sudden resolve, my anger igniting a fire within me. No more. No more would I allow him to manipulate me or use our shared moments against me. I wouldn't let his coldness freeze my spirit. I had my own battles to fight, and this revelation felt like the start of a war. I would confront him, demand answers, and reclaim my power, no matter how deep the pain cut.

As I stormed out of his office, my heart pounding with purpose, I found Reid leaning against the wall, arms crossed and an unreadable expression etched across his face. He looked like a statue, chiseled and unyielding, but inside, I could feel the tension radiating off him.

"Hey," I said, my voice steady, though the tremor of betrayal lingered in my chest. "We need to talk."

He arched an eyebrow, the corner of his mouth twitching into a half-smile that felt like a taunt. "I thought you were busy."

"Enough games, Reid," I shot back, my patience worn thin. "I found something today. Something you've been hiding from me."

His expression hardened, and for a fleeting moment, I saw a flicker of something—fear, perhaps? Or was it guilt? "You need to drop it," he replied, his voice dropping to a low murmur, but the tension in his shoulders betrayed his calm facade.

"I can't just ignore it. You've been lying to me, and I deserve to know the truth." My heart raced as I confronted him, each word infused with raw emotion. "What have you been hiding?"

He shifted, his gaze darting away, and I could see the gears turning in his mind, calculating his next move. For a heartbeat, I thought he might confess, the walls he had built starting to crumble. But then, he straightened, the cold veneer slipping back into place. "You don't understand what you're asking for. You're in over your head."

I bristled at his dismissiveness. "In over my head? You're the one who dragged me into this!" My voice rose, echoing through the empty office, the air crackling with unresolved tension.

"Do you really want to know?" he asked, stepping closer, his eyes darkening. "Because once you do, there's no going back. You could lose everything."

"Everything? You've already taken that from me," I shot back, my resolve hardening. "So go ahead. Spill it."

For a moment, the air hung heavy between us, charged with unspoken words and simmering emotions. The battle lines were drawn, and I was ready to fight, to reclaim the narrative of our partnership. But as Reid's expression shifted, a blend of anger and something softer, more vulnerable, crossed his features. I sensed the struggle within him, a conflict that mirrored my own.

With each passing second, I could feel the tension swell, a storm brewing in the air between us. He was a riddle wrapped in an enigma, and I was determined to unravel him, even if it meant tearing down the walls he had so carefully erected.

"Why do you keep pushing?" he asked, his voice steady but laced with a tension that vibrated through the air like a taut string ready to snap. The sharpness of his words felt like daggers, each one aimed to cut through the haze of my frustration.

"Because I deserve answers," I shot back, my heart thundering as the weight of the truth loomed large between us. "You think shutting me out will protect me? I'm already in the middle of this mess."

Reid's expression darkened, shadows flickering across his face like ghosts of secrets long buried. "This isn't a game, Elise. People could get hurt."

"People are already hurt!" I replied, my voice rising with each word, fueled by a mix of fear and anger. "You're acting like you're some kind of lone wolf, but we're supposed to be a team. You can't just isolate yourself and expect me to follow blindly."

His jaw clenched, the muscles tightening like a coiled spring. I could see the struggle in his eyes, the way they darted away from mine as if he were searching for an escape. "You think you want the truth? I don't think you can handle it," he retorted, frustration seeping into his tone.

"Try me," I challenged, crossing my arms defiantly. "I've dealt with enough chaos in my life to know how to navigate the storm."

In a sudden burst of movement, he closed the distance between us, his frustration palpable. "This isn't a storm you can just weather, Elise. This is a hurricane, and it'll rip you apart if you're not careful."

For a moment, the air crackled with unspoken feelings, tension thickening until it felt as if the very walls were vibrating with our unresolved emotions. I could sense his fear, not just for me, but for himself, for the truth that he was so desperately trying to keep hidden.

"Then let's face it together," I urged, my voice softening. "You don't have to do this alone. I'm here, whether you want me to be or not."

The flicker of vulnerability returned to his eyes, and I could see him weighing my words, considering the possibility of letting someone in. Just when I thought he might relent, the facade hardened again, and he stepped back, putting distance between us.

"You don't understand," he said, almost to himself, his voice barely above a whisper. "If you knew what I was really capable of, you wouldn't want anything to do with me."

His admission hung in the air like a taunting specter, and a chill ran down my spine. "You're not some villain in a movie, Reid. You're a man. A flawed, complicated man, but not evil."

He scoffed, the bitterness in his laugh cutting through me. "That's easy for you to say. You don't know what I've done."

"Then tell me!" I implored, my patience fraying at the edges. "Stop hiding behind your walls and let me in. Whatever it is, we can deal with it together."

He ran a hand through his hair, a gesture that spoke volumes of his inner turmoil. "You really think you want that? You're so naïve, Elise. This isn't just about us. It's about consequences, about lives that hang in the balance. People I've had to manipulate, intimidate... even betray."

The honesty in his words struck a chord deep within me, reverberating like a thunderclap in the stillness of the room. I took a deep breath, searching for the right words. "We all make mistakes, Reid. But we don't have to let those mistakes define us. You can still choose to do the right thing."

He seemed to flinch at my words, the air between us heavy with unsaid thoughts. "What if doing the right thing puts you in danger? What if it puts everyone I care about in jeopardy?"

"Then we figure it out together," I insisted, my voice firm. "You're not alone in this, no matter how hard you try to push me away."

A long silence followed, and I could see the battle waging in his mind, the flickering of hope battling against years of hardened resolve. He took a step toward me, his eyes finally meeting mine with a depth of emotion that sent shivers down my spine. "What if I'm too far gone?"

I shook my head, feeling a fierce determination rise within me. "Then we'll bring you back. But you have to trust me, Reid. Trust that I won't run away just because things get messy."

With that, he seemed to deflate slightly, the sharp angles of his demeanor softening. I could see the crack in his armor, the glimpse of a man who wanted to be better but didn't know how to escape the tangled web he had woven.

"I want to tell you everything," he murmured, his voice low, almost vulnerable. "But I need you to understand—once I do, there's no going back. You'll be in danger."

"Then let me make that choice," I replied, heart pounding as I stepped closer, my resolve hardening. "I'd rather know the truth than live in this constant state of confusion and mistrust. Whatever you've done, it doesn't change how I feel about you."

He studied me, his gaze intense, as if trying to decipher the labyrinth of my heart. Finally, he took a deep breath, and for the first time, I saw a flicker of hope. "Alright. But you have to promise me that you won't regret this."

"Promise," I said, my voice steady.

As Reid began to open up, I leaned against the edge of his desk, feeling the electric tension of the moment pulsing through the air. The darkness of his past spilled out, a torrent of secrets that seemed both daunting and liberating. He spoke of choices made in desperation, alliances forged in the shadows, and a web of corruption that snaked through the very foundation of our investigation.

The revelations shook me to my core, each confession a jagged edge against my heart. But through it all, I remained anchored, determined to hold on to the connection we had forged, no matter how complicated the truth became. We stood on the precipice of something profound, a fragile bond that could either shatter or bloom in the face of adversity.

As Reid shared the depths of his entanglement in a world of deceit, the air between us pulsed with an intensity that felt almost alive. He recounted clandestine meetings with figures I had only read about in the newspapers—men with power and connections, names that echoed with an authority that chilled me to the bone. The web he had spun was intricate, a dizzying maze of manipulation that left me reeling. "I didn't have a choice, Elise," he said, desperation creeping into his voice. "I was in too deep."

"Too deep?" I echoed, my heart aching as the pieces fell into place. "What were you thinking, playing both sides? We were supposed to expose the corruption, not become part of it!"

His frustration flared, and for a moment, I thought he might lash out. Instead, he ran a hand through his hair, a gesture of surrender. "I thought I could keep you safe. I thought I could control it."

The irony of his words hung heavy between us. Control was a delusion, and he knew it as well as I did. "You've been lying to me this whole time, Reid. How could you think that would keep me safe?"

"Because I thought if I could just get us to the finish line, I could make it right," he insisted, his voice growing steadier. "I thought you could trust me."

Trust. The word felt like a knife twisting in my gut. "And now? What do you expect me to feel?" I challenged, my voice trembling with a mix of hurt and fury. "You think I can just overlook everything? You're implicated in the very system we're trying to dismantle!"

He stepped closer, the heat of his body radiating against mine, and for a heartbeat, I was caught in the storm of his eyes. "I didn't want you to see this side of me, Elise. I didn't want you to be part of my mistakes."

"Too late for that," I shot back, my heart pounding. "I'm already in this, whether you like it or not."

The silence stretched taut between us, charged with emotions we couldn't fully articulate. "So, what now?" he finally asked, the vulnerability creeping back into his tone.

I took a breath, trying to compose my racing thoughts. "We confront it. We go after the evidence, the truth. But this time, we do it together, without any more secrets."

"Together," he repeated, the word hanging between us like a lifeline. "But I can't guarantee your safety. You could become a target."

"Then we'll be targets together," I replied, a fierce determination igniting in my chest. "I'm not backing down now, Reid. Not after everything that's happened."

He nodded slowly, a reluctant acceptance of my resolve. "Alright. But you need to promise me that if it gets dangerous, you'll walk away."

"I can't promise that. Not anymore." I stepped back, trying to put some space between us. The reality of what lay ahead was daunting, and the stakes were higher than I had ever imagined. "We need to gather everything we have, all the evidence, and then we'll take it to the authorities. We can't just sit back and let this happen."

Reid looked at me, the shadows of doubt still flickering across his features. "And what if they don't believe us? What if we're the ones who end up in trouble?"

I shook my head, pushing the fear down. "We'll figure it out. We've come this far; we can't let them win."

Just then, the soft ping of a notification from my phone broke the tension, cutting through the haze of uncertainty. I pulled it from my pocket, my heart racing as I saw the message flash across the screen. It was from an unknown number, a single sentence that sent icy fingers creeping up my spine: "You need to stop digging."

"What is it?" Reid asked, his voice low, concern etched across his face.

I held the phone out to him, my hands trembling. "Someone just warned me to back off."

His expression shifted, a mix of concern and determination flashing across his face. "Did they say who they are?"

"No. Just... stop digging."

Reid took a step back, scanning the room as if the walls might yield some answer. "We need to be careful. They know we're onto something, and they won't hesitate to silence us."

"Then we'll have to move quickly," I replied, my heart pounding with a blend of fear and adrenaline. "We can't let them intimidate us."

He nodded, the fire returning to his eyes. "Let's gather what we have and meet up later. We'll plan our next move."

I felt a surge of resolve as we began to gather the papers and files scattered across the desk, the physical evidence of our shared mission weighing heavily in my hands. With each document I tucked away, I felt the reality of our situation settling into a harsh truth: this was no longer just a fight against corruption; it was a battle for our lives.

As we finished, Reid paused, his gaze lingering on me. "Whatever happens, I want you to know I'm glad you're in this with me."

The sincerity in his voice sent a thrill through me, mingling with the fear of what lay ahead. "Same here. Just... stay close."

"Always," he promised, his eyes steady as he stepped back.

With one last look, I turned to leave, the weight of our shared mission pressing down on my shoulders. As I exited the building, a chill swept through the air, a premonition of the storm brewing just on the horizon.

The streets outside were dimly lit, shadows stretching like fingers reaching for me as I hurried to my car. I had barely unlocked the door when I heard a rustling sound behind me, a soft crunch of gravel that sent my heart racing.

I spun around, scanning the area, but the street was empty, the cool night air whispering secrets I couldn't decipher. Just as I turned back, a figure emerged from the shadows, a flash of recognition striking me like lightning.

"Reid!" I shouted, but it was too late. The figure lunged, and before I could react, the world around me dissolved into chaos, leaving me grappling with the terrifying realization that the game had changed, and the stakes were higher than I ever imagined.

Chapter 15: A Game of Shadows

The rain pattered softly against the window, a symphony of droplets weaving a rhythm that danced around the tension crackling in the room. Each droplet seemed to echo my heart's frantic beat as I faced him, the man I had trusted more than anyone. The shadows cast by the flickering candlelight played tricks on my eyes, morphing his familiar features into something foreign, something unrecognizable. His once-warm gaze felt like shards of ice piercing through the haze of my anger.

"What do you mean, protect me?" I demanded, my voice barely above a whisper, trembling with the weight of unshed tears. "Protect me from what? From whom? You've been lying to me, hiding everything. What kind of protection is that?" I could feel the heat of betrayal curling around my heart, squeezing tightly until I was almost breathless.

He took a step closer, the distance between us shrinking, yet the chasm of his secrets yawned wide. "I did what I had to do. You don't understand—there are forces at play here that are far beyond anything you can comprehend. I thought keeping you in the dark would keep you safe." His voice was low, almost pleading, but I was far beyond placating words.

"Safe? Is that what you call this? You've made a mockery of my trust." The accusation hung heavy in the air, filled with the weight of every secret I had unearthed in the last few days. It had begun as a whisper in the shadows, a hint of something amiss in our world, but now it felt like a dark storm gathering strength. I could feel it in my bones, the undeniable truth that this was only the beginning.

His brow furrowed, a flicker of desperation crossing his features. "I never wanted this for you. I wanted to keep you away from all of it—the threats, the danger that lurks in every corner of our lives. I thought I could shield you from the darkness." The sincerity in his voice caught me off guard. There was no denying the depth of his feelings, but they were laced with something else—fear, perhaps, or guilt.

"Shield me?" I echoed, my tone dripping with disbelief. "You've wrapped me in chains of your own making. I'm drowning in your lies." I turned away, not wanting him to see how deeply his words cut. Each accusation felt like a dagger twisting deeper into the fabric of our relationship, unraveling it thread by thread.

"Please," he said, his voice softer now, almost broken. "Just listen to me. I didn't want to involve you in this world—this game of shadows that I've been thrust into. But now, I can't protect you anymore. You're already in it, whether you like it or not."

I turned back to him, my eyes narrowing. "In it? I was blissfully ignorant, and you pulled me into this chaos. Don't you see? You can't protect me from what you've created." The fire in my words reflected the tempest swirling in my chest, but beneath the anger lay something else—fear, a fear that his secrets might unravel everything I had come to know and love.

His gaze fell to the ground, shoulders slumping under the weight of unspoken burdens. "I know. I just thought... if I could keep you away from it a little longer, maybe things would change. I thought I could fix it." The vulnerability in his admission cracked through my hardened resolve. I had never seen him so defeated, and for a fleeting moment, I felt the urge to reach out, to comfort him despite the chaos we were ensnared in.

"Fix what?" I pressed, my heart racing as the truth lay tantalizingly close, just beyond my grasp. "What are you even talking about? You can't fix something you've broken."

He stepped back, the space between us widening again. "I can't go into detail, not yet. But you need to trust me. I need you to understand that everything I've done—every choice I've made—it was to keep you safe. This isn't just about us anymore; it's bigger than that."

A swell of emotions crashed over me, each wave stronger than the last. "Bigger than us?" I laughed bitterly, the sound hollow. "You've made this into a game of secrets and lies. Do you think I can just sit here and play the victim? I'm not some damsel in distress waiting for you to ride in and save the day. I want the truth, and I deserve it."

The silence stretched between us, thick with unspoken words. I could see the flicker of conflict in his eyes, the battle between his instincts to shield me and the growing realization that I was no longer the naïve girl he had once known.

"I never wanted to keep you in the dark forever," he finally said, his voice barely a whisper. "But I was afraid. Afraid of what this world would do to you if you knew the whole truth."

"Then let me choose my own battles," I implored, taking a small step towards him. "Let me fight alongside you instead of hiding in the shadows. I'm done with the secrets."

He searched my eyes, looking for something—maybe a sign that I would retreat, that I would back down and let him handle everything as he always had. But the fire in me refused to dim.

"I can't promise you won't get hurt," he said, finally letting his guard down. "But I can promise that whatever happens next, we'll face it together."

And in that moment, the darkness that had cloaked us began to lift, revealing the path ahead. It was a dangerous road, fraught with unknown perils, but it was ours to navigate. I could feel my resolve hardening, a sense of purpose igniting deep within me. No more secrets. No more shadows.

"Together," I repeated, my voice steadier now, filled with newfound determination. The road ahead was shrouded in uncertainty, but one thing was clear: we would face whatever came our way, side by side.

The tension in the room hung like thick fog, wrapping around us as we both fought for control. I could hear the soft tick-tock of the old clock on the wall, each second stretching into eternity as I contemplated his words. "You're in deeper than I thought," I finally said, breaking the silence, my voice steadying as the truth settled in. "How long have you been living this double life?"

He ran a hand through his hair, the gesture so familiar yet now filled with layers of meaning. "Longer than I care to admit," he replied, his gaze falling to the floor as if it held the answers he couldn't quite articulate. "But I never meant to drag you into it. I thought I could handle it alone."

"Handle it alone?" I echoed incredulously. "And how's that working out for you? Because from where I stand, it looks like your 'handling' has put both of us in danger." The fire in my words lit a spark in him, and he looked up, a flicker of defiance breaking through his shadows.

"It's not that simple!" he snapped, frustration boiling over. "You have no idea what I'm dealing with. The people I'm involved with—they don't play by the same rules. You think I wanted any of this? I wanted to keep you safe, to give you a life far removed from this chaos. But now it's too late."

"Too late?" I repeated, the incredulity rising in my voice. "You've kept me in the dark while the storm raged around us! Don't you think it's a little too late for that excuse?" The anger surged within me, a powerful wave crashing against the walls of his carefully constructed defenses.

He took a step forward, his eyes darkening with an intensity that made my breath hitch. "I know I've messed up, but I need you to trust me now. There are things I can't explain, but I'm trying to protect you from them. We have to leave—tonight."

"Leave? Just like that?" I couldn't help the incredulous laugh that escaped my lips. "What, are we fleeing to some romantic hideaway in the mountains? This isn't a fairy tale, and I'm not about to be whisked away like some damsel waiting for her knight."

He moved closer, urgency etched in every line of his face. "This is serious. They've been watching us, and if we don't act fast, we'll be caught in the crossfire. I won't let that happen to you."

My heart raced, the reality of his words sinking in like a stone in my stomach. "Caught in the crossfire of what, exactly? You still haven't told me who 'they' are."

A pained expression crossed his face, and he hesitated, his jaw tightening. "I can't reveal everything yet. Just know that I have enemies—powerful ones. I thought I could outsmart them, but I was wrong."

"Outsmarting them sounds like a game, and I'm tired of playing games." I crossed my arms, unwilling to back down despite the rising tide of fear threatening to overwhelm me. "If we're in this together, I deserve to know the full story."

His shoulders dropped, and he let out a slow breath, the weight of his secrets pressing down on him. "I can't tell you everything right now, but I promise I will. I need you to trust me until then. I'll explain as we go."

"Trust you? It's hard to do that when your version of trust comes with half-truths and cryptic warnings." I shifted my weight, frustration bubbling just beneath the surface. "You're asking me to jump into the unknown without a safety net."

"Do you think I want to drag you into this mess?" He was practically pleading now, desperation seeping into his voice. "But the truth is, you're already in it. If we don't leave, we're going to be swallowed whole."

An uneasy silence settled over us, thick and heavy, and for a moment, the only sound was the relentless rain, tapping against the window like an anxious heartbeat. I could feel the walls closing in, the reality of our situation pressing down on me. I didn't want to leave; I didn't want to abandon everything I had built. But the truth echoed in my mind, relentless and unyielding: staying would mean putting myself directly in the path of danger.

"What do we need to do?" I finally asked, my voice steady despite the turmoil within. "If we're going to do this, we need a plan. I'm not just going to run away without knowing where we're going."

His expression shifted, a flicker of hope sparking in his eyes. "We'll need to gather some supplies—just the essentials. I have a car parked a few blocks away, and it's equipped for a quick getaway. We need to move fast."

I nodded slowly, adrenaline coursing through my veins as I mentally prepared myself. "And what about your enemies? Are they just going to let us walk away?"

"They might try to stop us, but if we're smart about it, we'll get a head start." He reached for my hand, his grip firm yet gentle. "I know it's a lot to ask, but we need to trust each other completely right now."

"I'll trust you, but only because I don't have another choice," I replied, my heart pounding with uncertainty. "Just remember: this is a two-way street. I'm not your pawn."

"Understood," he said, the corners of his mouth twitching into a small smile. "I wouldn't dream of treating you like one."

With a shared glance of determination, we turned towards the door, ready to step into the unknown. The storm outside raged on, mirroring the tumult of emotions swirling within me. As we crossed the threshold, the world beyond was a blur of rain and shadows, but beneath the uncertainty lay a flicker of hope. Together, we would navigate the darkness, refusing to be defined by the secrets that had threatened to tear us apart. In that moment, I realized I wouldn't let fear dictate my choices anymore. Whatever lay ahead, we would face it together, even if it meant plunging headfirst into chaos.

The city lay before us, cloaked in shadows and shrouded by the relentless rain, its streets slick with uncertainty. The air buzzed with the scent of wet asphalt and distant thunder, an ominous backdrop to our hurried escape. As we sprinted down the alley, the harsh glow of the streetlamps flickered, illuminating our path with an almost eerie glow, casting elongated shadows that seemed to twist and reach for us.

"Is it always this dramatic?" I quipped, half out of breath and half in disbelief at the unfolding chaos. I could feel the adrenaline surging through my veins, a heady cocktail of fear and excitement. "You should really consider a more subtle approach next time."

He glanced at me, a smirk breaking through the tension. "Subtlety isn't exactly an option when you've got enemies lurking in the dark. Besides, I thought you liked a little adventure."

"Adventure? Sure. A death-defying escape from a life I didn't ask for? Not quite the thrill I was hoping for." I shot back, trying to keep the mood light even as my heart raced. The irony wasn't lost on me; I had always craved excitement, but not like this—not under the specter of danger.

We reached the car, a nondescript sedan parked under the shelter of a nearby awning. As he fumbled with the keys, I stole a glance over my shoulder, scanning the darkness for any sign of pursuit. My instincts buzzed like a swarm of bees, alerting me to the imminent threat that seemed to pulse in the very air around us. "Are you sure this is going to work?" I asked, a sliver of doubt creeping into my voice.

He looked up, eyes glinting with determination. "It has to. We'll be out of here in no time." With that, he threw the door open and slid into the driver's seat, his expression a mix of urgency and resolve.

I followed suit, slamming the door behind me as if that single act could seal us off from the chaos we were leaving behind.

As he started the engine, the car rumbled to life, a low growl that felt reassuring in the tense silence. "Where to?" I asked, trying to sound casual, though my heart felt like it was tap dancing in my chest.

"Anywhere but here," he replied, shifting the car into gear and pulling away from the curb. "We need to find a place to lay low for a bit, somewhere off the radar."

"Off the radar, huh? So, like a cabin in the woods? Are we about to star in our own romantic thriller?" I shot him a teasing grin, but my stomach churned at the thought of the isolation.

"More like a safe house," he countered, the corner of his mouth lifting. "But I like the sound of 'romantic thriller.' Maybe we'll write our own script."

I laughed despite the situation, the tension breaking just a little. "Great, as long as I get to choose the ending."

The streets blurred past us, each turn pulling us further away from the life I had known, closer to an uncertain future. As we drove, the rain began to let up, giving way to a murky twilight that wrapped the city in a veil of mystery. The familiar landmarks I had taken for granted slipped away into the shadows, replaced by an unknown landscape filled with endless possibilities—or perhaps dangers.

"Tell me more about these enemies," I urged, trying to anchor myself in something I could understand. "You can't just toss me into this without context. I need to know what we're dealing with."

His jaw clenched, and I could see the wheels turning in his mind, contemplating how much to share. "They're part of a larger network—powerful people who don't take kindly to betrayal. When I decided to step away from the game, I made a lot of enemies."

"Betrayal?" I echoed, feeling a chill race down my spine. "What game are we talking about here?"

"The kind of game where people play for keeps," he replied, his tone darkening. "I was involved in something much bigger than either of us realized. And now that I've pulled you into it, I can't let you go."

I blinked, trying to absorb the gravity of his words. "So, what exactly did you do? Were you a spy? A criminal?" My mind raced with possibilities, each more sinister than the last.

"Something in between," he admitted, his voice steady but laced with tension. "I was an operative, but I went off-script to protect you. It's a long story, one that I hope to tell you when it's safe."

"Operative, huh?" I mused, feeling both impressed and unnerved. "So this isn't just about you protecting me. It's about you protecting yourself too."

"Exactly." He glanced at me, and I could see the vulnerability behind his bravado. "I've made choices I'm not proud of, and now those choices are catching up with me—and with you. I need to find a way to get us out of this mess."

The car slipped into a quieter neighborhood, the streets lined with tall trees whose branches whispered secrets to the wind. As we turned a corner, my breath caught in my throat. There, looming ahead, was a dilapidated house, its windows dark and foreboding. It looked like a relic from another time, a stark contrast to the bustling city we had just fled.

"Is this where we're laying low?" I asked, my voice rising in disbelief. "Because if it is, I'm not sure it's the best choice for a romantic getaway."

"Trust me," he said, his tone firm. "It's safe, and it'll keep us off the radar for a while." He parked the car and turned to me, his expression grave. "But we need to move quickly. They could be following us."

I nodded, pushing down the unease that flared at the thought of stepping into the unknown. As we stepped out of the car, the air grew thick with anticipation, and every sound—the rustle of leaves, the distant echo of thunder—seemed to amplify the weight of the moment.

"Stay close," he instructed, his hand brushing mine, a spark igniting between us. "We'll go in through the back."

We crept around to the rear of the house, the damp earth squelching beneath our feet. The door creaked open at his touch, revealing a dark interior that smelled of mildew and abandonment. As he stepped inside, I hesitated, the thrill of the chase giving way to the unsettling silence that enveloped us.

Just then, my phone buzzed in my pocket, breaking the stillness like a gunshot. I pulled it out, heart racing as I saw the name flashing on the screen—an unknown number. The hairs on the back of my neck stood on end. "Who is it?" he asked, his voice tense.

"I have no idea," I replied, my voice barely a whisper. "Should I answer?"

Before I could react, the phone buzzed again, the screen illuminating the darkness with an eerie glow. My fingers trembled as I pressed the green button, bringing the device to my ear. "Hello?"

Silence. Then a low, menacing voice slithered through the line, sending chills racing down my spine. "You shouldn't have run. Now you'll pay the price."

The connection went dead, leaving only the echoes of my racing heart and the suffocating darkness around us. I turned to him, my breath hitching in my throat, but before I could speak, the distant sound of tires screeching filled the air, slicing through the stillness like a knife.

"We need to go," he said urgently, grabbing my hand and pulling me deeper into the shadows of the house.

As we moved through the darkness, I couldn't shake the feeling that we were being watched, that the game had just taken a turn for the worse, and whatever lay ahead was waiting, poised to strike.

Chapter 16: The Thin Line Between Love and Hate

The evening air was thick with tension as I sat across from him in that dimly lit office, the faint hum of the city barely penetrating the thick glass walls. Outside, the world thrived, oblivious to the chaos simmering within. Shadows danced around us, wrapping us in their embrace as we poured over endless files that detailed our crumbling partnership. The papers lay strewn across the mahogany desk, like the pieces of our lives slowly unraveling before us. His brow furrowed in concentration, a stark contrast to the charming smile I once found irresistible. The line between love and hate blurred with each heated argument, each moment of silence stretched taut between us like a coiled spring, ready to snap.

I could feel the weight of betrayal sitting heavily in my chest, a relentless ache that had become all too familiar. It was maddening, really, how he could infuriate me with one breath and ignite a wildfire of longing with the next. "Do you really think you can just fix this with paperwork?" I shot at him, my voice sharp, laced with venom. He glanced up, his blue eyes piercing through the haze of anger that clouded my mind.

"Maybe it's not about the paperwork," he replied, his tone steady but soft, almost pleading. "Maybe it's about us." The silence that followed was deafening, stretching like an elastic band ready to snap. I could see the flicker of a challenge in his gaze, and despite the fury that bubbled within me, I felt a spark of something else—a wild, reckless yearning.

With a huff, I leaned back in my chair, crossing my arms tightly over my chest as if it would shield me from his gaze. "You think we can just sweep everything under the rug? Pretend it didn't happen?"

I shot back, my heart racing as he inched closer, invading my space with an intensity that sent shivers down my spine.

He reached for my hand, his warmth penetrating the cold shell I had wrapped around myself. "Sometimes, pretending is the only way to survive," he said, his voice dropping to a whisper, and in that moment, the room spun around us, the weight of unspoken words crashing down like an avalanche. The cool air of the office felt stifling, thick with the aroma of coffee and a hint of his aftershave that made my heart race despite my best intentions.

For a fleeting second, the tension shifted. We weren't rivals or enemies; we were just two souls tangled in a web of emotions we were too stubborn to untangle. I stared into his eyes, searching for the truth behind the mask he wore. Was it arrogance? Ignorance? Or was there a flicker of vulnerability hidden beneath his bravado?

"Do you remember how we used to be?" he asked, a ghost of a smile curling at the corners of his lips. "Back when we weren't constantly at each other's throats?" My breath hitched as memories of laughter and late-night conversations flooded my mind. The way he'd toss his head back in laughter, eyes bright and carefree, made my chest ache with a longing that was both beautiful and devastating.

I scoffed, shaking my head, but the smile threatened to break free. "Yeah, and then you decided to betray my trust," I countered, trying to keep my tone steady. "You don't get to just reminisce while I'm still trying to pick up the pieces."

"Maybe I was wrong," he said, his voice earnest, drawing me in like a moth to a flame. "Maybe I should have told you the truth from the beginning. But I didn't want to lose you."

My heart twisted at his admission, and I felt the walls I had built around my emotions begin to crumble. "And look where we are now," I said softly, my voice barely above a whisper. "Lost in this mess."

The silence stretched between us, thick and heavy, filled with all the things we hadn't said. His thumb brushed over my knuckles, sending shockwaves of sensation coursing through me, reminding me of the tender moments we once shared. Just when I thought I could escape the storm of emotions raging within me, he leaned closer, his breath warm against my skin. "I never stopped caring, you know. Not even for a moment."

The sincerity in his voice disarmed me, and suddenly, the office felt too small, the distance between us too great. I could taste the bitterness of our past, but beneath that, there was a sweetness I couldn't deny. The air crackled with something electric, a pull that was both terrifying and intoxicating. My heart raced, not out of anger this time, but from the sheer force of my feelings threatening to consume me.

"Maybe we should stop pretending," I breathed, the words slipping out before I could snatch them back. His eyes widened slightly, and for a moment, I saw a glimmer of hope in his gaze. But just as quickly, the fear crept back in, clawing at my resolve.

"We can't just ignore what happened," I continued, my voice stronger now, as if to steady my wavering heart. "It's not that easy."

"Life rarely is," he shot back, a playful challenge in his tone. "But isn't it worth trying? Isn't it worth fighting for?"

As I stared into his eyes, the walls around my heart began to dissolve, and I found myself teetering on the precipice of a choice that could change everything. My heart whispered to me, urging me to take a leap, to trust in the flicker of hope igniting between us, but my mind screamed caution. Was this the moment I would finally surrender, risking everything I had built to embrace the chaos of love?

The moment hung between us like the delicate strands of a spider's web, each quiver echoing with the uncertainty of what lay ahead. His fingers lingered over mine, an anchor in the storm of emotions swirling around us. I could feel my heart pounding, each thud a reminder of the line we danced on, a perilous tightrope strung high above the depths of unresolved feelings. The air in the room thickened, charged with the energy of everything left unsaid, every hurt and every hope coiling together into a singular moment that felt as fragile as glass.

"Let's not make this harder than it is," I said, forcing my voice to remain steady, though the tremor in my hand betrayed me. "You can't just touch me and expect that everything will magically fix itself." My words came out sharper than I intended, but they held the truth I was struggling to articulate. The pain of betrayal lingered like a ghost at the edges of our conversation, haunting the spaces between us.

"I'm not trying to fix it," he replied, his voice a low rumble, deep and earnest. "I'm just trying to understand how we got here." He leaned back slightly, his gaze piercing mine, as if he could peel away the layers of my defenses with sheer will alone. "You mean something to me, and I can't pretend that doesn't matter."

"You mean something to me too," I admitted, my heart a traitor to my resolve. "But that doesn't change the fact that you kept secrets. You made choices without me, and those choices hurt." The weight of my words hung heavily in the air, each syllable a reminder of the gulf that lay between us.

"Maybe I thought I was protecting you," he countered, his expression shifting, vulnerability flickering in his eyes. "Or maybe I was just scared of losing what we had."

"Scared?" I echoed, incredulous. "You think hiding the truth was the right way to handle things? You turned everything into a game." I tried to keep my voice steady, but it cracked under the strain of all that simmering rage and sorrow. "And now we're here, playing this twisted version of cat and mouse where every moment feels like a ticking clock."

"Then let's stop playing," he challenged, his eyes narrowing slightly, that familiar spark of defiance igniting the air around us. "Let's be honest. For once."

His insistence ignited a fire in me that I thought had dimmed. "Fine. I'm listening." My heart raced, bracing for whatever truths he was about to unveil, knowing full well that the revelations could shatter what was left of our fragile bond.

"I never meant for it to go this far," he began, his tone serious but laced with an edge of something almost playful. "I thought I could manage it all—work, the partnership, and... you."

The way he said "you" made my breath hitch. It was the kind of inflection that suggested so much more than mere attraction. "You should have known better," I snapped, although a part of me warmed at the implication, a flicker of hope igniting in my chest.

"Maybe I was too busy trying to keep my head above water," he said, leaning forward as if the distance between us was suffocating him. "Or maybe I thought you wouldn't want to be tangled up in this mess."

"Maybe you underestimated me," I shot back, my bravado giving me the courage to lean closer as well. The room felt electric, charged with possibility and danger. "I'm not the one who's scared here."

"Is that so?" He raised an eyebrow, the corner of his mouth quirking up in that infuriatingly charming way that used to make my heart flutter. "You think you can handle whatever I throw your way?"

"Try me," I dared, my pulse racing in a mix of fear and exhilaration. His gaze bore into mine, a silent battle of wills playing out as we exchanged words sharp enough to cut glass.

But just then, the spell was broken by the shrill ring of his phone, slicing through the atmosphere like a knife. We both jumped, the moment shattering as the reality of our situation crashed back in. He glanced at the screen, his face darkening as he read the name flashing in bold letters. "It's my brother," he muttered, frustration evident in his voice.

"Do you need to get that?" I asked, attempting to mask the disappointment creeping into my tone. The unspoken tension between us hung like a veil, but reality always had a way of intruding.

"No," he said, his expression hardening as he silenced the call. "Not right now." His focus shifted back to me, determination etched across his features. "I need to figure this out. You're not the only one who feels trapped in this."

"Then let's talk," I urged, my voice softer now, as if the fracture in our connection had opened a path for honesty to seep through. "We can't keep dancing around the real issues."

He nodded, taking a deep breath as if steeling himself for a confession that had been too long in coming. "There's more to this than just us, you know. My family, my brother... they're involved in things I never wanted you to know about."

"What kind of things?" I asked, a knot of anxiety forming in my stomach. "You're not talking about anything illegal, are you?"

"Not illegal, but definitely complicated," he replied, his voice low and grave. "They've made some choices that could impact everything. And I didn't want you to be part of that."

The gravity of his words weighed heavily between us, shifting the dynamics of our fragile truce. My heart raced with a blend of dread and curiosity. "And now? Now that I know, what happens?"

He took a moment, the tension between us crackling like static electricity. "Now, we figure it out together," he said, a hint of resolve creeping into his tone. "If you're willing to trust me. Because I can't promise it'll be easy."

"Easy was never on the table, was it?" I replied, a wry smile creeping onto my lips despite the seriousness of the situation. "But that doesn't mean we shouldn't try."

With a shared glance, an unspoken agreement hung in the air, binding us together against the looming storm. Whatever lay ahead, I knew one thing for sure: we were no longer just players in a game of deception. We were allies, ready to face the truth, no matter how jagged or painful. And somehow, that felt like the first step toward healing, toward finding our way back to each other amid the chaos.

The air grew thick with tension as we hovered on the brink of a revelation that could alter the course of our lives. His admission hung between us like a promise, glimmering with hope yet tinged with uncertainty. "We can face this together," he urged, determination coursing through his words. The weight of the world felt heavy on his shoulders, but as I gazed into his eyes, a mix of determination and vulnerability flickered beneath the surface.

"Together, huh?" I replied, my voice laced with skepticism, a lingering caution from the past. "You make it sound so easy. Just trust you and ignore the mess?" My heart thudded in my chest, unsure whether I was ready to dive deeper into this unpredictable waters.

"I know it sounds like a lot," he admitted, running a hand through his hair, tousling it further. "But I want to be transparent. The last thing I want is for you to feel trapped or used."

The sincerity in his voice tugged at something deep within me, a longing for honesty amid the chaos. "So, what's the plan? We expose the family secrets over coffee?" I asked, my tone playful yet edged with seriousness.

He chuckled, the sound a balm to my frayed nerves. "Not quite. But there are people who need to know the truth. We need to confront this head-on."

The thought of stepping into the chaos of his family's world sent a shiver of anxiety racing down my spine. "You do realize that this could blow up in our faces, right? I mean, what if it backfires?"

"Then we'll handle it," he said, his eyes sparkling with that familiar defiance that always drew me in. "I've faced worse. Trust me."

"Trust seems to be the issue here," I murmured, more to myself than to him. But even as the words left my lips, I couldn't shake the instinct to lean into the unknown.

A sudden knock at the door jolted us back into reality, the moment suspended like a tightrope stretched too far. He looked at me, eyes wide with surprise, as if the interruption had come from another world entirely. "Who the hell could that be?"

"I guess we're about to find out," I said, my voice a mixture of apprehension and curiosity. The knock came again, more insistent this time, and before I could protest, he stood and opened the door.

A woman stood in the doorway, her expression unreadable, framed by a halo of dark curls that cascaded over her shoulders. The faint scent of jasmine wafted into the room, mingling with the lingering aroma of coffee. "I'm sorry to interrupt, but I need to speak with you—both of you," she said, her voice steady yet tinged with urgency.

I exchanged a quick glance with him, confusion etched on our faces. "Do we know you?" he asked, his tone cautious.

"I'm Isabelle," she replied, taking a step closer, her eyes darting between us like a bird assessing its next move. "I'm here about your brother."

My heart raced as I glanced at him, the color draining from his face. "What about him?"

"Let's just say he's in deeper trouble than you realize," she said, her gaze locking onto his with an intensity that sent chills skittering down my spine. "And if you're involved, you need to know what you're walking into."

"What do you mean?" I asked, my voice sharper than intended. "What kind of trouble?"

Isabelle took a deep breath, her demeanor shifting from urgency to grim determination. "Your brother is mixed up in something dangerous. He's been trying to protect you, but his choices could put you both at risk."

He stepped forward, his expression fierce. "What are you talking about? He would never—"

"Never what?" she interrupted, her tone incredulous. "Never get involved in a situation that could endanger his family? You don't know the half of it."

The revelation hung heavy in the air, spinning a web of confusion and dread. I could see the tension coiling between them, the raw energy crackling like a storm on the horizon. "What do you know?" I pressed, needing clarity amid the chaos that threatened to engulf us.

"Enough to know that you're in the crosshairs," she said, her voice softening as she turned to me. "And if you don't get involved now, it might be too late."

I felt a cold wave wash over me, the reality of the situation setting in like an ice-cold shower. "What do you want us to do?"

"First, we need to get to him. He's been hiding something, and it's only a matter of time before it blows up in his face. We have to act fast."

The urgency in her voice propelled me into motion, the adrenaline coursing through my veins like wildfire. I glanced at him, and the unspoken agreement surged between us once more. This was our moment, our chance to confront the tangled web of lies and truths that had ensnared us.

"Okay," I said, my voice steadier than I felt. "What's the plan?"

Isabelle stepped fully into the office, the door clicking shut behind her as if sealing us in with the weight of our choices. "First, we need to gather the right information. There are people who know more than they're letting on. We can't just charge in without knowing who we're up against."

"And then?" he pressed, the determination in his voice igniting a fire within me.

"Then we confront your brother, and we find out the truth once and for all," she said, a fierce glint in her eyes. "But you need to understand—this won't be easy. Once the truth is out, there's no going back."

"I'm in," I declared, my heart pounding with a blend of fear and excitement. I glanced at him, waiting for his response, knowing that the path ahead was fraught with danger.

He looked at me, and in that moment, I saw a flicker of something fierce—a shared resolve to navigate the storm ahead. "I'm in too," he said, his voice steady, but I could sense the turmoil bubbling just beneath the surface.

Isabelle nodded, her expression serious. "Then let's move. We don't have much time."

As we made our way out of the office, I couldn't shake the feeling that we were stepping into the unknown, each moment pulling us deeper into a world woven with secrets and shadows. My heart raced with a mixture of dread and exhilaration, and just as we reached the door, the blaring sound of sirens echoed from the street outside, piercing the stillness like a warning bell.

"What the hell is that?" I asked, my heart skipping a beat.

"Trouble," Isabelle said, her expression hardening as she glanced back at us. "And we need to be ready for anything."

With that, the world outside shifted, the air thick with impending danger, and I knew in that moment that everything was about to change. As we stepped into the chaos, uncertainty clung to me like a second skin, and my mind raced with possibilities—some hopeful, others terrifying. We were no longer just fighting for our partnership; we were fighting for our lives.

Chapter 17: The Trap Tightens

The stench of old paper mixed with the metallic tang of fear hung thick in the air as Reid and I sifted through the chaos of his office. Stacks of files teetered precariously, threatening to topple like the very foundation of the world we were stumbling through. I could feel the weight of our investigation pressing down on us, heavy as lead. Each file held whispers of betrayal, shrouded in the minutiae of corporate espionage and double-crosses that sent chills racing down my spine. Reid sat across from me, his usually composed demeanor cracking like ice underfoot.

He ran a hand through his hair, frustration etching lines into his brow. "We need to find the original documents," he muttered, half to himself and half to me, the intensity in his voice as palpable as the dust motes dancing in the dying light. The sun was sinking low, casting long shadows that crept along the walls like fingers of impending doom.

I nodded, though my thoughts were a jumbled mess. Every moment spent unearthing layers of deceit felt like navigating a treacherous minefield. One wrong step could detonate a bomb we were not even aware existed. My fingers brushed against the edge of a folder labeled "Confidential," the word practically glowing in the dim light. It beckoned me closer, promising secrets buried beneath the mundane.

"Reid," I said, the urgency in my voice breaking through the thick air. "What if we're looking in the wrong place? What if the answers are right under our noses?"

He glanced up, his sharp blue eyes narrowing in thought. "You might be onto something. Maybe it's not about the files themselves, but the people connected to them. What if we—"

The sound of a heavy thud interrupted him, the noise ricocheting off the walls like an omen. My heart stuttered, and I froze, my breath catching in my throat. Reid stood up abruptly, the chair scraping against the wooden floor as he moved towards the door. I followed closely, my instincts screaming for caution, the tension coiling tighter in my chest.

He pressed his ear against the door, and I felt a swell of unease ripple through me. The silence was oppressive, the kind that stretched until it threatened to snap. Just as I was about to suggest we retreat, a soft, ominous rustle came from the hallway. Reid's expression hardened; he reached for the doorknob, and before I could protest, he swung it open.

The hallway was empty, yet a chill swept through, chilling the air around us. Shadows danced at the edges of the fluorescent lights, and I could almost hear the whispers of secrets lurking just beyond our sight. "Stay close," he instructed, his voice low and gravelly, a command that made my pulse quicken. I nodded, trailing behind him as we ventured into the unknown.

As we made our way down the corridor, the atmosphere felt charged, electric with anticipation. Each creak of the floorboards beneath our feet echoed like a countdown. I stole glances at Reid, whose jaw was set in determination, the sharp angles of his face illuminated in stark relief against the harsh lighting. He was the kind of man who radiated strength, but I could sense the undercurrent of fear—an emotion that mirrored my own.

Suddenly, a door at the end of the hall swung open, and a figure stepped out. The resemblance was uncanny—long, dark hair cascading around her shoulders, eyes that seemed to absorb the light. It was Claire, Reid's estranged sister. The tension in the air thickened as recognition crashed over us like a wave.

"What are you doing here?" Reid demanded, his voice taut, masking the whirlwind of emotions beneath. Claire shrugged, a smirk dancing at the corners of her lips. "Just visiting my favorite brother. Heard you were playing detective."

I caught Reid's sharp intake of breath, the way his eyes darted between her and me, a silent struggle for control unfolding before me. "You need to leave," he said, his tone sharp. "This isn't safe for you."

"Safe? Oh, please." Claire stepped closer, the light illuminating the defiance in her stance. "You think I don't know what you're up to? You're digging into things that are better left buried, Reid. You have no idea what you're messing with."

"Maybe you could help us then," I interjected, trying to bridge the chasm of animosity growing between them. "If you know something—"

"Know something?" She laughed, the sound tinged with bitterness. "I know plenty, but it's not the kind of information that comes without a price." Her gaze flickered to the shadows, a flicker of unease betraying her bravado.

"Claire, this isn't a game," Reid warned, his voice low and urgent. "People are getting hurt."

"Right. Like you care," she shot back, eyes narrowing. "You abandoned us for your precious job, and now you expect me to jump in and save the day?"

The tension crackled in the air as they squared off, a storm brewing in the small corridor. I could sense the depths of their history—decades of unspoken grievances simmering just beneath the surface. It was like watching a collision of worlds, each one vying for dominance.

"Enough!" I interrupted, unable to bear the standoff any longer. "We're all in this mess together, whether we like it or not. So how about we focus on what really matters?" The words hung in the air, the weight of truth settling over us like a heavy blanket.

Claire's expression shifted, uncertainty flickering across her features. "Fine," she relented, crossing her arms defensively. "But don't expect me to trust you, Reid. Not after everything."

DUAL FLAME 179

Before Reid could respond, the envelope we had found earlier slipped from my pocket, fluttering to the ground. The photograph inside it had been an unsettling reminder of our precarious situation, a stark reminder that someone was watching us. I bent to retrieve it, my heart pounding, feeling the eyes of both Reid and Claire on me.

"Let's not forget why we're here," I said, holding up the photograph, the threat etched in its words still fresh in my mind. "We have to keep moving. Whoever did this isn't going to wait for us to get our act together."

Reid's jaw tightened, and Claire's eyes widened as she caught a glimpse of the photograph. "You really think they're watching?" she asked, skepticism mixing with concern.

"Absolutely," I replied, my voice steady despite the tremor in my heart. "And if we don't act fast, the trap is going to close around us. All of us."

Reid's eyes darted from the photograph to Claire, the tension thickening like a summer storm, crackling with unspoken words and unresolved issues. "We need to get out of here," he said, his voice strained. I could see him wrestling with the precarious balance between family loyalty and the looming threat that hung over us like a guillotine. Claire folded her arms tighter, a defensive posture that mirrored the shadows gathering in her eyes.

"Running won't solve anything," Claire shot back, her tone sharp enough to cut glass. "You think they care if we bolt? If they're watching us here, they're already two steps ahead."

I felt a surge of frustration. "Then we need to outsmart them. Let's regroup and come up with a plan that actually gives us the upper hand."

"Plan? You've just been handed a warning, and you want to sit around strategizing?" Claire's voice was laced with disbelief. "You really think they'll give us that chance?"

I could feel Reid's tension radiating off him, a palpable force in the cramped space. He leaned against the wall, arms crossed, his thoughts hidden behind a veil of determination. "She's right, Claire. We need to find out who's behind this, and fast. If they know we're onto them, they won't hesitate to make their next move."

Claire's expression softened slightly, the sharp edges of her defensiveness dulling. "And what if it leads to more danger? What if it puts you both in the crosshairs?"

"Danger is the name of the game," I replied, the words tumbling out before I could think them through. "If we stay in the shadows, we're dead ducks. But if we can bring the fight to them—"

Reid straightened, an ember of hope igniting in his blue eyes. "You're right. But we can't do this alone. If we're going to expose whoever is behind this, we need allies we can trust."

Claire rolled her eyes, but the tension in her shoulders eased. "Trust? That's rich coming from you, Reid. The last time we spoke, you practically disowned me."

"Let's not make this a family therapy session," I interjected, sensing the conversation veering into dangerous territory. "We need to focus on the task at hand."

"Fine," Claire relented, pushing a loose strand of hair behind her ear. "But don't think for a second that I'm going to let you two throw me into the fire without some guarantees. I'm not going to be collateral damage in this."

Before Reid could respond, a shrill ringing cut through the charged atmosphere, a sound that echoed off the walls like an alarm. My heart skipped as I fished my phone out of my pocket, the screen lighting up with a number I didn't recognize. "What now?" I muttered, the instinct to ignore it battling with curiosity.

"Answer it," Reid urged, his gaze focused on me. "It could be important."

I hesitated, then pressed the button, holding the phone to my ear. "Hello?"

A voice, smooth as silk yet laced with an underlying menace, slithered through the receiver. "Is this our little detective?"

My stomach dropped, every instinct screaming that this was not going to end well. "Who is this?" I demanded, trying to keep my voice steady.

"Let's just say I have an interest in your investigation," the voice replied, dripping with insincerity. "And I think it's time for you to reconsider your approach. You're digging into matters that don't concern you, and that can be... dangerous."

"Dangerous?" I echoed, my heart racing. "What are you trying to imply?"

"Consider it a friendly warning. Leave the past buried, or you might find yourself buried with it." The line went dead, the ominous finality of their words hanging in the air like a fog that wouldn't lift.

I stared at Reid and Claire, both of their faces pale, the reality of our situation crashing down around us. "That was a threat," I said, voice barely above a whisper.

"I think we've crossed a line," Reid murmured, his brow furrowing with concern. "This is bigger than we thought."

"Bigger how?" Claire asked, her voice steadier than I expected. "We're already on the brink here. What could possibly be more dangerous than this?"

Reid rubbed his temples, as if trying to massage some clarity into the chaos. "If they know we're investigating, it means we have a mole. Someone on the inside feeding information."

"Great. Just what we need." I threw my hands up in frustration. "So now we're not only being watched, but someone we thought we could trust might be betraying us?"

"Exactly," Reid said, his eyes darkening with determination. "We need to figure out who we can rely on and who we need to eliminate from our circle."

"That's going to be fun," Claire said dryly. "A social experiment of who gets the axe."

"Can we be serious for a moment?" I snapped, my patience wearing thin. "If we're going to get out of this alive, we need to think strategically. Who do we know that could help us without revealing our hand?"

Reid hesitated, a flicker of realization crossing his features. "There's Sarah. She's been in the industry long enough to have her ear to the ground. If anyone can help us uncover the truth without tipping off whoever's tailing us, it's her."

"Sarah?" Claire repeated, skepticism lacing her voice. "You trust her?"

"Trust? No. But she's our best shot at getting inside information without putting ourselves at further risk," Reid replied, his gaze piercing. "It's either that or we sit here and wait to be cornered."

"Then let's move," I urged, adrenaline coursing through me. "We can't waste any more time."

As we left Reid's office, the weight of uncertainty hung heavy around us, but a flicker of hope ignited in the darkness. The air outside felt electric, charged with anticipation and danger. We hurried down the street, the glow of the streetlamps casting eerie shadows that danced along the pavement, a constant reminder that eyes were always watching.

"Is it too late to change my mind?" Claire asked, glancing around nervously as if expecting someone to leap out from behind a nearby car.

"Absolutely," Reid replied with a half-smile that didn't quite reach his eyes. "Besides, I'm sure they'd find you regardless of your decision."

I smirked at their banter, a small warmth in my chest as we moved together. Whatever dangers lay ahead, we were united by a shared goal. As we approached Sarah's office, the thrill of the unknown coursed through me, awakening a fierce determination to unravel the threads of deceit and bring the shadows into the light. We were running toward danger, yes, but we were also running toward the truth—and nothing could hold us back now.

The pavement shimmered under the glow of streetlights, each step resonating with the urgency of our mission. Reid led the way, a determined silhouette against the night, while Claire and I flanked him, our collective energy coiling tightly around us like a taut wire. The adrenaline coursing through me blended with the anxiety that had become our constant companion. Every shadow seemed to pulse with the threat of unseen eyes, every whispered breeze hinted at lurking danger. It was as if the city itself was conspiring against us, a dark backdrop for our precarious play.

"Do you think Sarah will even see us?" Claire asked, her tone a mixture of skepticism and hope. "I mean, she's always been a little... preoccupied with her own affairs."

Reid shot her a sideways glance, his expression half-amused, half-exasperated. "If anyone can sniff out trouble, it's Sarah. Trust me, she'll be more than willing to help if it means keeping her own secrets safe."

"Fabulous," Claire said dryly. "Nothing like a little self-interest to bring people together."

As we approached the office building that housed Sarah's consulting firm, a sleek glass facade loomed before us, reflecting the chaotic energy of the city. Inside, the flickering lights suggested life was still pulsing through the otherwise deserted halls. I felt a flutter of nerves in my stomach. What if this was another trap? What if Sarah was just a piece of the puzzle that was leading us deeper into darkness?

"Stick to the plan," Reid reminded us quietly, his voice firm yet low enough to avoid drawing attention. "We need information, and we need to keep our wits about us. No impulsive moves."

"Right, because that's my specialty," I replied with a wry smile, grateful for the banter that helped relieve the tension swirling around us.

We stepped through the glass doors, the scent of fresh coffee mingling with the faint aroma of burnt toast wafting from the break room. The dimly lit reception area was eerily quiet, save for the soft hum of the air conditioning and the distant tapping of keyboards echoing like whispers of conspirators. I could feel my heart thrumming in sync with the beat of uncertainty, each pulse a reminder of the stakes we were playing for.

Reid approached the front desk, where a weary receptionist glanced up, her expression barely masking her annoyance at our intrusion. "Can I help you?" she asked, barely hiding a yawn.

"We're here to see Sarah Thompson," Reid replied, his voice smooth and confident. "She's expecting us."

The receptionist raised an eyebrow, clearly skeptical. "Doesn't look like she has any appointments right now. You'll have to wait."

"Just tell her it's Reid," he said, a touch of impatience creeping into his tone. "She'll want to see me."

The receptionist hesitated, her finger hovering over the keyboard as she weighed her options. Finally, with an exasperated sigh, she picked up the phone and dialed. "Yeah, Sarah? You have some visitors..."

While she relayed our names, I exchanged a glance with Claire, who wore an expression of cautious optimism. The seconds stretched, each one feeling like an eternity. Finally, the receptionist hung up and waved us through. "You can go in."

Reid led the charge, and I followed closely, taking a deep breath to steady myself. The door swung open, revealing Sarah's office, an oasis of organized chaos. Papers were strewn across her desk, and the faint scent of cinnamon lingered in the air from a half-finished cup of tea. She sat behind the desk, her brow furrowed in concentration, but her expression shifted to one of surprise as she looked up.

"Reid! What are you doing here?" Her voice was bright, but the moment she spotted Claire and me, her demeanor cooled. "And you brought friends."

"Friends is a strong word," Claire quipped, her trademark sarcasm surfacing. "We prefer the term 'accomplices.'"

"Right," Sarah said, shooting her a pointed look. "What's going on? You both look like you've seen a ghost."

"More like we're being haunted," Reid replied, his voice low and serious. He stepped forward, leaning against the edge of her desk. "We're in deep, Sarah. We need your help."

The lightness in her expression vanished as she studied us, the tension in the room palpable. "I don't have much time. What's the situation?"

"We've uncovered something big," I started, my voice steady despite the chaos swirling in my mind. "Someone's watching us. We found a photograph of the three of us together, along with a threat. Whoever is behind this knows we're investigating."

"Fantastic," Sarah muttered, running a hand through her tousled hair. "You've attracted attention, and that's never good news. You should have been more careful."

"Tell me something I don't know," I shot back, the weight of anxiety creeping back in. "We need to figure out who's behind this and how deep it goes."

Sarah's eyes narrowed, the wheels in her head visibly turning. "There's a rumor about a mole in the system, someone feeding information to the higher-ups. But I thought it was just that—a rumor."

"Then it's time to dig deeper," Reid urged, his eyes blazing with determination. "We can't let them keep pulling the strings."

"Who do you trust?" Sarah asked, folding her arms, her expression wary. "Because if this is as dangerous as you say, then we need to proceed with caution. You can't just throw yourself into the fire without knowing who's holding the match."

"I trust you," Reid said, the sincerity in his voice cutting through the tension like a knife. "You've always been the one with the connections."

"I can get you information, but I need something in return," Sarah replied, her tone shifting to a more transactional air. "What do you know about the project files? The ones connected to the merger?"

"The merger?" I echoed, confusion flooding my mind. "What do those have to do with us?"

"Everything," she replied, leaning forward, urgency radiating from her. "Those files are connected to a network of corruption that goes all the way to the top. If you're being targeted, it's likely tied to someone involved in that deal."

"Then we need to see those files," I asserted, a flicker of determination igniting within me. "Where are they?"

Sarah hesitated, her gaze darting toward the door as if she could sense the danger lurking just beyond. "I can get you access, but we have to move quickly. If they know you're onto them, they'll make their next move sooner than you think."

Reid and I exchanged a look, the weight of the moment sinking in. "Let's do this," he said, his voice steady, infused with resolve.

As Sarah began typing furiously at her computer, I felt a strange thrill coiling in my stomach—a mix of fear and exhilaration. This was it, the precipice of something larger than any of us had anticipated. Just as Sarah was about to share the information, the lights flickered ominously, plunging the room into darkness.

A crash echoed outside, the sound of glass shattering reverberating through the air. My heart raced as I felt the unmistakable weight of dread settle in the pit of my stomach. "What the hell was that?" Claire asked, her voice edged with panic.

Before any of us could react, the door burst open, and a figure cloaked in shadow stepped inside, a gleaming weapon drawn and aimed straight at us. "I suggest you all come with me," the voice commanded, cold and authoritative, shattering our fragile sense of safety in an instant.

The air grew thick with tension, and in that moment, I knew we were standing at the edge of an abyss, teetering between the known and the unknowable, and the only way forward was into the unknown.

Chapter 18: Close Quarters

The air was thick with the scent of coffee and the faintest hint of something sweet, lingering from the pastries we had hastily devoured earlier. Reid's living room, illuminated by a single lamp that cast a warm glow, felt like a sanctuary amid the chaos that loomed just beyond the door. Bookshelves lined the walls, filled with tomes that seemed to hold the weight of untold stories, much like us. Each title was a testament to a life lived in between the pages, an invitation to dive deeper into someone else's reality. I was painfully aware of my own story, unwritten yet rife with conflicts and uncertainties, as I sat across from him on the well-worn couch, the fabric soft against my skin.

Reid's eyes flickered with something unnameable, a mixture of concern and curiosity. They were an unusual shade, caught somewhere between the depths of a forest and the cerulean sky just before dusk. As he spoke, his voice rumbled like distant thunder, drawing me in with each syllable. He shared tales from his childhood—stories of mischievous pranks and wild adventures that made me laugh, but also tales that hinted at the shadows he had battled over the years. Each anecdote was a brushstroke on the canvas of his life, revealing layers of complexity beneath that rugged exterior. In turn, I revealed pieces of my own past, the fragments I usually kept hidden, as if exposing them would leave me vulnerable to the elements of my life I wished to escape.

I could see the way he listened, his attention unwavering, as if he were a sailor navigating uncharted waters, carefully plotting each course. "It's funny," I said, a small smile playing on my lips, "how we both ended up here. In this moment, of all moments." The laughter that bubbled up between us felt like a breath of fresh air, a welcome distraction from the looming storm outside.

"Yeah," he replied, his smile softening the hard edges of his demeanor. "Who would've thought I'd be stuck with a runaway artist in my living room, sharing secrets over half-eaten croissants?" His playful tone, underlined by a sincerity I had not expected, sent a shiver of warmth through me.

"Runaway artist, huh? Maybe I should add that to my résumé," I teased, leaning forward slightly, an unspoken challenge hanging in the air between us. He raised an eyebrow, a grin breaking through the tension that had built around us.

"Don't sell yourself short. You might be more than just a runaway. You could be a mastermind in hiding."

As we exchanged banter, the atmosphere shifted, and I felt the invisible threads between us tighten, pulling us closer. His hand brushed mine, tentative yet deliberate, as if he were testing the waters of my trust. That fleeting touch sent a rush of electricity up my arm, igniting something deep within me that had lain dormant for too long. My breath caught as his fingers lingered, the air charged with an intensity I could no longer ignore.

"Reid, I—" My words hung in the air, half-formed and laced with uncertainty.

"Hey," he interrupted gently, his gaze steady and searching. "You don't have to say anything if you don't want to. Just know that I'm here."

There was an honesty in his eyes that pierced through my defenses, igniting a spark of courage I didn't know I possessed. The very act of being seen by him felt both exhilarating and terrifying. With him, I was no longer just the artist escaping her past; I was a woman grappling with her choices, her fears, and a burgeoning sense of hope.

And in that moment, I made a choice. I leaned closer, letting the barriers I had constructed dissolve like sugar in warm tea. "Maybe I do want to," I whispered, each word heavy with intention.

His breath hitched, and in the quiet that followed, the world outside faded into insignificance. It was just us—a pair of souls entwined in this cocoon of vulnerability and possibility. As I fell into his embrace, every ounce of tension slipped away, replaced by a warmth that spread through my entire being. I could feel the rhythm of his heartbeat, a steady drumbeat that seemed to match my own.

In his arms, the past seemed less daunting, and for the first time in ages, I felt a flicker of trust blossoming within me, fragile yet persistent. But even as I surrendered to the moment, a gnawing fear whispered in the back of my mind, warning me that this kind of closeness came with its own set of risks. It was intoxicating, yes, but it was also a dangerous game we were playing.

Yet, as I pulled away just enough to meet his gaze, I saw something in his eyes—an echo of the same hope that resided in my chest. We both carried burdens, but perhaps together we could lighten the load. I took a breath, steadied by the warmth of his presence, and found the courage to lean in again, not just physically, but emotionally.

"Reid, if we're going to do this, whatever 'this' is, I need to know I can trust you," I said, my voice barely a whisper, fragile yet firm.

He nodded slowly, his expression serious. "You can. I promise. But you also need to know that I have my demons too. Just like you."

"Demons?" I echoed, a wry smile returning. "I thought we were just sharing croissants and secrets, not exchanging horror stories."

His chuckle was deep and resonant, shaking the tension that still clung to the air. "Fair point. But we might need those stories if we're going to navigate what's ahead."

And just like that, the weight of what lay beyond the safety of those walls pressed in once more. A reminder that while we were creating something beautiful here, shadows still loomed, ready to pounce on our newfound connection.

The gentle hum of the city outside seemed to fade as Reid and I sat cocooned in the warmth of his living room, our shared breaths mingling in the charged atmosphere. The flickering shadows cast by the lamp danced on the walls, creating an intimacy that felt both comforting and precarious. In that moment, I wanted to believe that the outside world—the threats, the chaos—could simply vanish, leaving just us in our little bubble. But reality had a way of creeping in when least expected, like a cat burglar slipping through an open window.

"Can you imagine what it would be like if we could just... escape?" I ventured, my voice soft and contemplative. "Just pack our bags and drive until the roads end, leaving everything behind."

Reid tilted his head, an amused grin breaking across his face, that boyish charm turning the serious into playful. "And then what? Get lost in some sleepy town where the biggest drama is who makes the best apple pie? I don't know about you, but I need a little more excitement in my life than that."

"Excitement?" I chuckled, rolling my eyes. "You mean like this? Huddling in your living room while the shadows outside plot our doom?"

"Fair point," he conceded, but the glimmer in his eyes suggested he wasn't entirely against the idea of a quiet life, perhaps even one with me. "But at least you'd have the best company. I make a mean cup of coffee. And I've been told I'm quite the conversationalist."

"Oh, so now I'm a captive audience for your coffee-making skills?" I teased, raising an eyebrow. "What's next? A PowerPoint presentation on your life as a barista?"

"Don't give me ideas," he said, his laughter infectious, filling the space with an energy that made the shadows feel less threatening. "I could show you my latte art. I've been known to create a mean heart. Or, you know, a dinosaur if you're feeling adventurous."

I laughed harder, the kind of laughter that felt like sunshine breaking through clouds. "A dinosaur? Now that I must see. But I have to warn you; I'm a tough critic. If it looks like a lizard with a bad haircut, we're going to have a problem."

"Challenge accepted," he replied, leaning back as if pondering his future culinary masterpieces. The moment stretched between us, filled with an undeniable connection, yet the reality of our situation loomed just beyond the door, a constant reminder that danger was still lurking.

Suddenly, a sharp knock at the door shattered the moment, sending adrenaline coursing through my veins. Reid's expression shifted, the playful banter giving way to alertness. He glanced at me, his smile replaced by a serious intensity that made my heart race.

"Stay here," he instructed, his voice low, like a whisper shared between conspirators. "I'll check it out."

Before I could protest, he was up and moving, his silhouette stark against the warm light of the room. I felt a rush of frustration but understood the necessity. It was in moments like these that his protective instincts flared, a primal urge to shield me from whatever darkness lurked outside.

I sat frozen on the couch, the laughter still echoing in my mind but now overshadowed by a dread I couldn't shake. The knock came again, louder this time, a heavy thud that reverberated through the silence. I clenched my fists, nerves jangling like a guitar string pulled too tight.

Moments later, Reid returned, his face taut with concentration. "It's just the mailman," he said, trying to ease my tension, but his eyes betrayed him, still wary. "He must have missed our usual drop-off. I'll get it."

"Do you really think it's safe?" I asked, my voice barely above a whisper.

"Safe is a relative term right now, but I'll be quick." He opened the door, and the bright flood of streetlights illuminated the entryway, casting long shadows that danced across the floor.

I held my breath as he stepped outside, the door barely creaking shut behind him. I could hear him talking, a quick exchange with the mailman, but anxiety thrummed through me like a live wire. I needed to know he was safe, to feel the solidity of him beside me once more.

When he finally reentered, the tension in his shoulders seemed to dissipate slightly, though I could see the weight of the world still pressing on him. He held a small stack of envelopes, and I was struck by the absurdity of normality intruding on our chaotic lives.

"Looks like the universe is sending us junk mail," he said, a touch of lightness returning to his tone. "And one very interesting postcard." He held it up, a vivid image of a beach at sunset splashed across the front.

"Where's that from?" I asked, curiosity piqued despite the earlier tension.

"An old friend. She's living her best life in Bali," he said, turning it over. "And here I am, hiding from the world."

"You could join her," I suggested impulsively, my heart racing at the thought. "Who says you can't be the next mysterious stranger with a penchant for surfboards and sunset views?"

He smirked, but it didn't quite reach his eyes. "And leave all this behind? I don't think so. Besides, I'm pretty sure my surfing skills would make for a catastrophic display."

"Ah, but think of the stories! The beach bum life could be quite the adventure," I said, trying to coax that smile back into his gaze. "You could create latte art for surfers. It'd be a hit."

"Right," he chuckled, but the laughter didn't reach the depths of his being. "While I'd be pouring heart-shaped foam, you'd be creating masterpieces, probably featuring a colorful dinosaur. We'd be the talk of the island."

The banter was a momentary balm, but the weight of unspoken fears hung between us, a palpable tension that reminded us both of the urgency of our circumstances. I leaned back, attempting to absorb the playful atmosphere, but the gnawing sensation in my gut refused to be quieted.

"Reid," I said, a softness returning to my voice, "I know we've only just begun to unravel our stories, but... I want to be in this. Whatever this is."

He paused, his expression shifting as if weighing my words carefully. "You do realize what that means, right? This isn't just a game for me. I'm not exactly in a position to offer safety and stability."

"I'm not looking for a fairytale," I replied, my voice steadier than I felt. "But I am looking for something real. Something worth fighting for, even if that means facing down the shadows together."

For a moment, silence enveloped us, heavy yet charged with possibility. The darkness outside still loomed, threatening to break through, but in that moment of honesty, I felt the stirrings of something profound—a bond forged in vulnerability, a connection that hinted at resilience.

The lingering scent of coffee and warmth filled the air, but now it felt tinged with something sharper, an undercurrent of urgency that crackled between us. I leaned back slightly, searching Reid's face for answers, but his gaze was focused, assessing the shifting shadows just beyond the window. The city outside hummed with life, but inside, we were cocooned in a silence that felt heavy with unspoken promises and fears.

"Do you ever wonder if we're being too reckless?" I asked, my voice barely above a whisper, the weight of my question hanging in the air like a storm cloud. "I mean, we're playing with fire here."

He turned to me, his expression serious, the flicker of playfulness dimmed by the reality of our circumstances. "Sometimes, you have to be reckless to feel alive," he said, his voice low but steady. "And right now, I'd rather face the danger head-on than cower in fear. I'd rather have you by my side than hide away."

There was a sincerity in his words that sent a shiver down my spine, igniting a warmth that spread through me like wildfire. Yet, the shadows outside felt closer now, more menacing, as if they were inching toward us, hungry for our moments of joy.

"Reid, if we're going to do this—whatever this is—we need to be prepared. I mean really prepared," I said, my heart racing. "We can't just throw ourselves into this without a plan."

His brow furrowed, the tension in his shoulders reappearing as he considered my words. "What do you suggest? A strategy meeting? Perhaps we could create a PowerPoint, complete with bullet points and pie charts."

"Very funny," I shot back, crossing my arms. "I'm serious. We can't afford to be naive about what's out there."

"I get it," he said, his expression softening slightly. "But we also can't let fear dictate our choices. We need to find a balance."

As the night deepened, we fell into a rhythm, discussing potential next steps with a mix of levity and gravity. Every now and then, laughter broke through the tension, easing the tightness in my chest. I felt a strange comfort in our banter, a sense of safety wrapped in the chaos surrounding us.

"I think our first move should be getting some intel," I said, a plan forming in my mind. "We need to understand what we're up against. Knowledge is power, right?"

"True, but information can also lead to paranoia. Are you ready for that?" he asked, a hint of concern lacing his words.

"More than I ever thought I would be," I admitted. "I've been running from my past for too long. It's time to confront it, and to confront whatever is threatening us now."

Reid nodded, a flicker of admiration in his gaze. "You're brave," he said, his voice low. "It's not easy to face the darkness."

"I guess bravery is all I have left," I replied, a bittersweet smile gracing my lips. "It's either that or stay stuck in the shadows."

Just as the atmosphere lightened again, a sudden crash echoed from outside, shattering the fragile peace we had built. I jumped, adrenaline flooding my system, my heart hammering against my ribcage. Reid's expression shifted instantly from relaxed to vigilant as he moved toward the window, his body tense and alert.

"What was that?" I asked, my voice trembling slightly.

"I don't know, but it doesn't sound good," he replied, peering out cautiously. The streetlights cast eerie shadows, and I could see flickers of movement in the darkness. The hairs on the back of my neck stood on end, the air thick with foreboding.

"Should we call the police?" I suggested, a chill creeping down my spine.

"No time for that," he said, his tone clipped. "Whatever's out there, we need to know now."

He turned back to me, a fire igniting in his eyes. "Stay close, okay? If anything happens—"

"I know the drill," I interrupted, swallowing hard. "Keep my head down and stay quiet."

He offered a small nod, a reassuring gesture that both calmed and unsettled me. As he opened the door just a crack, the night air rushed in, bringing with it the faint sounds of a scuffle and the sharp ring of metal against concrete. My heart raced as he slipped outside, leaving me in the dim glow of the living room, a haunting stillness enveloping me.

I strained to hear what was happening, my breath catching as the tension thickened like fog. The shadows outside moved again, and I dared to peek through the crack of the door. My stomach dropped as I caught a glimpse of two figures—tall and menacing—engaged in a struggle that felt all too familiar.

"Reid!" I whispered, panic rising within me. I rushed to the door, barely keeping my voice steady. "Come back!"

Just then, one of the figures turned, their face partially obscured by a hood, but I could see the glint of something sharp in their hand. It was a knife. My blood ran cold, the fear I had tried to suppress surging back to the surface.

The other figure—a man, Reid—struggled against the grip of the attacker, his face a mask of determination and fear. In that instant, I felt as if the ground beneath me was crumbling, the safety I had felt moments ago slipping away.

"Reid, no!" I shouted, throwing open the door, the urgency propelling me forward.

Time slowed as I rushed into the chaos, adrenaline pushing me beyond my limits. I grabbed a nearby flowerpot, my heart racing with the absurdity of my actions but fueled by the need to protect him.

"Get away from him!" I shouted, my voice rising above the fray.

The attacker turned, surprise flickering in their eyes for just a moment before I swung the pot with all my might, aiming for their head. It connected with a satisfying thud, and the figure stumbled back, momentarily dazed.

"Reid, get out of there!" I yelled, my pulse pounding in my ears.

But as he regained his footing, the attacker recovered faster than I anticipated, lunging toward Reid with a swift, deadly intent. I felt my stomach drop as I realized I had made a terrible mistake—what had I just done?

In the chaos of it all, I heard a gunshot ring out, echoing against the night, and everything froze for a heartbeat. The world around us came crashing back into focus, but it felt like I was moving through molasses. The realization hit me like a wave: the danger was no longer lurking; it had arrived.

"Run!" Reid shouted, his eyes locking onto mine, a fierce protectiveness emanating from him.

Just as I turned to flee, I caught sight of the hooded figure again, advancing with a menacing resolve. The shadows that had once felt like a comforting cloak now morphed into a suffocating veil, and I knew, without a doubt, that we were on the brink of something terrifyingly unpredictable.

As I sprinted back into the house, my heart thundered in my chest, the world spinning around me, filled with the harsh reality that our moment of refuge had shattered. The door slammed shut behind me, but I could still hear the chaos outside—a cacophony of violence that told me we were no longer safe, and whatever came next would determine our fate.

Chapter 19: The Enemy Within

The rain drummed softly against the window, each drop a tiny reminder of the tempest swirling inside me. I curled my fingers around a mug of lukewarm coffee, the bitter taste barely cutting through the sweetness of my thoughts. Reid sat across the table, his eyes glued to the screen of his laptop, the flickering glow illuminating the sharp angles of his face. It had been a long few weeks since we'd teamed up, and the once electric chemistry between us now crackled with an unsettling tension.

"Hey," I said, my voice tentative, like a kid approaching a sleeping bear. "You've been awfully quiet lately. What's going on in that head of yours?"

He didn't look up. The muscles in his jaw tightened, and for a moment, the air between us thickened with unspoken words. "Just trying to piece everything together," he replied, his tone casual but clipped, like a door being slammed in my face.

My heart sank, but I pushed forward. "You can talk to me, you know. We're in this together." I tried to keep my voice light, even as unease coiled tighter around my chest.

Reid finally looked up, but there was an intensity in his gaze that made me want to pull back. "It's complicated, okay?" His words were edged with frustration, a stark contrast to the warmth I had come to expect from him.

"Complicated how? Are you in some sort of trouble?" I leaned in, curiosity mingling with concern. The way he was behaving, so shut off from me, was unlike him. Reid was the type who confronted problems head-on, his characteristic bravado never allowing fear to take the wheel. But now, he was retreating, like a deer in headlights, and I was left grasping at shadows.

He ran a hand through his tousled hair, a gesture that always sent a thrill through me. But today, it only made me anxious. "It's just...

the investigation is more than I anticipated. We're not just up against petty corruption. There are bigger players involved, and I need to make sure we don't get in over our heads." His words hung between us, heavy with the weight of something unspoken.

I wanted to push further, to peel back the layers of his guarded demeanor, but the fear of what I might uncover froze my tongue. Instead, I nodded, feeling the flicker of disappointment swell within me. "Okay. Just... promise you won't shut me out."

Reid's gaze softened, just for a heartbeat. "I promise."

But the promise felt fragile, like the last strands of a spider's web glimmering under a hesitant sun. I returned to my coffee, swirling it absently, its bitterness a poor reflection of the turmoil brewing beneath my calm exterior.

Days passed, each filled with the same uncomfortable silence. The tension between us thickened, wrapping around my thoughts like a fog, suffocating yet somehow familiar. Each time I glimpsed Reid, that familiar warmth tugged at my heart, yet the shadows lurking behind his eyes pushed me away. I was caught in a dance of desire and distrust, my instincts screaming that something was off, while my heart yearned for him to lean in, to let me in.

It was late one night when I discovered the truth, hidden beneath layers of uncertainty. I had stayed behind at our shared workspace, sifting through documents we had gathered in our pursuit of justice. A file slipped from the edge of my desk, tumbling to the floor like an unwelcome secret. As I bent to pick it up, I froze. There, scrawled in Reid's unmistakable handwriting, were notes outlining our investigation. But as I scanned further, my heart sank.

There, among the hastily scribbled thoughts, was a name that made bile rise in my throat: a name tied to the corruption we had been trying to expose. Reid had connections—dangerous ones. The realization hit me like a punch to the gut, each breath becoming a laborious effort as panic clawed its way to the forefront of my mind.

I stumbled to my feet, adrenaline surging as I replayed our recent conversations. The evasiveness, the sudden change in demeanor—everything snapped into place with alarming clarity. It wasn't just that Reid had been distracted; he had been concealing his involvement in the very corruption we had sought to dismantle.

Storming into the common area, I found him staring at his laptop again, illuminated by the blue light that felt far too cold for comfort. "We need to talk," I demanded, my voice a tense whip.

He turned, surprise flickering across his features before they hardened into something unreadable. "What's wrong?"

"Don't play dumb with me, Reid. I found your notes." The words spilled out like venom, laced with disbelief and hurt. "You're connected to this, aren't you? How long have you been hiding this from me?"

His expression shifted, shadows flickering across his face as if the truth were a monster lurking just out of sight. "I can explain," he started, but I cut him off, anger igniting the air between us.

"Explain? You've been keeping secrets, Reid. Do you think I'm just going to stand here and let you sweep this under the rug?"

"Listen to me!" he snapped, his voice sharper than I had ever heard. The desperation in his eyes pierced through my outrage, a chink in the armor he had built around himself. "You don't understand what I'm dealing with. This goes deeper than either of us anticipated."

My chest tightened, the weight of his words settling uncomfortably in my gut. "Then enlighten me! Because right now, all I see is betrayal."

Reid's face fell, anguish mixing with the frustration that churned within him. "I didn't want you to get dragged into this. I was trying to protect you!"

"Protect me? Or protect yourself?" I shot back, the betrayal spiraling into an agonizing ache that gripped my heart. The foundation of our partnership, once steadfast and reassuring, now felt like quicksand. I was caught in a storm of conflicting emotions, desperation clawing at my throat as I realized the man I had come to trust was not who I thought he was.

He took a step closer, the space between us crackling with unfulfilled tension. "You have to believe me, I was trying to gather evidence without putting you in danger. But things spiraled out of control."

"By lying to me? By hiding the truth?" My heart pounded like a drum, echoing the chaos swirling inside me. "What else have you kept from me?"

The silence hung heavily, laden with unanswered questions and fears. I wanted to scream, to shake him until the truth spilled out like a river, but instead, I stood frozen, waiting for him to make the next move. The night had turned dark, and so had the bond we once shared. It was only a matter of time before everything unraveled, revealing the hidden truths lurking just beneath the surface.

"Do you really think I'm going to just accept that you were trying to protect me?" The words tumbled out, laced with incredulity as I fought to keep my voice steady. "You could have told me, Reid. Instead, you've kept me in the dark while you play both sides."

His expression shifted, anguish contorting his features. "It was never meant to be like this," he insisted, his voice low, almost pleading. "I didn't want to involve you until I knew more, until I could protect you properly."

The sincerity in his eyes was both comforting and infuriating, pulling me into a tumultuous wave of emotions. "Protect me? Is that what you call this?" I gestured wildly, the mug in my hand trembling dangerously. "You've turned my world upside down while pretending everything was fine."

"I thought I could handle it!" he shot back, frustration edging into his tone. "But it's bigger than I anticipated, and I didn't want you to be a target."

I took a step back, feeling the chill of his words seep into my bones. "You're making it sound like this was some sort of noble quest. You could've involved me, Reid. I've held my own against threats before. We could have tackled this together."

"I didn't want to put you in danger," he repeated, his voice rising just enough to match the turmoil swirling between us. "There are people involved who won't hesitate to silence anyone who gets too close."

A shiver ran down my spine, the weight of his confession crashing into me like a wave of ice. "So, you thought lying would keep me safe? Keeping me in the dark was your grand plan?" My heart raced, each beat echoing the mounting tension. "If you didn't want me involved, why even team up in the first place?"

"Because I thought I could figure this out without dragging you into the muck," he admitted, the rawness of his frustration illuminating the stark reality between us. "But every time I think I'm getting closer, it feels like the ground shifts beneath my feet."

"And now?" I challenged, crossing my arms, the warmth of our earlier camaraderie fading into an uncomfortable void. "What do you want from me now? Am I supposed to just forget everything you've hidden from me and trust you?"

"Trust?" he echoed, disbelief threading through his words. "That's rich coming from someone who's questioning everything." The fire in his gaze sparked something fierce in me, igniting a desire to push forward, to break through this wall he'd erected.

"You can't just pull the trust card now," I countered, feeling my pulse quicken. "You've been lying to me. You've put our entire investigation at risk!"

"Do you honestly think I wanted this?" He stepped closer, the space between us dwindling, the energy shifting as he reached for me. "I wanted to keep you safe, and now I'm risking everything, including your trust."

We stood inches apart, the air thick with unspoken words and unresolved tension. In that moment, the world outside faded into a muted blur, leaving only us and the fragile thread holding our partnership together. But trust was a currency I wasn't willing to spend lightly, especially now, when shadows loomed large over everything I thought I knew about him.

"I need time," I finally said, my voice barely a whisper. "Time to process this." I turned away, feeling the sting of tears prickling at the corners of my eyes. This wasn't just about betrayal; it was about the sinking realization that everything I had believed in—the partnership, the promise of uncovering the truth together—had begun to crumble.

The next few days dragged on, each one stretching the tension between us tauter than a bowstring. I kept my distance, pouring myself into research, filling my days with data and leads while my mind wrestled with the reality of Reid's deception. The documents we had amassed became a refuge, a tangible connection to the truth we were chasing, even as the specter of his betrayal loomed in the background.

At night, I would lie awake, the shadows in my room whispering doubts as they danced along the walls. I replayed our conversations, the spark of our initial camaraderie now dulled, leaving only the echoes of laughter replaced by accusations and secrets. Each moment felt like a reminder of the trust that had slipped through my fingers, leaving nothing but the cold grasp of uncertainty.

The following week, I received an anonymous tip that sent my heart racing. It came through a mysterious email, a single line offering a lead: "Follow the money trail; the answer lies within the boardroom." My pulse quickened as adrenaline coursed through me. This could be the breakthrough we needed, a way to expose the corruption Reid had stumbled upon and ultimately vindicate our efforts.

Without thinking, I dashed into the office, intent on uncovering more. I pulled out the financial documents we had gathered and laid them out on my desk. My fingers brushed against the papers, each one heavy with implications. It was time to put the pieces together, to reclaim the narrative that had been twisted by deceit.

As I sifted through the data, the door creaked open behind me. I didn't need to turn to know it was Reid. I could feel the tension radiating from him, a palpable energy that hung in the air like static. "You're working late," he said, his voice soft but firm.

"I have leads to follow," I replied, not bothering to hide the edge in my tone.

"Can we talk?" he asked, stepping further into the room.

"About what? How you've been lying to me?" I snapped, the bitterness spilling out before I could reign it in. "You want to sit down and discuss the ways you've kept me out of the loop? Or maybe you want to explain why I should even trust you again?"

"I'm not asking for your trust," he said quietly, a weight in his words that tugged at something deep within me. "I just want a chance to explain. There's something I need you to see."

I hesitated, torn between the instinct to shove him away and the undeniable pull of my own curiosity. "Fine. But you'd better make it good."

He moved closer, urgency in his stride, and pulled out his phone. "I received some intel that could change everything. It's about the boardroom meeting—who's involved and what's really at stake."

As he began to explain, I felt the walls I had erected slowly start to crack. Perhaps the truth was still within reach, hidden behind the tangled web of lies. I listened, my skepticism battling against the hope fluttering to life. With every detail Reid unveiled, the pieces of our investigation began to shift into a new arrangement, one that might yet lead us to the truth we sought, together.

I leaned back in my chair, trying to absorb Reid's hurried words about the boardroom meeting, a knot of anxiety twisting in my stomach. The energy in the room crackled with unresolved tension, and I could almost feel the weight of our unspoken doubts pressing down on us like a storm cloud. He paced in front of me, his hands animated, the urgency of his revelations both intoxicating and infuriating.

"They're planning something big, something that could jeopardize everything we've worked for," Reid said, his voice low but charged. "I intercepted a message that names key players who will be at the meeting. If we can get inside, we could expose their plans."

I blinked, my mind racing to catch up. "You intercepted a message? When did you have time for that?" Skepticism laced my words, though curiosity flared like a match in a dark room.

"I've been keeping an eye on their communications. It's a tightrope walk, but I've managed to gather enough to know they're up to something sinister. If we're going to make our move, we need to do it soon." He leaned closer, his eyes gleaming with fervor, and I couldn't help but feel a rush of adrenaline at the prospect of action.

"Sinister how?" I pressed, needing details, wanting to know exactly how deep the rabbit hole went this time.

He hesitated, and for a brief moment, the flicker of doubt crossed his face. "There's talk of eliminating those who might stand in their way, and—" He stopped abruptly, his gaze darting to the door as if expecting someone to burst in at any moment.

"Reid, what are you not telling me?" I demanded, frustration bubbling to the surface. "If you know something, you have to spill it all."

"It's not just the boardroom," he admitted, running a hand through his hair, a gesture I recognized as a sign of his rising stress. "There are people involved who are willing to kill to protect their interests. They've got connections that run deeper than we imagined."

A shiver ran down my spine. "Kill? You're saying there are lives at stake here?"

"Exactly," he replied, urgency threading his voice. "And if we're not careful, we could be next."

The implications of his words hit me like a punch to the gut. I leaned back in my chair, struggling to process the reality of what we were up against. "So what's the plan, then? We just waltz into the meeting, flash our badges, and demand answers? Sounds like a recipe for disaster."

Reid shook his head, a faint smile playing at the corners of his lips, though it didn't reach his eyes. "I was thinking more along the lines of sneaking in, gathering intel, and then exposing their plans to the authorities. But we'll need to move fast."

I frowned, feeling the gravity of our situation. "And what if we get caught? If they're willing to kill to protect their secrets, we're walking straight into a lion's den."

"Then we make sure we're prepared for anything," he replied, the determination in his voice igniting a flicker of hope within me. "We've come this far. We can't turn back now."

His conviction tugged at something deep inside me—a desire for justice, for the truth. Despite the betrayal, despite the doubt that still lingered, I felt myself leaning toward the fire of our shared purpose. "All right," I said slowly, weighing my words. "Let's say I'm in. What do we do first?"

Reid straightened, his posture shifting from defensive to resolute. "We need to find out where the meeting is taking place. I have a contact who might be able to help."

"Great. And how do you plan to approach this contact without raising suspicion?" I raised an eyebrow, the skepticism bubbling back to the surface.

"Leave that to me," he said with a wink, the spark of mischief igniting in his eyes, reminding me of the man I had once trusted so completely. "I'll handle it. You just focus on gathering whatever intel you can from our existing documents. We need to know everything."

As we fell into a rhythm, I felt the tension of our previous arguments begin to ebb, replaced by a shared sense of purpose. It was easy to forget the shadows between us as we huddled over the papers, piecing together the evidence like detectives on a mission. But even as I lost myself in the work, the lingering doubts about Reid's motives simmered just beneath the surface, waiting for a moment to resurface.

The next few hours flew by, each tick of the clock echoing in my mind as I scanned through spreadsheets, emails, and financial reports, searching for patterns and connections that could lead us closer to the truth. My mind whirred, each detail merging into a complex tapestry of deceit and corruption.

"Here!" I exclaimed, pointing at the screen. "Look at this. There's a series of transactions that coincide with dates tied to board meetings. They're funneling money through different shell companies. It could lead us straight to the heart of the operation."

Reid leaned over my shoulder, the warmth of his presence sending a jolt through me. "That's brilliant," he said, the admiration in his tone making my heart flutter despite the chaos surrounding us. "If we can connect these dots, we might have enough evidence to take them down."

Just as I was about to dive deeper into the implications of my discovery, my phone buzzed on the desk, breaking the focused silence. I grabbed it, glancing at the screen to see an unknown number flashing ominously. My heart raced; my instincts screamed that this could be the breakthrough we needed—or a trap.

"Reid," I murmured, "do you think I should answer this?"

"Only if you're prepared for anything," he replied, a guarded look crossing his face. "It could be someone trying to warn us or something more sinister."

I took a deep breath, the weight of the moment pressing down on me. "Here goes nothing."

I swiped to answer, holding my breath as the line crackled to life. "Hello?"

There was a pause, and then a voice emerged from the other end, distorted and low. "You need to stop digging. You're in over your head."

My pulse quickened. "Who is this?"

"Someone who knows what they're capable of. Back off while you still can." The voice faded, leaving nothing but silence hanging heavily in the air.

I glanced at Reid, my heart pounding in my ears. "Did you hear that?"

He nodded, the color draining from his face. "We're not just dealing with corporate corruption. They know about us, and they're not afraid to threaten us."

"Great. Just great," I muttered, my mind racing. "What do we do now?"

Reid stepped closer, determination flashing in his eyes. "We don't back down. We push forward. We're closer than ever, and I won't let fear dictate our next move."

Just as I was about to respond, a loud crash echoed from outside, shaking the very foundation of our makeshift headquarters. My heart dropped as the sound reverberated through the room, followed by frantic footsteps echoing down the hall.

"Get down!" Reid shouted, instinctively pulling me behind the desk as the door swung open, revealing a figure cloaked in darkness. The world spun into chaos, and as I clutched the edge of the desk, my breath hitching in my throat, I realized that the danger we had been chasing was no longer just an idea—it had come to claim us, ready to snatch away everything we had fought for.

Chapter 20: Bound by Secrets

The rain drummed a relentless beat against the windowpane, blurring the outside world into a watercolor wash of gray. I paced the small living room, the floorboards creaking beneath my feet like a long-forgotten symphony. Each step brought me closer to a decision that twisted my gut with a nauseating mix of dread and anticipation. The aroma of brewing coffee lingered in the air, grounding me amidst the chaos swirling in my mind. I could almost hear Reid's voice cutting through the fog, teasing me about my overabundance of caffeine. It was a voice I both longed for and dreaded, a tether to a reality that felt increasingly tenuous.

The way he had looked at me last week, eyes a stormy sea of regret and unspoken words, haunted me. I couldn't shake the feeling that the secrets we were chasing together were woven tightly into the very fabric of his being. What was it about the thrill of the chase that left me breathless, teetering on the edge of revelation and ruin? I could almost convince myself that the taste of betrayal was nothing compared to the sweetness of the truth that lay just out of reach.

A knock echoed through the silence, sharp and demanding. My heart raced as I approached the door, each step punctuated by the mounting tension coiling in my chest. I hesitated, peering through the peephole, half-expecting to see Reid's familiar silhouette, a harbinger of both warmth and trouble. Instead, a stranger stood there, a silhouette cloaked in shadows, with a face obscured by the brim of a rain-soaked hat.

"Who is it?" I called out, my voice trembling slightly, betraying my apprehension.

"It's me," came the muffled reply. The deep timbre wrapped around me like an old favorite song, both soothing and disquieting. I flung open the door, and there he was—Reid, dripping wet, hair tousled and plastered to his forehead, eyes glinting with a mix of mischief and urgency that ignited an uncontainable spark within me.

"Do you always make a habit of appearing on my doorstep like a rogue in a storm?" I shot back, trying to maintain the façade of annoyance while my heart fluttered in response to his presence. He stepped inside, shaking off droplets like a wet dog, and a grin crept across his lips.

"Only when the opportunity arises," he said, his voice low, resonating with a warmth that made my skin tingle. "You look like you've been fighting a battle of your own."

"Just battling my over-caffeinated thoughts, thank you very much," I retorted, crossing my arms. But the tension hung between us, thick and electric, weaving through the air like the dampness from outside. "What do you want, Reid? If you're here to talk about the job... or last week..."

"I'm here to talk about the truth," he interrupted, stepping closer, his presence enveloping me in a whirlwind of conflicting emotions. I could see the shadows under his eyes, the weariness that came from too many sleepless nights filled with relentless worry. It mirrored my own.

"Does that mean you're finally ready to come clean?" I challenged, heart pounding as I faced him, the weight of our shared secrets pressing down like an anchor. "Because if it's just more half-truths, then I don't know if I can handle it."

Reid sighed, running a hand through his hair in a gesture of defeat. "I wish I could. But it's more complicated than that. You have to trust me, just a little longer."

"Trust? Trust is a currency I've spent too freely already," I snapped, my voice rising. The very mention of trust felt like salt on an open wound. "You've made me question everything, Reid. Everything we've built together."

His gaze softened, the intensity of his expression disarming me for a moment. "I know, and I hate that I've put you in this position. But we're close, you have to believe me. I'm here to help us figure this out, to find the truth together."

"Together," I repeated, testing the word like a prayer on my lips, the very idea both terrifying and exhilarating. "And what if the truth is something we can't handle?"

Reid stepped even closer, the space between us dwindling to a mere whisper of air. "Then we face it together, as we always have. You and me against the world, right?"

I searched his eyes, looking for the glimmer of sincerity I so desperately wanted to believe in. "You make it sound so simple."

He chuckled softly, a sound that warmed me even amid the chaos. "Nothing about this is simple, but isn't that what makes it worth it? The unpredictability? The danger? It's what brought us together in the first place."

"And what might tear us apart," I murmured, the weight of my words hanging heavily in the air. "We're already walking a tightrope. One misstep…"

"We'll find our balance," he assured me, his voice a steady anchor amidst the turbulence. "We can't turn back now. There's too much at stake, and I won't let you walk away from this, not when we're so close."

With a deep breath, I looked into his eyes, allowing myself to be swept away by the depth of his determination. The world outside might have been a storm of uncertainty, but here, in this moment, with him standing before me, I felt the stirrings of hope begin to unfurl.

"Okay," I whispered, a fragile agreement hanging in the air, "but this time, no more secrets. We either go all in or not at all."

Reid's smile returned, brightening the dim room, illuminating the shadows that had lingered too long. "Deal. But first, let's figure out who we're really up against. I have a lead."

He leaned closer, lowering his voice to a conspiratorial whisper that sent shivers down my spine. "And trust me, it's bigger than either of us imagined."

As I leaned in, curiosity igniting the fire within, the world outside faded into insignificance. The storm could rage, and secrets could twist in the dark, but in that moment, we were bound by a single unyielding truth: together, we would uncover the mysteries that lay ahead.

The rain had begun to ease, a soft patter that now sounded almost melodic against the roof, as if it were trying to soothe the tension that clung to me. Reid's presence filled the small room with an undeniable warmth, and yet, I could sense the heaviness in his shoulders, a burden that mirrored my own. The moment felt charged, a fragile truce forged amidst the chaos, and as we moved into the kitchen, the smell of fresh coffee mingled with the promise of revelations.

"Let's make a plan," I suggested, my voice steadying as I poured us both a steaming cup. I set the mug in front of him, watching as his fingers wrapped around the warmth, a brief moment of peace amid the brewing storm. "What do we know?"

Reid leaned back against the counter, his expression shifting from playful to serious. "We know that the files from the company are being moved, probably to cover up something big. My contact mentioned strange shipments going out at odd hours, and people disappearing for days. It's definitely worth investigating."

"Right," I replied, trying to suppress the swell of panic rising in my chest. "But why now? What are they hiding?" I could feel the adrenaline coursing through me, and I was all too aware that every moment spent pondering the 'why' could lead us down a rabbit hole we might not return from.

"Good question," Reid replied, a hint of a smile playing on his lips. "But first, we need to get our hands on one of those shipments. That's our best shot at uncovering what's really going on."

"And you have a plan for that, I presume?" I leaned closer, intrigued by the spark in his eyes.

"Of course. You remember the warehouse on Fifth? The one that used to be an old textile factory?"

I nodded, the name striking a chord. It had been abandoned for years, a hulking relic of a bygone era, its windows boarded up and covered in graffiti. "You think they're using it as a cover?"

"Exactly," he said, the excitement creeping back into his voice. "If we can get inside during one of those late-night shipments, we might catch them red-handed. But it won't be easy. We'll need to be careful."

"Careful, huh? That's rich coming from you," I quipped, attempting to inject some levity into the situation. "Do you even know the meaning of the word?"

He chuckled, the sound reverberating through the room. "Touché. But this time, I promise to keep my bravado in check."

"Good. I'd prefer to have you around for the next round of coffee," I said, taking a sip, the rich warmth grounding me even as my mind raced ahead.

"Right, because nothing says 'I love you' quite like caffeine," he shot back, winking. But then his smile faded as he leaned closer, his expression turning serious. "Listen, I know things have been... complicated. But I need you to trust me. No matter what happens out there."

"Trust you? That's the million-dollar question, isn't it?" I countered, a teasing lilt to my tone, though my heart wasn't entirely in it. "What if this is all one big setup? What if you're leading me right into a trap?"

Reid's brow furrowed, and for a split second, I caught a glimpse of the vulnerability hidden behind his bravado. "I won't let that happen. I promise. We're in this together, and I'd never put you in danger intentionally. You mean too much to me."

The weight of his words hung in the air, a potent reminder of the fragile bond we shared. I hesitated, letting the silence stretch between us, the tension coiling tighter around my chest. "Okay, fine. We'll do it your way. But you'd better keep that promise."

A flicker of relief washed over his face, and he grinned, the familiar light returning to his eyes. "Deal. We'll gather what we need and head out tonight. Just the two of us, like old times."

As we began to brainstorm a plan, gathering flashlights and a few supplies, a sense of purpose fueled me. My previous doubts faded into the background, overtaken by the thrill of the chase. It felt like a dance we had practiced many times before, the steps falling into place with an ease that belied the danger ahead.

But as the sun dipped below the horizon, casting long shadows across the room, an unsettling feeling crept in. It was a reminder that beneath our laughter and easy banter lay a web of secrets that could ensnare us at any moment. And yet, the more I fought against the rising tide of fear, the more determined I became to unravel the truth.

The old factory loomed before us like a giant sleeping beast, its darkened windows watching our approach. A chill danced along my spine as we stepped inside, the air thick with dust and memories of a time long past. Each echo of our footsteps felt amplified in the hollow space, a reminder that we were not alone; the shadows seemed to stretch and twist around us, holding their breath in anticipation.

"Remember, stay close," Reid whispered, his voice a low murmur that sent ripples of awareness through me. "We don't know what's waiting for us."

"I'm not exactly a stranger to danger, you know," I replied, forcing a bravado I didn't entirely feel. The thrill of the unknown coursed through my veins, and with it, a pulse of adrenaline that both terrified and exhilarated me.

"True, but let's avoid any unnecessary heroics," he shot back, a teasing glint in his eyes, and I couldn't help but smile at his attempt to lighten the mood.

As we navigated the shadows, I caught snippets of whispered conversations echoing through the rafters, the air vibrating with urgency. I glanced at Reid, who held up a finger to his lips, signaling me to remain silent. My heart raced, the thrill of discovery tinged with a sharp edge of fear as we pressed deeper into the heart of the factory.

What awaited us inside those crumbling walls? The answer hung just beyond the next corner, a mystery waiting to be uncovered, and I felt the spark of danger ignite my senses, weaving an unbreakable thread between us as we faced whatever darkness lay ahead.

The musty air of the factory wrapped around us like an old, tattered blanket, its chill seeping into my bones. The shadows loomed large, but they were nothing compared to the growing tension between us. With every step, the dust kicked up in puffs around our feet, mingling with the anticipation that hummed in the silence. We ventured deeper, inching past ancient machinery that creaked with age, remnants of a time when this place was alive with purpose.

"Do you think they're actually here?" I whispered, glancing over my shoulder. The fading light from our flashlights danced against the walls, revealing graffiti that told tales of youthful rebellion—hearts and names scrawled in haphazard strokes, echoes of laughter now swallowed by time.

"Only one way to find out," Reid replied, his tone both confident and cautious, a combination that sent my pulse racing. "Stick close. Remember, we're not just looking for answers; we're looking for the truth. Whatever that may be."

I nodded, my heart pounding like a war drum in my chest. The thrill of the hunt surged within me, but with each passing moment, I could feel the uncertainty threading its way into my thoughts. What if we stumbled upon something we weren't prepared to face? A flicker of doubt crossed my mind, but I pushed it aside. We had come too far to turn back now.

We rounded a corner, the sound of voices growing louder, an urgent murmur that prickled the hairs on the back of my neck. I could feel Reid tense beside me, the change in his posture a testament to the seriousness of our mission. "Let's listen," he suggested, dropping his voice to a hushed tone. We pressed ourselves against the wall, the cool concrete rough against my skin as I strained to hear the conversation ahead.

"—moving the shipment tonight. No delays this time," a gruff voice stated, the words laced with a sense of finality that made my stomach churn.

"Can't have anyone snooping around," another voice replied, the tone sharper, filled with an underlying threat. "You know how that turned out last time."

Reid and I exchanged a glance, the urgency of the situation striking like a lightning bolt. "They're talking about the shipment," I whispered, dread pooling in my stomach. "We need to find out what they're planning."

"Let's get closer," he replied, and before I could protest, he was leading the way, slipping through a narrow opening into what appeared to be an old storage room. The air here felt thick, saturated with the weight of hidden secrets, and I followed closely, trusting his instincts even as my heart raced with trepidation.

Inside, the shadows deepened, wrapping us in a cloak of secrecy. Crates piled high in disarray lined the walls, and I spotted a flickering light coming from a small window at the far end of the room. "There," I pointed, my excitement bubbling beneath the surface. "We can see what's happening from there."

Reid nodded, moving silently toward the light. I held my breath, every step feeling like an eternity as we approached the window, careful to avoid the splintered floorboards that threatened to betray our presence.

Peering through the grime-caked glass, I squinted to see the scene unfolding outside. Men moved in the dark, their silhouettes weaving around large crates. They were focused, intent on a purpose I couldn't yet decipher. "What are they unloading?" I whispered, my heart pounding as I tried to catch snippets of their conversation.

Suddenly, one of the men stepped into the light—a familiar face that sent a jolt of shock coursing through me. "No way," I breathed, feeling the color drain from my cheeks. "That's—"

"Who?" Reid asked, leaning closer, his breath warm against my ear.

"Derek. The guy from the finance department. I thought he was clean."

Reid's eyes widened as he processed the information. "This changes everything. We need to find out what he's involved in."

But before we could formulate a plan, a loud crash echoed through the room, followed by a series of hurried footsteps approaching our hiding spot. Panic surged through me, and I grabbed Reid's arm, pulling him back further into the shadows.

"What now?" he whispered, eyes darting around as he strained to listen.

"Hide," I hissed, our breaths synchronized in the thick air. We pressed against the far wall, hearts racing as we waited, the tension tightening around us like a noose.

The door swung open with a creak, and three men stormed into the room, their voices low but urgent. "We can't keep this up," one of them grumbled, his tone brimming with frustration. "If anyone finds out about the shipments..."

"We'll handle it," Derek interrupted sharply, his voice cutting through the air like a knife. "Just keep your heads down and stick to the plan. We're too close to let this fall apart now."

Reid and I exchanged a panicked glance, my mind racing as I struggled to piece together the implications of Derek's words. What was he involved in, and how deep did this rabbit hole go? I felt the weight of the situation pressing in on me, every second stretching into an eternity as the men continued their heated exchange.

"And what about the girl?" one of the newcomers asked, a hint of hesitation in his voice. "We can't risk her finding out."

My stomach dropped. They were talking about me.

"We'll take care of her," Derek replied dismissively. "She's just an obstacle, and we know how to handle obstacles."

The cold chill of dread washed over me, and I instinctively squeezed Reid's arm, the fear gripping me tightly. "They know about me," I whispered, my voice barely a breath. "We need to get out of here. Now."

Just as we began to back away, the floor creaked ominously beneath us, a sound that echoed like a gunshot in the tense silence. The men turned abruptly, their eyes narrowing as they caught sight of our movement.

"Who's there?" Derek shouted, his voice ringing with authority.

Time seemed to freeze, and in that heartbeat, I realized that we were no longer the hunters in this game—we were the prey. Reid grabbed my hand, pulling me back toward the door, but before we could make our escape, the weight of reality crashed down around us. The shadows that had once shielded us now felt like a tightening noose, and the panic ignited into a frantic race against time.

"Run!" Reid shouted, his voice cutting through the chaos.

We bolted from our hiding spot, the adrenaline surging as we sprinted toward the exit. The men's shouts echoed behind us, urgency threading through their words as they gave chase. Each step felt like a heartbeat away from capture, and the world around me blurred into a dizzying whirlwind of fear and resolve.

Just as we reached the door, a figure stepped into our path, blocking our escape. My breath caught in my throat as the dim light revealed the face of the last person I expected to see—the very embodiment of betrayal, standing between us and freedom.

"Going somewhere?" Derek smirked, a dangerous glint in his eye, and I knew in that moment that whatever secrets lay ahead, they would unravel faster than I could ever have prepared for.

Chapter 21: Into the Lion's Den

The heavy air was thick with secrets, each breath I took mingling with the acrid scent of rust and sweat. Shadows danced in the corners of the warehouse, stretching and contorting like the hidden truths we'd chased for weeks. My heart raced, not just from the adrenaline surging through me, but from the sheer weight of anticipation. Tonight, we would either uncover the story that had eluded us or become mere footnotes in someone else's sordid history.

I glanced at Reid, his jaw set in that determined way that made me both proud and terrified. His dark hair fell across his forehead in tousled waves, and his eyes glinted like steel, reflecting the faint light from the flickering bulbs above. "You ready for this?" he asked, a wry smile curling his lips, but I could see the tension radiating from him, an electric current that buzzed in the air between us.

"As ready as I'll ever be," I replied, though doubt gnawed at my insides like a hungry animal. The ledger was supposed to be here, buried among the rusting machinery and forgotten crates, its pages filled with the kind of names that could shake empires and expose the underbelly of the city's elite. But as I stepped deeper into the darkness, a sense of foreboding wrapped around me, tighter than a noose.

The beam of my flashlight cut through the gloom, illuminating the peeling walls and scattered debris. Each step echoed like a heartbeat, pulsing with the tension that hung thick in the air. I could almost hear the whispers of the past, stories that had long since been buried, all waiting for someone brave—or foolish—enough to dig them up.

We rounded a corner, and there it was. A battered wooden crate, partially hidden beneath a mound of dust and old tarps, stood defiantly against the decay around it. My breath caught in my throat, and I exchanged a glance with Reid, who nodded, his expression a mix of excitement and caution. Together, we approached, each footfall deliberate, as if any sudden movement would send our hard-won prize scurrying back into the shadows.

As I pried the lid open, the hinges creaked like the bones of a long-dead creature, and my heart thudded in my chest. Inside, the ledger lay nestled among a tangle of old papers, its leather cover cracked and worn. My fingers trembled as I reached for it, the sensation of destiny crackling through my veins. "This is it," I whispered, barely able to contain my awe.

"Be careful," Reid cautioned, his voice low, barely above a breath. "We don't know what else is here."

The pages were yellowed, but the ink was surprisingly fresh, as if the words had been scrawled only yesterday. As I flipped through, each name leaped out at me, a gallery of the city's hidden puppeteers, their strings tied tight to one another. I could almost hear the whispers of their machinations, plotting and scheming in the dark corners of their palatial offices.

But before I could fully digest the implications of what I was seeing, the sharp crack of boots against concrete sent a chill racing up my spine. Reid stiffened beside me, the atmosphere shifting from electric anticipation to palpable dread in an instant. We exchanged a quick glance, a silent agreement forming between us. We had to get out, and fast.

I tucked the ledger under my arm and started to back away, but the clatter of footsteps grew louder, closing in on us like a hunter stalking its prey. "Go!" Reid urged, his voice urgent.

With every instinct screaming for survival, I turned and ran, the world around me becoming a blur of shadows and echoes. I could hear Reid's footsteps pounding behind me, feel the heat of his presence as we darted through the maze of rusted machinery, desperate to find an exit.

The warehouse was a labyrinth, a twisted game designed to ensnare us. Each turn felt like a gamble, the stakes rising with every second. The footsteps behind us morphed into a chorus of threats, taunting us as we darted between old crates and towering stacks of boxes.

I could see the exit, a rectangle of dim light beckoning us like a distant star, but the path to it seemed to grow longer with every stride. Just as I thought we were clear, the sound of laughter echoed through the space, dark and mocking. A chill ran down my spine.

"Looks like the little mice have come out to play," a voice sneered, dripping with malice. I froze, recognizing the tone as belonging to Marcus, one of the city's most notorious figures. His face, etched with shadows, appeared at the entrance, flanked by men whose loyalty was as dangerous as their weapons.

"Trapped like rats," he continued, stepping forward, a predatory smile twisting his lips. "Did you really think you could steal from us and get away with it?"

I felt Reid's hand tighten on my arm, an anchor amidst the chaos. "We're not the ones in trouble here, Marcus," he said, his voice steady despite the danger surrounding us. "You're the ones who should be worried."

For a brief moment, time froze, and the world narrowed to just the four of us—the hunter and the hunted, the inevitable clash that had been brewing for so long. My heart thundered in my chest, a reminder of all that was at stake. In this moment, I could see it clearly: the truth we were fighting for was not just for ourselves, but for everyone who had been silenced, every soul crushed beneath the weight of corruption.

Then, without warning, the tension snapped. The air shifted, and chaos erupted. I barely had time to register the flurry of movement before Reid shoved me to the side, his body shielding mine as fists flew and the air filled with the cacophony of chaos. The warehouse became a battlefield, every surface a potential weapon, and I could feel the stakes rise higher than ever before.

Adrenaline surged as I scrambled to my feet, the ledger clutched tightly in my hands. This was more than just a fight for survival; it was a fight for the truth, a battle I was willing to face head-on. I glanced at Reid, whose fierce gaze met mine, and in that moment, we knew what we had to do.

With a surge of determination, we would not only escape this den of lions, but we would take the truth with us, no matter the cost.

Panic surged through me like a wildfire, but I forced myself to focus on the chaos unfolding around us. Reid and I ducked behind a rusted metal pillar, our breaths shallow as we strained to listen over the din of fists meeting flesh and the furious growls of our adversaries. Each thud echoed through the warehouse, a stark reminder of the stakes at play.

"Why does this always happen to us?" I muttered, the irony of our situation not lost on me. One minute, we were uncovering a web of deceit, and the next, we were the prey in a game we never intended to play.

Reid shot me a sidelong glance, his expression a mix of frustration and amusement. "Because we have a knack for finding trouble? Or perhaps we just have bad luck."

"Or excellent taste in adventure," I quipped, trying to inject some levity into our dire situation. "Who wouldn't want to face down a group of thugs in a decrepit warehouse?"

"Next time, let's aim for a coffee shop," he shot back, a wry smile teasing at the corners of his mouth. The banter felt like a lifeline in the midst of the chaos, grounding us in the moment.

But the laughter faded quickly as the commotion intensified. A particularly loud crash reverberated through the space, followed by a grunt from one of Marcus's men. It was clear we couldn't hide here forever. "What's the plan?" I whispered, urgency lacing my words.

Reid's brow furrowed as he scanned the area. "We need to create a diversion, something to buy us a little time. I'll distract them; you make a run for the exit."

"Absolutely not. We stick together," I insisted, the thought of separating sending a jolt of fear through me. "I'm not leaving you behind."

He opened his mouth to protest, but I shook my head, determination setting my jaw. "We'll make it out together. Besides, I'm pretty sure I can be convincingly obnoxious if it comes to that."

"Just what I need—my partner engaging in a grand performance," he replied, a mix of pride and exasperation in his tone. "Fine. But we do this quickly."

With a nod, I positioned myself to move as he stepped out from behind the pillar, calling out to Marcus and his crew with a defiance I didn't fully feel. "Hey, you overgrown cockroaches! Why don't you pick on someone your own size?"

Marcus turned, his brows knitting together in annoyance as he zeroed in on Reid. "Ah, the little firecracker returns," he sneered. "What's your plan, boy? Flirt your way out of this?"

Reid didn't flinch. "Just thought I'd remind you that you're the one in a warehouse full of junk, while I'm about to walk out the door with the only treasure worth having."

It was a risky gamble, but I had to admit, the man had a flair for the dramatic. I seized the moment, slipping away from my hiding spot while the attention was drawn away from me. My feet moved almost instinctively, darting toward the far side of the warehouse where I hoped the exit lay. I could hear Reid continuing his taunts behind me, his voice echoing off the steel walls, but I didn't dare look back.

My heart raced as I reached the back wall, where shadows flickered and danced like phantoms. I could see the dim light spilling from a door—freedom was tantalizingly close. I reached for the handle, my fingers trembling in anticipation, when a sharp noise cut through the air.

"Where do you think you're going?" Marcus's voice slithered into my ears like poison. I whipped around just in time to see him striding toward me, his minions regrouping behind him, a pack of wolves ready to pounce.

"Didn't anyone ever teach you not to corner a cat?" I shot back, adrenaline pumping through my veins as I prepared for a fight.

He laughed, a low, chilling sound that raised goosebumps on my skin. "Cats are nice and all, but we prefer to deal with the feral kind. Much more satisfying."

I braced myself, adrenaline flooding my system. The door was behind me, and I knew I had to reach it, but facing down Marcus and his henchmen felt like a death wish. Just as I was weighing my options, Reid lunged back into the fray, a wild look in his eyes. "You can't have her, Marcus!"

In that instant, everything shifted. The tension that had been simmering burst into flames, igniting the warehouse with energy. I darted to the side, ready to find a way past Marcus, but the room spun in a whirlwind of bodies and chaos.

Reid's fierce determination made me feel invincible, but that feeling quickly evaporated as Marcus advanced, a predatory glint in his eye. "Oh, so now we have a hero. How quaint," he sneered. "But you're outnumbered."

"Maybe. But I'm also more resourceful than you think," Reid replied, standing tall, as if daring Marcus to make a move. His bravery fueled my own.

Without thinking, I dove into the nearest pile of debris, scattering old machinery parts in all directions. "Reid, cover me!" I shouted, heart racing as I fumbled through the mess, searching for anything that could give us an edge.

"Always," he called back, and I could hear him engaging with Marcus, their voices a blend of challenge and bravado.

The clang of metal on metal rang out as I found a heavy piece of scrap. It wasn't much, but it would have to do. I gripped it tightly, steeling myself for what came next. Taking a deep breath, I rose, ready to spring into action.

Just then, I caught a glimpse of something shimmering under a fallen piece of machinery—a weapon left behind in the chaos. I scrambled toward it, adrenaline surging. But the moment my fingers closed around the cold metal, I realized I'd stumbled onto something more than just a potential weapon. This was a gun, and its weight in my hand felt both empowering and terrifying.

Before I could fully process what I held, a commotion erupted behind me. Reid was fighting valiantly, but I could see that the odds were rapidly turning against him. My heart twisted with fear; I couldn't let him down.

"Reid!" I yelled, brandishing the gun as I stepped into the fray. "Get out of there!"

His eyes widened as he caught sight of me, surprise flickering across his face. "What are you doing?" he shouted, grappling with one of Marcus's men.

"Something drastic!" I fired a shot into the air, the sound deafening in the cramped space. "Back off, or the next one won't be a warning!"

The chaos froze for a moment, stunned silence enveloping the warehouse as everyone processed the unexpected twist. Marcus's gaze flickered between me and Reid, confusion and irritation battling for supremacy.

"You're bluffing," he said, trying to regain control of the situation. "You think that makes you tough?"

"No," I replied, feeling the adrenaline coursing through my veins, emboldening me. "It makes me desperate."

The tension crackled in the air, each breath heavy with potential violence. I held my ground, knowing that in this moment, we had a slim chance to turn the tide. Reid's eyes met mine, a flicker of gratitude mingling with disbelief.

"Let's finish this," he said, his voice low and steady. And in that shared glance, we understood: we weren't just fighting for our lives; we were fighting for the truth, for every person silenced by corruption.

As the moment stretched into eternity, I realized we might just have the upper hand after all.

The stillness that followed the gunshot felt surreal, as if time had suspended itself in a breathless pause, holding its collective breath. Marcus blinked at me, his sneer faltering just a fraction, and I could sense the gears in his mind turning, calculating, re-evaluating the situation. His men hesitated, glancing back at their leader as if awaiting orders. I stood there, heart hammering in my chest, weapon clutched tightly, every nerve alive with a fierce mix of fear and resolve.

"Are we really doing this?" Reid's voice cut through the tension, a blend of disbelief and admiration. "I knew you were bold, but I didn't think you'd go for a gun."

"I didn't think I would either!" I shot back, adrenaline coursing through me like wildfire. "But here we are. So how about we take advantage of it?"

Marcus's bravado flickered for a heartbeat. "You're playing a dangerous game, girl. You think that little toy can save you?" He gestured dismissively, but I could see the calculations flashing behind his eyes—how to regain control, how to turn the tide back in his favor.

"I don't think it can save me. I know it can save us," I replied, my voice steady even as my hands trembled slightly. "But it will only work if you let us go. Walk away, Marcus. I won't ask again."

The challenge hung in the air, taut and electric, and for a moment, I thought I saw doubt cross Marcus's face. His men shifted uneasily, eyes darting between their leader and the makeshift weapon I held. I could feel the balance of power teetering, the scales threatening to tip, and I held my breath, praying it would lean in our favor.

"Get her!" Marcus barked, his bravado returning like a wave crashing over fragile cliffs. "Take the gun!"

Before I could react, the thugs surged forward, a wave of muscle and malice intent on reclaiming the upper hand. Instinct kicked in, and I fired again, this time aiming lower, hoping to startle them enough to create space for Reid and me to escape.

The shot rang out, echoing through the warehouse, and one of the men stumbled back, clutching his leg. The moment of hesitation was all I needed. "Now!" I shouted, darting toward the exit as chaos erupted behind me.

Reid was right at my heels, propelling us forward like a force of nature. We wove through the maze of debris, our footsteps a frenzied symphony of urgency. I could hear the shouts behind us, the sound of boots pounding against the concrete floor, and I knew we had to reach the door before they regrouped.

With a surge of hope, I threw myself toward the exit, bursting through the door into the cool night air. The sharp contrast of the outside world hit me like a refreshing slap, invigorating and terrifying all at once. We were free, but the battle wasn't over yet.

"Keep moving!" Reid urged, grabbing my hand and pulling me into the darkness beyond the warehouse. The fog had thickened, wrapping around us like a shroud, but the dim light of streetlamps glimmered in the distance, a beacon of safety—or so I hoped.

"What now?" I panted, adrenaline still coursing through me, making my heart race faster than my feet could carry me. The streets were eerily quiet, a stark contrast to the chaos we had just fled.

"Find a place to lay low, regroup, and figure out our next move," Reid replied, his expression focused and determined. The weight of the ledger pressed against my side, a reminder of the secrets we still held and the danger looming ahead.

We ducked into a nearby alley, shadows swallowing us whole as we pressed against the damp brick wall, our breaths coming in ragged gasps. The adrenaline was wearing off, replaced by a bone-deep exhaustion that settled in my bones like a heavy fog. "Did we lose them?" I whispered, peering into the murky darkness, half-expecting to see the glint of Marcus's eyes watching us.

Reid strained to listen, his gaze flicking toward the mouth of the alley. "For now, but we need to move. They won't stay down for long."

"Great. So we're not safe yet?" I said, trying to inject some humor into the tension that crackled between us.

"Not quite," he replied, a slight grin breaking through the tension. "But you're doing amazing. I mean, who knew you had it in you to hold a gun?"

"Desperation brings out the best in people," I quipped, but the reality weighed heavily on my shoulders.

Before we could formulate a plan, the distant sound of sirens pierced the night, growing louder by the second. I felt my pulse quicken, a sense of urgency washing over me. "We need to go, now!"

Reid nodded, and we slipped deeper into the shadows, moving away from the cacophony of police sirens and the chaos we'd left behind. We navigated the labyrinthine streets, weaving through alleys and side roads, our hearts racing in unison as we sought refuge.

"Do you have any idea where we're going?" I asked, trying to catch my breath.

"Not a clue," he admitted, his eyes scanning the dimly lit street ahead. "But anywhere is better than here."

Just as we turned a corner, a sudden flash of headlights cut through the fog, illuminating us in stark relief. I froze, my breath hitching as a sleek black car skidded to a halt a few feet away, tires screeching against the pavement. The back door swung open, and a familiar figure emerged, silhouetted against the glow of the headlights.

"Get in!" a voice shouted, sharp and commanding. I squinted, recognition dawning as the figure stepped into the light. It was Tom, our ally, the one person I hadn't expected to see at this hour.

"Are you serious?" Reid said, stepping protectively in front of me. "What are you doing here?"

"We don't have time for questions!" Tom urged, glancing over his shoulder as if sensing danger closing in. "They're coming. Get in!"

Without thinking, I grabbed Reid's hand, and together we dove into the back seat, the door slamming shut behind us. The moment we were inside, the car lurched forward, speeding away from the danger that threatened to engulf us.

"I thought you were out of town," I gasped, turning to Tom, who gripped the wheel with white knuckles, his expression serious.

"Plans changed. I got a tip-off that things were going south for you two. Good thing I did," he replied, shooting a glance in the rearview mirror, anxiety etched across his features.

"Where's the ledger?" he asked, turning back to face us, urgency threading his voice. I instinctively placed a protective hand over it, feeling the weight of its significance.

"It's right here," I said, and for a brief moment, the enormity of our discovery settled over us like a warm blanket. But before I could feel triumphant, Reid's voice broke through my thoughts.

"Do you think Marcus is still after us?"

Tom grimaced, adjusting his speed as we sped down the dimly lit road. "He doesn't give up easily. We need to get somewhere safe, fast."

The car flew through the night, the fog swirling around us like an ominous omen. My mind raced with thoughts of the ledger, of the names it contained, and what it could mean for the corrupt system that had plagued our city for too long. But just as hope began to blossom, a piercing realization struck me.

"What if we're walking into another trap?" I said, my heart sinking as the thought took hold. "What if Tom is working for Marcus?"

The silence that followed felt heavy, thick with tension. Tom's expression hardened, and Reid's gaze flicked between us, confusion knitting his brows together. "You think I'd lead you into a trap? After everything?"

"Trust can be hard to come by in our line of work," I replied, my heart racing. The stakes had never felt higher, and every instinct screamed that we weren't out of danger yet.

Before Tom could respond, a loud crash erupted behind us, metal screeching against metal as another vehicle collided with us, the impact jarring. The car spun, skidding out of control as screams erupted from my throat, chaos consuming the world around us.

As we careened into the night, I locked eyes with Reid, terror mirrored in his gaze, and I realized this fight was far from over. With the weight of the ledger still in my grasp, I knew the truth was out there waiting for us, but the question remained: would we survive long enough to uncover it?

Chapter 22: Broken Vows

The air was thick with unspoken words, the silence between us heavy enough to suffocate. I glanced at Reid as we walked side by side through the dimly lit alley, the streetlights flickering like old memories. His jaw was clenched, and I could sense the turmoil bubbling beneath his skin, a tempest that mirrored my own. I wished I could reach out, lay a hand on his arm, and anchor him back to reality. But every inch of me felt like a porcelain doll, teetering on the brink of shattering.

"Are we just going to pretend that didn't happen?" I finally ventured, my voice barely above a whisper, afraid that even the air around us would crack under the weight of our shared burden. I needed to know if the connection we had forged in the heat of battle still held any warmth, or if it had frozen into something cold and unyielding.

He didn't meet my gaze, instead focusing on the ground ahead, as if it held all the answers. "What do you want me to say?" The bite in his tone stung, but I didn't flinch. This was Reid, after all. Beneath his rough exterior, there was always a vulnerability that he kept buried deep. I had seen glimpses of it before, but now it felt like I was standing on the precipice of a cliff, waiting for him to leap or retreat.

"I want you to say you're still here. That we're still us." My heart raced as I spoke, the words spilling from my lips like a confession. "Because it doesn't feel like that right now. It feels like we're both just...existing. Surviving, but not really living."

He finally turned to me, his eyes dark pools reflecting the chaos within. "And what do you think we're supposed to do? Pretend it didn't happen? Pretend we're not both terrified?" His voice softened, a hint of the Reid I knew creeping back in, but the tension remained, thick and palpable.

"Maybe we should stop pretending we can handle everything alone," I suggested, the warmth of honesty filling the cracks between us. "We can't fight every battle without help. We can't shoulder this alone." I took a step closer, closing the distance, hoping to weave our fragmented pieces back together.

He exhaled sharply, a sound filled with frustration and longing. "I don't want to drag you into this. I thought I was protecting you." His gaze drifted to the shadows, and I followed his eyes to a distant street corner where a couple laughed, oblivious to the darkness we had just escaped. I envied their lightness, their ignorance of the scars that lingered just beneath the surface.

"Protecting me?" I scoffed, feeling a fire ignite within me. "You think shutting me out will keep me safe? You're wrong. You're not the only one who has faced the darkness. I'm here too, Reid. I've fought my own battles." My voice trembled with the weight of my words, a raw honesty that seemed to hang in the air between us, a tenuous thread linking our souls.

He stepped closer, his brow furrowing as if he were piecing together a puzzle that had eluded him for too long. "You don't understand," he said softly. "I've made mistakes. I've hurt people. And I don't want to do that to you." There was a vulnerability in his confession that cut through the tension, a moment of clarity that I desperately clung to.

"Neither do I," I replied, my heart pounding in my chest. "But we can't move forward without each other. We need to face our fears together, not apart." I reached for his hand, the warmth of his skin grounding me in that chaotic moment. His fingers hesitated, then intertwined with mine, a silent agreement that sent a jolt of electricity through my veins.

A flicker of hope ignited in his eyes as he squeezed my hand, the first real connection we'd shared since everything had unraveled.

"Okay," he said, the word escaping his lips like a promise. "But we have to be honest. No more hiding."

"Deal," I said, my heart racing. "But first, let's get out of this alley before I start feeling like a character in a bad noir film." The tension broke, laughter bubbling to the surface, lightening the air between us. I had missed this—his laughter, the way it danced with mine, weaving a tapestry of shared moments that defined our bond.

As we stepped back into the world, I could feel the energy shifting. The air felt charged, alive with possibility. Perhaps this was the beginning of something new—a chance to rebuild what had been broken, piece by piece. But as we moved forward, I couldn't shake the nagging feeling that shadows still lurked in the corners, waiting for the opportune moment to strike.

"Let's grab a coffee," I suggested, desperately craving something warm to cradle in my hands. "I need caffeine to process everything." I could see the ghost of a smile tug at his lips, and for the first time in what felt like forever, the heaviness in my chest began to lift.

"Fine, but only if you promise to share your infamous chocolate croissants," he teased, the lightness in his voice like a balm to my weary soul. "I'm not above bribery when it comes to baked goods."

"Deal," I replied, the laughter flowing freely now, unearthing a sense of camaraderie that I feared we had lost forever. With each step, we forged a path through the chaos, ready to face whatever came next, together.

But beneath the laughter, the undercurrents of doubt lingered. I couldn't shake the feeling that our past would always be a shadow, lurking just behind us, waiting for an opportunity to pull us back into darkness. Yet, as I glanced at Reid, the resolve in his eyes ignited a flicker of hope that perhaps, just perhaps, we could rise from the ashes stronger than before.

The café's warmth enveloped us like a soft blanket, the rich aroma of freshly ground coffee mingling with the scent of pastries that danced tantalizingly in the air. I perched on a stool at the counter, trying to shake off the chill that had settled into my bones, remnants of the darkness we had escaped. Reid leaned against the wall, arms crossed, eyes scanning the room as if looking for threats lurking among the scattered tables. His tension was palpable, a tightrope stretched between us, but I hoped this place could serve as a sanctuary, if only for a little while.

"Okay, Mr. Brooding," I said, trying to inject some levity into the atmosphere. "I'll have you know that this place makes the best chocolate croissants in the city. You might even smile." I grinned, gesturing toward the glass display filled with golden-brown pastries. He glanced my way, one eyebrow raised, skepticism etched on his face.

"Smile? In a café? Sounds like something out of a rom-com," he quipped, his lips twitching slightly, hinting at the flicker of amusement beneath his stoic exterior. "What's next? You're going to tell me to order a fruity drink with an umbrella in it?"

"Only if you promise to wear a Hawaiian shirt," I shot back, unable to suppress a chuckle. He rolled his eyes, but I could see the corners of his mouth soften, the tension in his shoulders easing just a bit.

"I'll pass, but I'll take a black coffee and one of those croissants, if you insist," he said, finally approaching the counter. As he ordered, I watched the barista's expert hands working with the dough, kneading and shaping it with an artistry I envied. There was something comforting in the ritual, a reminder that beauty could be created even amid chaos.

With our orders secured, we settled at a small table near the window, the sun spilling golden light onto the surface, casting playful shadows. I took a deep breath, inhaling the warmth and sweetness of the café, a stark contrast to the bitter memories clawing at the edges of my mind.

"Here's to sugary carbs saving the day," I declared, lifting my croissant in a toast. Reid chuckled softly, the sound a welcome balm to my anxious spirit.

"Just what I need to combat my existential dread," he replied, tearing into his pastry with exaggerated gusto. I couldn't help but laugh at the sight. He was like a child discovering something delightful for the first time, his serious facade momentarily cracking.

As I watched him, the realization hit me like a jolt. This was the Reid I remembered, the one who could find humor in the darkest of times. Beneath the weight of everything that had transpired, there was still a flicker of light within him, a spark I desperately wanted to fan into a flame.

"Okay, let's talk about it," I said, my voice steadier than I felt. "The darkness. What happened?" I leaned forward, my heart racing, prepared to peel back the layers we had wrapped around ourselves. It was time to confront the specters haunting our steps.

He paused, the laughter fading from his eyes as the gravity of my question settled over us. "I thought we'd left that behind," he muttered, his gaze dropping to the table, tracing the delicate patterns etched into the wood.

"Maybe not," I pressed gently. "We can't just bury it. Not if we want to move forward." The atmosphere shifted, thickening with unspoken truths. I could feel my pulse quicken as the moment hung heavy in the air, a pivotal moment teetering on the edge of revelation.

Reid sighed, running a hand through his hair, the movement laden with frustration. "It's complicated. I thought I could handle it. I thought I could protect you, but..." His voice trailed off, and I felt the space between us grow again, filled with all the words left unspoken.

"Reid, I'm not made of glass," I said, my tone firm but tender. "I'm stronger than you think. You can lean on me too."

His eyes flicked up to mine, and I saw the turmoil swirling within them, like a storm ready to break. "It's not just about you. There are things I can't talk about. Things that could put you in danger." His words hung like a noose, tightening around my throat.

"Is that what you think? That I'd break under pressure? You don't know me at all." I leaned closer, driven by a mix of anger and desperation. "You think by keeping secrets you're protecting me? But all you're doing is building walls, and I can't reach you through them."

He studied me for a moment, something flickering in his gaze—doubt, maybe, or fear. "It's easier to keep things to myself. It's safer." His voice was low, barely above a whisper, as if the very act of admitting vulnerability could shatter him.

"Is it, though?" I challenged, leaning back in my chair, crossing my arms defiantly. "What happens when the darkness finds you alone? When it comes knocking and you have no one to answer?"

For a moment, silence enveloped us, the clatter of cups and laughter of patrons fading into a distant hum. The weight of my words settled over the table, a shroud of tension palpable between us. Reid's expression shifted, the edges of his resolve softening just a fraction.

"I don't want to lose you," he finally admitted, his voice thick with emotion. "But maybe I'm the one who needs to learn how to share the burden."

I felt my heart swell at his admission, a flicker of hope igniting the darkness that had threatened to swallow us whole. "Then let's do this together. Whatever it is, we face it side by side. You don't have to do this alone."

His gaze locked onto mine, and for the first time, I saw a glimmer of acceptance—a willingness to let me in. "Alright," he said, his voice steadier now, imbued with a newfound determination. "But you have to promise to keep your head down. I can't lose you."

"Deal," I replied, my heart racing with anticipation. "And if you ever think about going all lone wolf again, just remember the power of croissants."

We shared a smile, the tension between us beginning to ease as laughter bubbled back to the surface, an effervescent reminder of our bond. It was a tentative truce, but one I hoped would grow stronger as we began to unravel the threads of our past and weave them into a future that was ours to define.

The moment of clarity between us, however fleeting, filled the air with a tentative sense of relief. We sat together, our laughter mingling with the sounds of the café, and the shadows that had loomed over us began to retreat. I took a sip of my coffee, the rich bitterness grounding me as I tried to imagine a world where Reid and I could stand shoulder to shoulder against whatever darkness awaited us. But lurking behind that thought was the creeping realization that the battles ahead might not be fought with mere words and pastries.

"I've been thinking," I said, breaking the silence that followed our moment of levity. "What if we didn't just wait for the next threat to come to us? What if we took the fight to them?" The idea hung in the air, bold and daunting, as I watched Reid's brow furrow in contemplation.

"Are you suggesting we become some sort of vigilantes?" His voice was laced with a mix of incredulity and intrigue. "Because if we're planning on jumping into the fray, I need to know if you're really ready for that."

"I've been ready for a long time, Reid. I didn't choose this life, but I can't keep hiding in the shadows," I replied, meeting his gaze with unwavering determination. "We can't let our past define us any longer. We have to take control."

The flicker of admiration in his eyes made my heart race. "I admire your courage, but it's not just about us anymore. There are others involved now, people who could get hurt." His tone was cautious, but the steel behind it showed he was considering my proposal.

"Then let's bring them into the light," I suggested, leaning in. "We can't fight this alone, and I don't want to. If we work together, gather our resources, we might stand a chance." The idea felt thrilling, like standing on the edge of a precipice, the wind whipping through my hair.

Reid remained silent for a moment, the weight of my words settling between us. Finally, he nodded, his expression a mixture of resolve and caution. "Alright, let's do it. But we need a plan. We need to be strategic. If we go in half-cocked, it'll be just like throwing ourselves into a lion's den with no exit."

"Then we'll make a map," I replied, a grin spreading across my face. "A treasure map for the bravest of adventurers." The idea of crafting a plan, of drawing lines and connecting dots, ignited a fire in me that I hadn't felt in ages.

Reid laughed, the sound lightening the tension that still hung around us. "Alright, Captain Adventure, what's our first step?"

I paused, letting the laughter settle, and leaned back in my chair, surveying the café as if it were a battlefield. "First, we need to gather intel. We need to know who we're up against."

"And how do you propose we do that?" he challenged, his eyes narrowing, clearly intrigued but still cautious.

"Remember that guy we saw in the alley?" I began, my mind racing. "The one who had been watching us? He seemed to know something. If we can find him again, maybe he can point us in the right direction."

Reid frowned. "That could be dangerous. We don't know what he's capable of. He could be working for them."

"Or he could be our only lead," I countered, the thrill of possibility coursing through me. "We need to take risks if we want to move forward."

As we discussed our next steps, a flicker of movement caught my eye outside the café window. A figure loomed near the entrance, shrouded in a dark hoodie, a face obscured by shadows. My heart skipped a beat as I recognized the unmistakable outline.

"Reid," I said, my voice barely a whisper, urgency creeping into my tone. "I think it's him." I pointed subtly, not wanting to alert the figure, but the adrenaline racing through my veins screamed for action.

"What do we do?" Reid asked, instinctively straightening, his body tensing beside me.

"Let's find out what he wants," I replied, gripping the edge of the table as I prepared to rise. My heart pounded in my chest, the stakes suddenly escalating. I had no idea what this confrontation could lead to, but I was ready to face it. I could feel Reid's hesitation, but he didn't stop me.

With each step toward the door, the world outside faded into a blur. The café's comforting chatter dimmed as the potential for confrontation loomed ahead. I pushed through the heavy door, the brisk air hitting me like a splash of cold water, jolting me into focus.

The figure stood motionless, the fabric of the hoodie drawing my gaze like a moth to a flame. "You've been looking for me," I said, attempting to sound braver than I felt.

He turned slowly, and as his face emerged from the shadows, recognition flooded through me. "You," I breathed, heart racing. "What are you doing here?"

"I came to warn you," he said, voice low and urgent, the weight of his words pressing against the chill of the air. "You're in deeper than you realize. They're coming for you."

Before I could process the implications, a sudden sound erupted from behind me. The unmistakable crack of glass shattered the air as someone pushed through the café door, rushing toward us with a force that sent shockwaves of fear rippling through my body. I turned, instinctively seeking Reid's presence, my heart pounding as the scene unfolded in front of me.

And then everything spun out of control.

Chapter 23: Shattered Illusions

Everything shifted that afternoon, the sky a bruised violet as storm clouds rolled in, their ominous presence mirroring the turmoil within me. I sat in the dimly lit café, the clinking of porcelain and muted conversations wrapping around me like a comforting blanket. Yet, the air felt charged, thick with unspoken truths and betrayal. I cradled my mug of lukewarm coffee, watching the steam curl like the ghosts of doubts swirling in my mind. The scent of rich espresso mingled with the sweet aroma of pastries, but all I could taste was the bitterness of impending loss.

Reid sat across from me, his usual confidence flickering like the candle at our table, shadows dancing across his features. I'd always admired that sharp jawline, the way his eyes sparkled with mischief and a hint of danger. But today, those eyes held a darkness I couldn't ignore. The world around us faded as he leaned in, his voice barely above a whisper, urgency threading through his words.

"Lila, you need to understand—this isn't just about us anymore. They're coming for everything we've built." His words were heavy with gravity, and I felt the weight of their truth settling in my chest like a stone.

I swallowed hard, the knot in my stomach tightening. "I know that. But what do we do? If we're going to fight, we need to know who we can trust." Trust had become a slippery concept, shifting like sand beneath my feet. The betrayal we'd uncovered had fractured the very foundation of our alliances. I thought I could rely on the connections I'd forged, the friendships that had blossomed in the chaos of this world we navigated, but now they felt like mirages, illusions crafted to deceive.

Reid exhaled sharply, his fingers tapping restlessly against the table. "I'm trying to piece it together. There's something bigger at play here, and I suspect it's not just the usual players. It's like a web, intricate and insidious, and we're caught in the center." His frustration mirrored my own, an unholy alliance against our better judgment.

"Who could it be?" I leaned closer, my heart racing as I processed the implications. "We've already lost so much. Are you saying there's someone among us?" The very idea sent a chill racing down my spine, like a gust of wind through an empty hall.

"Yes," he said, eyes darkening. "Someone we trusted. Someone you'd never expect." The implication hung heavy in the air, a spectral presence that loomed over our conversation, waiting to drop its final blow.

My mind reeled, racing through faces, memories clinging like ivy. I thought of Claire, my steadfast friend who always had my back, or Lucas, the ever-optimistic strategist who seemed to be two steps ahead of everyone. But then I remembered the cold glances exchanged in meetings, the subtle shifts in demeanor when Reid was around. "You think it's Claire?" I blurted out, horrified by the thought.

Reid shook his head, the lines of worry etched deeper on his brow. "I don't know. But whoever it is, they've played us both like a violin, and I can't let that continue. Not now, not when we're so close." His intensity was almost palpable, a storm brewing behind those dark eyes that held secrets I feared to uncover.

"What do we do then?" I asked, my voice barely above a whisper. The café felt like a sanctuary, but even here, I could feel the weight of the world closing in around us. I searched his face, looking for a sign, any sign, that everything would be okay. That the truth, whatever it was, wouldn't destroy us.

"We go deeper," Reid said, resolve hardening his features. "We dig until we unearth the truth. If we don't, we're left vulnerable, and I won't let that happen to you."

A chill ran through me, a mix of dread and anticipation. The stakes were higher than they had ever been, and I could feel the ground shifting beneath our feet. I wanted to believe in our fight, in the promise of a brighter tomorrow, but the specter of betrayal loomed large. The looming storm outside echoed my thoughts—was this the calm before the inevitable tempest?

As we left the café, the sky opened up, rain pouring down in sheets, a torrential reminder of the chaos we were wading into. I pulled my coat tighter around me, the fabric a flimsy shield against the elements. "We'll figure it out," I said, though doubt gnawed at my resolve. "We have to." Reid nodded, though uncertainty flickered in his eyes.

We made our way to my car, the streets slick and reflective, each puddle a shattered mirror reflecting our fractured trust. I couldn't shake the feeling that someone was watching us, lurking in the shadows, waiting for the right moment to strike. The thought was maddening, and I forced myself to focus on Reid's presence beside me, grounding me amidst the rising tide of panic.

"Lila," he said suddenly, halting in the rain-soaked street, the droplets clinging to his hair and clothes. "Promise me that whatever happens, you won't turn away. I need you in this." The earnestness in his voice pierced through the storm, and I met his gaze, feeling the raw emotion thrumming between us.

"I promise," I whispered, though the weight of that promise felt heavier than the rain. I wanted to believe in our strength, but doubt had a way of creeping in, whispering its dark tales in my ear. As we stood there, surrounded by the chaos of the world, I realized we were at a crossroads. The path ahead was fraught with danger, and with every beat of my heart, the stakes rose higher. I knew that whatever awaited us could either forge us into something unbreakable or shatter us completely.

And in that moment, under the relentless rain, I chose to fight.

The rain drummed steadily against the car roof as we drove, a relentless rhythm that mirrored my racing thoughts. Each raindrop felt like a warning, a reminder that our journey was fraught with danger. Reid glanced over at me, his expression a blend of determination and concern. "You good?" he asked, his voice cutting through the tension like a knife.

I forced a smile, though it felt like a brittle mask. "Just thinking about how to reinvent our lives as private detectives. You know, the whole trench coat and fedora vibe." I tried to inject some levity into the air, but the heaviness of our reality settled back in, weighing on my chest.

Reid chuckled, a low rumble that briefly lightened the atmosphere. "I think you'd pull it off, but we might need more than a hat and a coat to navigate this mess." He turned his attention back to the road, and I admired the way he focused, a soldier ready for battle. "We need intel, Lila. We have to identify who's pulling the strings."

The city lights blurred into streaks of color through the rain-slicked windshield, a kaleidoscope of chaos that seemed to echo my mind. "Right. Intel." I leaned back, letting the car's movement cradle me. "Any ideas on where to start?"

"I have a contact," he said, his voice steady. "Someone who knows the underbelly of this city better than anyone else." His tone shifted, a hint of caution creeping in. "But he's... unorthodox. We might need to grease some palms."

"Grease palms? Are we talking cash or something a bit more... creative?" I raised an eyebrow, a smirk tugging at my lips despite the seriousness of our situation.

"Let's just say he doesn't respond well to the usual channels," Reid replied, a smirk of his own forming. "But he can get us what we need."

I nodded, absorbing his words. It felt like we were slipping into a different world, one where shadows danced and secrets thrived.

"Do we have to go meet him in some shady bar? I mean, I have a reputation to uphold."

Reid laughed, a genuine sound that warmed the chill between us. "Oh, definitely. He'll be surrounded by people who have more tattoos than common sense."

The idea sent a shiver down my spine. "Tattoos and questionable judgment? Sounds like my kind of crowd." I leaned forward, caught in the excitement of the hunt. "What's his name?"

"Cruz," Reid said, his expression turning serious. "He's a bit of a wildcard, but he owes me a favor. I wouldn't trust him as far as I could throw him, but he might have what we need."

"Fantastic. Wildcards are my favorite," I deadpanned, a touch of sarcasm coloring my voice. "What's our play?"

"We need to approach him carefully," Reid advised. "He doesn't take kindly to surprises, and he can smell fear a mile away. But if we show him we're serious, we might just get him to spill."

The thought of meeting Cruz filled me with a strange mix of apprehension and thrill. This was a different kind of adventure, a step into a world I had only ever heard about in whispers and rumors. "Do I need to wear a leather jacket and sunglasses to fit in?" I joked, but the seriousness of our mission loomed large.

"No sunglasses. Just bring that killer instinct of yours," Reid replied, his smile infectious. "Trust me, you'll be fine."

As we pulled into the dimly lit parking lot of a bar that looked like it had been carved out of shadows and bad decisions, the atmosphere shifted. The air was thick with the scent of stale beer and something else I couldn't quite place. I turned to Reid, searching for reassurance in his eyes. "You sure about this?"

He nodded, the resolve in his gaze steadying me. "We've come this far, Lila. We need answers. Let's go see if Cruz can help us find them."

Stepping out of the car, the cool night air hit me like a splash of cold water, waking me up to the reality of our situation. As we approached the entrance, the pulsing music thumped like a heartbeat, and the cacophony of voices poured out into the street. The neon lights flickered, casting a kaleidoscope of colors across the cracked pavement.

Inside, the bar was a labyrinth of dim corners and raucous laughter, a chaotic symphony of life and desperation. I scanned the crowd, feeling the thrill of the unknown mingle with the fear coursing through my veins. "So, where's Cruz?" I asked, trying to sound nonchalant while my heart raced like a drum in my chest.

"Near the back, by the pool tables," Reid said, weaving through the throng with an ease that made me feel like I was the one stumbling in a foreign land. I followed closely, trying to adopt his confidence, but the clinking glasses and boisterous laughter felt like a reminder that I was a little fish in a big, murky pond.

As we approached the back, I caught sight of Cruz—a man with a lean frame, dark hair, and tattoos snaking up his arms like ivy. He leaned casually against the wall, a glass in hand, surveying the room with an air of someone who knew too much. I felt a shiver of anticipation run through me; he was exactly the kind of person I expected to find in a place like this, both fascinating and unnerving.

"Remember, let me do the talking," Reid whispered, his voice low as we stepped closer. "He can smell desperation."

"Yeah, because I'm radiating it right now," I muttered under my breath, the nerves churning in my stomach.

"Hey, Cruz," Reid called out, his voice cutting through the din like a knife. The man's gaze flicked toward us, his eyes narrowing, assessing.

"What do you want?" Cruz replied, his tone a mix of curiosity and challenge.

Reid stepped forward, his posture confident. "We need information, and I hear you're the one to talk to."

Cruz smirked, a knowing glint in his eye. "You've got that right. But information isn't free. What's in it for me?"

I held my breath, feeling the tension crackle in the air. Reid's response was quick, laced with a mixture of authority and urgency. "I can offer you a slice of something bigger than your usual fare. This isn't just about scraps, Cruz; it's about survival."

Cruz studied us, the flickering bar lights casting shadows over his face, making it hard to read his expression. "Survival, huh? You two really think you're playing with the big boys now?"

"Trust me," I chimed in, surprising myself with the confidence that bubbled to the surface. "We're not here to play games. We're looking to win."

Cruz raised an eyebrow, the challenge in his eyes sparking something deep within me. This was the kind of moment I had always wanted—raw and unfiltered, where stakes were high, and nothing was guaranteed. If we were going to dig deep, we had to prove ourselves, and I was ready to step into the fray.

Cruz took a sip from his glass, his gaze flitting between us, weighing his options like a predator sizing up its prey. "Alright, then. Let's see how far you're willing to go."

Cruz leaned against the wall, the flickering bar lights casting shadows across his face, illuminating the edges of a smirk that suggested he knew more than he was letting on. "So, you think you can just waltz in here, toss around some bravado, and expect me to spill my secrets?" His voice was laced with skepticism, but beneath that, I sensed a flicker of curiosity.

Reid remained unfazed, his posture straightening as he squared his shoulders. "We're not just any players in this game. We're here to take down some serious players, and we know you're caught in the middle. You might want to think about which side you want to be on."

The air crackled with tension, and I felt the weight of Cruz's gaze shift toward me, an unspoken challenge hanging between us. "And you," he said, his tone appraising. "What do you bring to the table? Just a pretty face?"

I straightened, refusing to let the insult slide. "You'll find I'm more than just a pretty face," I shot back, my voice steady despite the rush of adrenaline surging through me. "I'm not afraid of getting my hands dirty."

Cruz raised an eyebrow, clearly intrigued. "Is that right? You're willing to dive into the mess that is this city? You really don't know what you're asking for."

"Then tell me what I'm asking for," I replied, meeting his gaze head-on. "Give me something real. I'm tired of whispers and shadows."

He chuckled, a low, throaty sound that was more amused than offended. "You've got guts, I'll give you that. But guts don't mean much without a plan."

Reid interjected, sensing the shifting dynamics. "We need information about the syndicate. Their plans, their connections. We're not looking for gossip; we want actionable intel."

Cruz regarded us with a newfound seriousness. "You're playing with fire, and I'm not talking about the kind that gets you a nice warm glow. This is the kind of fire that burns everything to the ground."

"Then let's burn it down," I replied, surprising myself with the fierceness in my voice. "I'm not going to sit back while everything we've built crumbles. We're in this together, whether you like it or not."

He leaned in, curiosity glinting in his eyes. "Alright, let's say I help you. What's in it for me?"

Reid, sensing the opportunity, stepped closer, his voice lowering conspiratorially. "We can offer you protection, a chance to distance yourself from the chaos. You don't want to be caught on the wrong side of this when it all goes down."

Cruz's gaze hardened, contemplating the offer. "And what makes you think I trust you? You're both just two kids trying to play with the big boys."

"Because we've been through hell and back, and we're still standing," I countered, my voice rising above the chatter of the bar. "You think we're just some naive kids? We're willing to risk everything to end this."

The corner of Cruz's mouth twitched, a reluctant smile breaking through. "I like you. You've got spirit. But that spirit could get you killed."

"Good thing I'm not easily scared," I shot back, matching his playful challenge with a determined stare.

Cruz considered us for a moment, and then his expression shifted. "Alright, but I'm only giving you this once. If you cross me, I won't hesitate to put you on the other side of the law."

"Fair enough," Reid replied, the tension easing just slightly. "What do we need to do?"

Cruz leaned in closer, his voice lowering to a conspiratorial whisper. "There's a shipment coming in next week. High-value goods—money, weapons, the works. They'll be using the old docks, and that's where you can get your answers. You'll need to move fast. Get in, get what you need, and get out."

I felt a rush of excitement mixed with dread. "And if we get caught?"

"Then you better pray to whatever god you believe in," Cruz said, his eyes gleaming with mischief. "Or be prepared to bargain your way out."

With the deal struck, we spent the next hour gathering more details, the weight of the impending mission sinking deeper into my bones. Cruz was a fount of information, but every piece felt like a double-edged sword. The more we learned, the more I realized just how deep the rabbit hole went.

As we left the bar, the cool night air hit me with a sense of clarity. I turned to Reid, a mix of exhilaration and anxiety swirling within me. "We have a plan. Now we just need to execute it."

Reid nodded, his expression serious. "But we need to be careful. If Cruz is right, this is going to be more dangerous than we anticipated."

"I can handle danger," I replied, trying to project confidence even as my stomach twisted in knots. "I'm tired of running from shadows. It's time to face them head-on."

But as we stepped onto the street, a creeping sensation slithered down my spine. The night felt heavier, the air charged with uncertainty. A distant shout echoed from the alley, followed by the unmistakable sound of a scuffle.

"Did you hear that?" I said, my heart racing.

"Yeah, let's check it out," Reid replied, his voice low as he led the way toward the alley.

The shadows deepened as we approached, the dim light from the street lamps barely penetrating the darkness. The sounds grew louder, muffled voices and the thud of bodies hitting the ground. I could feel the adrenaline surging through my veins, my instincts kicking in.

As we turned the corner, a scene unfolded before us—three figures were grappling in the narrow space, their movements frantic and desperate. One of them, a tall man with a hood pulled low, pushed another against the wall, his fist raised in a menacing arc.

"Get away from him!" I shouted, the words bursting from me before I could think.

The man paused, glancing back, and in that split second, I saw his face—the sharp angles, the glint of recognition. It was one of our supposed allies, a trusted face from our recent past.

"Lila!" he yelled, panic flooding his voice. "Run! They're—"

Before he could finish, a third figure emerged from the shadows, a flash of metal gleaming in the dim light. My breath caught in my throat as realization crashed over me. This wasn't just a random fight; this was orchestrated chaos, and we were walking straight into a trap.

Reid's hand tightened around my wrist as he pulled me back, but it was too late. The sound of a gunshot rang out, sharp and deafening, slicing through the night like a knife.

The world around me seemed to freeze as I turned to Reid, our eyes locking in a moment that felt suspended in time. In that instant, everything we fought for hung in the balance, teetering on the edge of the abyss. I knew we had to make a choice: run, or confront the darkness head-on, and the consequences could alter everything we had built.

Chapter 24: A Reckoning at Dawn

The morning air was thick with anticipation, a coolness that clung to the skin like a whisper of ghosts. Each breath I took was a reminder of the stakes involved, of the lives teetering on the precipice of uncertainty. Reid stood beside me, his presence a steady flame against the encroaching chill, his grip on my hand a promise—unbreakable, unwavering. As the sun began its slow ascent, spilling light like molten gold across the horizon, I felt a stirring within me, an echo of the battles we had fought, a reminder that the fiercest storms often birthed the brightest days.

Our eyes met, his a stormy gray that flickered with determination. There was an unspoken understanding between us, a bond forged in the heat of chaos and tempered by trust. We had been pushed to our limits, our hearts laid bare under the weight of secrets and betrayals, yet here we were, ready to face whatever darkness lay ahead. My heart raced with the knowledge that this was it—our final stand against the forces that had sought to tear us apart, to keep us shackled in a web of lies.

"Are you ready?" Reid's voice was low, a quiet strength that anchored me. It was a question layered with gravity, a weighty acknowledgment of all we had endured. I nodded, swallowing the lump in my throat, my resolve crystallizing.

"Ready as I'll ever be," I replied, the sound of my voice stronger than I felt. I could taste the adrenaline on my tongue, the metallic edge of fear mixing with determination. The sun burst forth, illuminating the clearing where we had chosen to confront our adversaries, casting long shadows that danced like specters in the dawn light.

The place was a battleground—a stark contrast to the serene beauty that surrounded us. Tall, ancient trees loomed overhead, their branches swaying gently as if whispering their encouragement. The scent of damp earth mingled with the sweet aroma of blooming wildflowers, a cruel reminder of nature's indifference to the chaos of humanity. The air was electric with tension, charged with the remnants of a conflict that had raged in the dark corners of our lives.

I could hear the distant sounds of footsteps, a cacophony of hurried movement, and the gruff voices of those who had betrayed us. They were coming, and with them, the shadows of doubt crept into my mind. Would we be able to stand against the tide? As if reading my thoughts, Reid squeezed my hand tighter, his gaze unyielding.

"We've got this," he said, a flicker of mischief breaking through the seriousness. "Besides, I'm not letting anyone take you away from me. Not today, not ever." The words hung between us, a spark igniting the flicker of hope deep within me.

I took a deep breath, inhaling the rich scent of the earth and exhaling the fear that threatened to overtake me. The sun rose higher, casting a golden glow over the clearing, illuminating the path that lay ahead. With each passing moment, I felt the weight of my decisions, the choices that had led me here, and the realization that I was not alone. The air buzzed with possibilities, and the adrenaline coursed through my veins like fire.

And then they appeared, emerging from the treeline like wraiths. A group of figures, clad in dark clothing, their expressions twisted with malice and disdain. Their leader, a man with eyes like shards of ice and a smile that dripped with arrogance, stepped forward, the embodiment of everything we had fought against.

"So, the lovebirds have decided to play hero," he sneered, his voice smooth as silk yet laced with venom. "How quaint."

Reid's posture shifted, a barely contained fury emanating from him. "We're not here for your games," he shot back, his tone sharp as the blade hidden beneath his jacket. "We're here to end this."

I stepped forward, my heart pounding, a rush of courage surging within me. "You think you can control our lives? That your web of lies can keep us in the dark?" I called out, my voice steady despite the whirlwind of emotions battling within me. "We're taking back our power."

A low chuckle erupted from the leader, and the sound sent a chill down my spine. "Power? You think you have any power here? This isn't a fairy tale, sweetheart. This is reality."

But reality felt fluid in that moment, shaped by our choices and our refusal to back down. Reid and I exchanged a glance, an unspoken pact sealing our fate. Together, we would rewrite the narrative that had been thrust upon us.

As the confrontation escalated, the air crackled with tension. Words turned into shouts, accusations flared, and suddenly, the space transformed from a mere clearing into a battleground of wills. I could feel the pulse of adrenaline, the rush of anticipation, as I braced myself for the chaos that was about to unfold.

The first strike came swift and unexpected, a blur of motion as Reid launched himself at the leader, their bodies colliding with a force that sent shockwaves through the ground. I followed instinctively, my heart racing as I leaped into the fray. The world narrowed, the chaos melting away into a singular focus—protecting what mattered most.

Each movement was a dance of survival, the kind that bound us in a primal rhythm. I ducked and weaved, the adrenaline amplifying my senses, every sound sharper, every scent more vivid. The clash of bodies, the grunts of exertion, the cracking of branches underfoot—it all swirled together in a visceral symphony.

And amid the frenzy, I felt a fierce clarity. This was our reckoning, a moment that would define us. As we fought side by side, I knew that our love was more than a refuge; it was our greatest weapon.

The aftermath of the skirmish left the clearing charged with a strange energy, a mix of victory and disbelief swirling in the air like autumn leaves caught in a gust of wind. My breaths came heavy, each inhalation carrying with it the weight of everything we had just endured. I turned to Reid, who stood with his back straight, eyes scanning the remnants of our battle like a soldier surveying a battlefield. The sunlight filtered through the trees, illuminating his features, casting him in a glow that made him seem almost ethereal. In that moment, I couldn't help but admire him—a warrior and a lover, all at once.

"Looks like we left quite the impression," I said, attempting to lighten the tension, my voice slightly breathless.

Reid smirked, a teasing glimmer dancing in his eyes. "What can I say? We do have a flair for the dramatic." He swept a hand to encompass the chaos—the fallen branches, the scattered remnants of the confrontation. "Who knew we could turn this quaint little spot into a combat zone?"

I chuckled softly, grateful for the levity in our shared aftermath. But beneath the humor lingered a quiet anxiety. The enemy might have been vanquished, yet I knew we had merely scratched the surface of the labyrinthine treachery that threatened our lives. "Do you think they'll come back?" I asked, the worry creeping into my voice, sharp as a shard of glass.

Reid's expression shifted, his playful demeanor giving way to steely determination. "If they do, we'll be ready. But right now, let's focus on what we've gained." He looked around, eyes glinting with a fierce pride. "We've reclaimed our power, and there's no going back."

The beauty of the sun rising higher began to seep into my heart, dispelling some of the darkness that had clung to me for so long. Reid was right; we had emerged victorious against those who sought to control us, and for the first time in what felt like forever, I could breathe without the weight of constant fear. I stepped closer, brushing my fingers against his. "Together, then?"

"Always." His promise was as solid as the ground beneath our feet.

As we stood together, absorbing the magnitude of our triumph, a soft rustling from the edge of the clearing pulled my attention. My heart raced, a reflexive response to the sudden shift in atmosphere. I turned to see a figure emerge from the underbrush, the familiar silhouette of someone I had never expected to see again. It was Grace, her expression a mixture of relief and uncertainty, as if she had stumbled upon a scene from a dream.

"Grace?" I whispered, half in disbelief. "What are you doing here?"

Her eyes darted between Reid and me, as if gauging our state before answering. "I heard the commotion. I was worried." The vulnerability in her voice made my heart ache.

Reid took a step forward, his protective instincts kicking in. "You shouldn't be here. It's not safe."

Grace held up her hands, a gesture of peace, but her eyes burned with a fierce determination. "I'm not leaving you again. Not after everything."

A silence hung between us, heavy with unspoken words. I felt a swell of affection for her, an understanding that despite our complicated history, she was willing to fight alongside us. "You have every right to be here, Grace. We could use your help."

The tension in Reid's shoulders eased slightly, though I could sense his lingering doubt. "Fine. But if anything happens, you're out of here. No arguments."

"Understood." Her lips curled into a smirk that reminded me of the fierce girl I had once known. "You can't get rid of me that easily."

With Grace's presence solidifying our ranks, we began to strategize, plotting our next move against the unseen enemies lurking in the shadows. I felt a sense of camaraderie swell between us, a triad of resilience formed from shared experience and a collective refusal to yield.

"We need to gather intel," I proposed, leaning into my newfound confidence. "There are still loose ends we need to tie up, people who might be working with them. We can't let our guard down."

Reid nodded, a fire igniting in his eyes. "There's a safe house I know of, a place we can regroup and plan. It's hidden away, far from prying eyes."

"Lead the way," Grace said, her spirit unfaltering.

As we moved through the underbrush, the forest transformed around us, shadows dancing between the sun-dappled leaves. The air was thick with anticipation, and each step felt like we were forging a path into uncharted territory. I felt the warmth of Reid's hand at my back, a steadying presence, while Grace walked beside me, her footsteps echoing our collective resolve.

"Did you really think you could get away from this life?" Grace teased, a playful edge to her voice as we maneuvered through the dense foliage. "You know you've made quite the mess of things, right?"

"Mess?" I replied, incredulous laughter bubbling up. "This is just the beginning! I think I'm more of a 'grand adventure' kind of girl."

Reid shot me a sideways glance, an amused smile tugging at his lips. "You have a flair for understatement."

"Look, I'm just trying to keep things light." I retorted, mock-innocence weaving through my tone. "It's either that or spiral into existential dread."

"Spiraling can be fun too," Grace chimed in, a glint of mischief in her eyes. "Maybe we should plan a dramatic exit next time, complete with fireworks."

As laughter echoed through the trees, I felt the tension begin to fade, replaced by the warmth of friendship and the thrill of rebellion.

We had battled darkness together, and the light of the morning seemed to push away the shadows that threatened to encroach upon our joy.

Finally, we reached the safe house—a modest cabin, nestled among the trees like a well-kept secret. It exuded an inviting charm, with ivy creeping along its weathered walls and smoke curling from the chimney like an old friend. My heart lightened at the sight.

As we stepped inside, the familiar scent of pine and aged wood enveloped us, grounding me in the reality of our choices. "This is it," Reid declared, surveying the room with a fierce pride. "This is where we make our stand."

We gathered around a battered table, the surface etched with years of stories waiting to be told. With every map unfolded and every plan devised, I felt the pieces of our lives aligning, the weight of uncertainty morphing into a sense of purpose. The shadows that had once loomed so large began to retreat, slowly but surely.

As the sun streamed through the windows, illuminating our determined faces, I felt an unshakable sense of belonging. Together, we would rewrite our destinies, crafting a narrative rich with resilience and defiance. The battle was far from over, but we were ready to face it head-on, our hearts intertwined and our spirits unbreakable.

As the sun poured through the window of the cabin, it warmed the space and illuminated the remnants of our makeshift war room. The morning light flickered across the table strewn with maps, papers, and our collective hopes. I felt a sense of belonging that had eluded me for so long, the weight of uncertainty slowly lifting like mist under the sun's embrace. We were no longer just individuals tangled in a web of deceit; we were a team, ready to confront whatever threat loomed on the horizon.

Reid leaned back in his chair, his expression thoughtful. "We need to figure out who's still out there. They won't stop just because we won a fight."

Grace was flipping through a folder, her brow furrowed in concentration. "What about those who were working with them? We need to find out who has information, who might still be loyal to the cause."

I nodded, my mind racing with possibilities. "If we can get to the root of their network, we might be able to dismantle it before it grows back. Like a weed."

"Not a weed, more like a horde of angry raccoons," Reid interjected, a smirk tugging at his lips. "The kind that raiding your trash and scuttling off with your secrets."

"Charming imagery," I replied, unable to suppress my smile. "But effective nonetheless. We'll need a plan that's smarter than a raccoon and sneakier than a cat burglar."

"We'll channel our inner ninjas," Grace added, her voice teasing. "Cloaks and daggers all the way."

As the banter continued, a shared sense of purpose began to solidify among us. The trepidation of the past few days morphed into something vibrant and alive—a spark igniting the air between us, filling the cabin with energy. We discussed strategies and formulated a plan, our voices rising in animated discussion.

Hours slipped away, the sun now casting long shadows across the floor. I took a moment to reflect, watching my friends as they immersed themselves in the logistics of our plan. Reid's brow furrowed in concentration, a rare sight that I found both endearing and intimidating. Grace was animated, her hands moving expressively as she explained her ideas, laughter ringing through the air like music. In these moments, I felt more at home than I ever had, a sense of belonging that both thrilled and terrified me.

Suddenly, the atmosphere shifted, the door creaking open to reveal a figure silhouetted against the fading light. My heart raced as I turned to face the newcomer. A tall man, clad in a long coat, stepped into the cabin, his face obscured by the dim light. The air thickened with tension, the camaraderie we had built fading into uncertainty.

"Who are you?" Reid's voice cut through the silence, low and commanding.

The stranger stepped forward, revealing a face that sent a chill racing down my spine. It was Victor, the man whose machinations had set our lives spinning into chaos. His smile was as disarming as ever, but the glint in his eyes spoke of danger.

"Missed me?" he drawled, a mockery dancing on his lips. "I'd hate to crash your little gathering, but we need to talk."

"Talk?" Reid scoffed, stepping protectively in front of me. "You think we'd ever want to listen to you?"

"Oh, I'm not asking for your permission." Victor's gaze flickered to me, his expression shifting to one of feigned concern. "I'm here to warn you, actually. This fight isn't over."

"Why would you warn us?" I challenged, taking a step closer, unwilling to back down. "You've already tried to ruin our lives. What do you stand to gain by this?"

He chuckled, a sound that sent a shiver down my spine. "I'm not the villain in your story. I'm just a player in a much larger game." His eyes sparkled with a knowing glint that made my skin crawl. "And I believe I owe you a debt of gratitude for stirring things up. You see, things are changing, and I happen to know that you're about to be thrown into the storm."

"What storm?" Grace demanded, crossing her arms defiantly.

Victor leaned against the doorframe, casual yet calculated. "A storm of your making, my dear. You've put yourself at the center of a power struggle that runs far deeper than you can imagine. There are forces at play that you've yet to comprehend, and I can help you navigate it—if you're willing to listen."

"Why should we trust you?" Reid growled, his muscles coiled with tension.

"Because, my friend," Victor replied smoothly, "I know who's coming for you next. And trust me, they won't play by the same rules. You might be able to handle a few bruises, but you're facing a war now. One that's already been set in motion."

A heavy silence enveloped us as his words sank in. I exchanged glances with Reid and Grace, the air thick with uncertainty and a hint of dread. The stakes had suddenly escalated beyond anything we had anticipated.

"What do you want from us?" I asked, my voice steady, though my heart raced.

"Only to offer you an opportunity," Victor replied, his tone silkily persuasive. "Join me, and you might just come out of this alive. Or continue to fight blindly against a tide you can't control. The choice is yours."

Before I could respond, a loud crash erupted from outside the cabin, splintering the air like thunder. The sound reverberated through the walls, sending an icy chill coursing through my veins. My heart raced, panic clawing at the edges of my mind.

Reid's eyes darted toward the door, his instincts honed. "What was that?"

"Trouble," Victor said, his tone shifting to one of dark amusement. "And it seems your little safe haven is about to be compromised. I suggest you make a choice quickly—before the storm breaks."

With that, he turned on his heel and vanished into the shadows, leaving us reeling in the wake of his ominous words. The crash echoed again, louder this time, accompanied by the unmistakable sound of footsteps closing in.

"Prepare yourselves," Reid commanded, adrenaline surging through his voice. "Whatever comes next, we'll face it together."

The words barely left his lips when the door flew open, and figures poured into the cabin, dark silhouettes filled with menace and intent. The world outside erupted into chaos, shadows spilling over the threshold, and I felt the weight of our choices crashing down around us.

I took a deep breath, adrenaline surging through me, and braced myself for the fight of our lives. The storm had arrived, and with it, the uncertainty of our fate hung heavy in the air, waiting to unfold.

Milton Keynes UK
Ingram Content Group UK Ltd.
UKHW030948261124
451585UK00001B/136